FIGHTING FOR SURVIVAL

MEL SHERRATT

Also in The Estate Series

Somewhere to Hide (Book 1)
Behind a Closed Door (Book 2)

PROLOGUE

Ruth Millington covered her ears with her hands, the screams around her getting louder. She tucked herself into the corner of the kitchen and pulled her knees up to her chest.

Shut up. Shut UP. SHUT UP!

But Mason and Jamie Millington continued with their games, screaming as one stabbed the other, squealing as one grabbed the other in a rugby tackle. Down Mason went onto the floor with his brother; play but with real meaning.

'Shut up,' Ruth whispered. She banged her head on the wall behind her, again and again, but the noise didn't lessen.

As Jamie ran past her he took a biscuit from the open packet, knocking a carton of milk over in the process. Liquid ran off the worktop, drip, drip, dripping down the kitchen unit and onto the cheap, scratched flooring. Turning back to glance at his mother, Jamie covered his mouth with his hand. Then he laughed. It was the sound of an eight-year-old who had the upper hand; evil, cruel, taunting.

His older brother, ignoring the milk pooling on the floor, grabbed for a biscuit too. Then he turned up the dial on the radio. The tinny sound raised dramatically, the beat of the bass reverberating around the walls. He ran back into the living room, screaming as he did, Jamie hot on his heels.

'I am such a bad mother.' Ruth grabbed fistfuls of her hair and pulled as hard as she could. 'I am such a bad mother.' She banged her head against the wall again. 'I am such a bad mother. Always have been, always will be. They'll be better off without me.'

Ruth knew she could no more control them than she could herself. But she had to do something to stop them from growing up into anti-social thugs.

'Shut up, shut up, shut up!' Her voice rose with each word until it turned into a screech. 'Will you two shut the FUCK UP!'

She jumped to her feet and ran into the living room after them. Grabbing for Mason, he avoided her in the nick of time, quickly following his brother back through the kitchen and out into the garden.

Neither of them were laughing as their mother tore after them.

CHAPTER ONE

Gina Bradley swallowed two tablets with the help of a mouthful of water, knocking back the rest afterwards. It spilt over the rim and down her chin in her haste to get rid of the pounding inside her head. Bang, bang, bang.

It took her a moment to realise that the noise was actually from someone knocking at the front door. She shuffled through the living room, careful not to trip over Pete's boots splayed in the middle of the floor, and squeezed around the boxes of knock-off paraphernalia piled up along the narrow hallway.

'What the fuck do you want?' she snapped, looking down at Josie Mellor from her vantage point of three steps up.

'Good morning to you too,' said Josie. 'Don't say that you weren't expecting me. Are the twins at home? I need to talk to them about –'

'All right, all right, keep your voice down.' Gina opened the door and moved to one side. 'You'd better come in. I don't want the whole of Stanley Avenue to know my bleeding business.'

Josie moved past her. Before shutting the door, Gina looked up and down the road to see who was nosing at her. She watched for curtains twitching: it was bound to be one of the neighbours who had complained, although for once, it didn't seem to have anything to do with her and Pete making a racket after a late night argument.

She followed Josie into the living room and dropped onto the settee, not bothering to move the pile of magazines and a pair of men's jeans. Josie sat down on the armchair next to the gas fire.

'What do you want to know?' Gina asked as she reached for a packet of cigarettes from the coffee table.

'Where were your girls last night?'

'That depends.' She lit a cigarette and took a deep drag.

'In that case, you can't be certain that they weren't involved in the altercation across on the square.'

Gina leaned back and placed her feet onto the dusty coffee table. 'In that case,' she mimicked Josie, 'they were here with me all night.'

Josie sighed. 'Mrs Bradley, have you any idea of the serious nature of the attack?'

'Nope.' In truth, Gina hadn't a clue what Josie was referring to. She'd fallen asleep on the sofa, long before the twins had come home. They might have mentioned some sort of a fight when they'd nudged her awake and she'd gone up to bed but she couldn't recall anything now.

'There were two incidents, in fact,' said Josie. 'At half past seven, Rachel and Claire were seen riding like the clappers along Davy Road after a woman was knocked to the floor and her handbag was stolen.'

'Not my girls,' said Gina with a slow shake of the head. 'Besides, they know better than to get caught on CCTV.'

Josie frowned: damn the government cutbacks. Manning the cameras on the Mitchell Estate had been the first thing to suffer after the local council cut their staff by twenty per cent. Since then, things had started to slide again; people realised they couldn't be seen as much as before.

'The woman suffered a broken nose and a dislocated shoulder, Gina,' she said.

'And you think my girls are capable of that?' Gina stared back at her.

'They're not girls anymore, they're sixteen. And the mess they made of Melissa Riley last year, I dare say they are more than capable.'

'That was a teenage misunderstanding. You know how catfights can start when boys are involved.'

'Actually, I don't recall any when I was their age.'

'No, you would have been Miss Fucking Perfect at school, wouldn't you? I see you haven't changed now, apart from becoming a jobsworth.'

'At least I have a job,' muttered Josie.

'What?'

'Nothing.'

Gina watched as Josie lowered her eyes. Josie hardly ever retaliated, no matter what she spat out at her. What had rattled her cage?

'You mentioned two episodes?' she said.

'Yes.' Josie tried to regain her professionalism. 'There was another mugging half an hour later. This one was particularly brutal. A young lad was pushed down the steps on Frazer Terrace. He says he fell but –'

'He must have fallen if he said he did! Bleeding hell, Josie, can't you take anything at face value?'

'Not when I know he's lying.'

'And exactly how do you know that?'

'I just do, that's all.'

Gina glared at Josie, wondering as she did what she really thought of her – not her professional opinion but deep down inside. Josie was thirty-seven and had been working on the sprawling Mitchell Estate for the past eighteen years. More recently, she'd been splitting her time between the role of housing officer and manager of the new business enterprise centre, The Workshop, that opened the previous month. She was known as a fair, firm person, always offering a word of encouragement. But she wasn't a pushover; Josie would help for a while, giving anyone the benefit of the doubt until she realised that her advice wouldn't be taken, and then she'd resort to stronger methods to get things done. All the time, she would try; often she would fail. But she still cared, whatever the outcome.

There were twelve hundred houses on The Mitchell Estate. Until recently, Josie and her work colleague, Ray, had shared the responsibility of the properties that belonged to Mitchell Housing Association, but since The Workshop had opened, Josie was mostly based there. However, she always liked working out in the community and couldn't wait to get back to more casework when the time was right. For now, she was keeping old cases open and only visiting when requested to – like today.

Gina put herself in Josie's place and imagined what she would see. A small, fat woman who had let herself go - someone who looked much older than her thirty-five years, someone who couldn't be bothered to move her fat ass from the settee. She knew she looked a mess compared to the woman sitting opposite her, with her perfectly-styled bobbed hair, fresh make up, and the waft of perfume filling the room.

'Give me a break,' Gina pleaded. 'You ought to try living my life for a week. I have a lazy bastard for a husband who's never done a day's work in his life. My eldest son is heading the same way – either that or he'll end up inside again. I have daughters who happen to be the bane of everyone's life. Wherever they go, they cause mayhem. It's not exactly a barrel of laughs for me.'

'My life is in no way perfect,' said Josie, 'but I do try my best to get things right.'

Gina yawned. 'I'm bored with this conversation. Have you finished?'

'No, I haven't. Your girls are heading for a big come down. You know they think they rule the roost with this stupid gang they're part of.'

Gina giggled. 'Yeah. The Mitchell Mob, they call themselves. So funny.'

'It isn't funny at all!' Josie's voice rose slightly. 'Do you want them both to be locked up like Danny was last year? Then you'll be on your own and...'

'And?' Gina taunted when Josie had been silent for a few seconds.

'You know what I mean. They're heading for meltdown.'

Gina stood up quickly. 'I think you'd better sling your hook. I'm sick of you poking your nose into my family's business all the time. Who do you think you are?'

'I have a file on your family this thick,' Josie indicated an inch between her thumb and index finger, 'so you need to be careful. I can't keep shielding you and your girls from eviction.'

'Eviction?'

Josie said nothing.

'You can't be serious?' Gina continued. 'I've been a tenant here for seventeen years. You can't just turf us out.'

'I – I can,' said Josie, 'and I will, if I have to.'

Gina grabbed Josie's arm and pulled her up roughly. 'Get out of my house. And don't come back accusing my family of allsorts until you have the proof that they were involved.'

Josie tried to shrug Gina off but she held on tight. 'Could you at least try and talk to them?' she asked. 'They might listen to you.'

Gina sneered. 'What makes you think they'll listen to me? Like you said, they're sixteen now.'

'Which means we have more rights to lock them up if they're caught.'

Gina pushed Josie across the living room and along the hallway. She yanked open the front door and shoved her through it. Josie just about kept her balance as she flew down the steps.

'I'm warning you, Josie Mellor, stay away from here. Stay away from me and stay away from my family. Because if you don't, I'll come after you. Just you remember that.'

'Gina, you're making a big mistake! I can help you –'

'Just keep your nose out of my fucking business!' Gina slammed the door so hard that paint chips fell to the floor. She stomped back through to the kitchen, grabbed the whisky bottle from where she'd left it the night before and took a huge swig. Then another. And another.

She wiped her mouth with the back of her hand and took in a huge gulp of air. How dare Josie come round here and accuse her girls! Oh, she knew deep down that they must have had something to do with the drama last night. If not two incidents, they would more than likely be involved in one of them – probably the boy falling down the steps.

Damn that Josie Mellor. And damn that stupid housing association and its rules. No one would turf her family out. They wouldn't dare mess with the Bradleys.

Caren Williams shivered involuntarily, her legs feeling heavy as she leaned her back against the windowsill. She glanced around the large, family kitchen that she'd painted a welcoming yellow earlier that year but its brightness was wasted on her: this was the last morning she'd be walking into it.

Holding back tears, she realised that in less than three hours she and John had to be out of there. The bailiffs were calling at 2pm: neither of them wanted to be there when the locks would be changed and a notice pinned to their front door. Even though they'd voluntarily given the keys back to their mortgage company rather than wait for the inevitable, it still amounted to the same thing. They were being slung out because they couldn't afford to pay. Besides, Caren didn't want to see the pitying looks that were bound to come from their neighbours.

Bankruptcy – not a word she thought she would ever need to speak aloud in her life. She cast her mind back two years. John's plumbing and heating business had been going strong. It had been a struggle at first, as were most businesses during their first years, but as time went by, regular customers came on board and gradually it grew into a resounding success. Caren, who had worked full-time with John, taking care of the administration, the accounts, a little sales and a lot of PR, had even been able to reduce her working days to four a week, freeing time up to think about starting her own business. But then one of John's major clients had gone under. Not only did it leave them owed thousands of pounds, it created a cash flow problem that the bank wasn't willing to help them out with. The business also lost a vast percentage of its incoming work. John cut staff down to the bare minimum but in the end, the loss was too much to bear. Within months, everything they'd worked so hard to achieve was gone.

John walked into the room a few minutes later, sagging shoulders indicating his mood. Caren felt her heartbeat quicken again. She watched as he buried his face in his hands.

'John, don't –'

He opened his arms and she ran into them. He smelt of shower gel, his short, dark hair still wet. It was so comforting.

'I can't believe this is happening,' he cried. 'I'm so sorry.'

'It wasn't your fault,' she told him, tears running down her face.

'I should have seen it coming; shouldn't have put all my eggs into one basket. I should have reached out for more clients when I had the opportunity but I didn't think it would get this bad – to the point of no return.'

'We weren't to know that Carrington's would go into administration.'

'I know, but –'

'We'll get through this; in time you can start up again and I can get my business idea up and running.'

'It took us years to build up what we had! And now, look at us – at the bottom of the pile again.'

'Look on the bright side,' she encouraged. 'The only way is up; we can't get any lower than this.'

Despite their gloomy prospects, John smiled. 'You can always see the positive,' he said. 'I wish I shared your optimism.'

'We'll pick ourselves up and start again, you'll see.'

But John's buoyancy soon died. 'Sure, we only need a few thousand pounds that we don't have.'

'We'll find it again.' Caren wouldn't let him slide down – because if he did, she would no doubt go down with him. 'Besides, anything is better than sitting rocking in a corner thinking nothing will change. It will – eventually, it has to.'

John shook his head. 'Where would I be without you?'

There was so much pain in his eyes that Caren had to look away for a moment. She and John had been an item during her last year at high school. He was two years older than her at thirty-seven and she'd had a crush on him since the first time she'd seen him. Once she'd walked out of the school gates for the very last time, she'd done her utmost to keep him on the straight and narrow. The Mitchell Estate could drag even the most positive of people down with it after a while. She wasn't going to let that happen to them.

It took them two years to save for a deposit on a house and as soon as Caren finished her hairdressing and beauty course at college, they were on their way. Their first had been a two-up two-down terraced in a long, long row of ex-miners houses. Four years later, they'd swapped that for a semi-detached property that was hardly bigger but had three bedrooms. Next had come the three bed pre-war semi, closely followed by the four bedroom detached house they were going to lose today. It was her pride and joy, and it had all gone in a blink of an eye.

John looked at her. It was twenty years ago that she'd first fallen for those eyes; the blue-grey speckles in the dark ponds of sapphire, and those long, black lashes. There were a few faint laughter lines around them – not that she'd heard him laughing much since the eviction notice had arrived. Until recently, he'd always been her knight in shining armour. This had ruined him – it wasn't fair – but she wouldn't let it ruin them.

'We'll get through this,' she reiterated. 'You and me; we'll survive.'

Gently, he cupped her face in his hands. 'Do you think so?' he whispered.

'I know so.'

Caren lowered her eyes then, before she gave away how tense she was feeling. John enveloped her in his arms again, where she felt strong in his embrace.

She loved him with all her heart.

No matter what happened, they'd get through this mess.

CHAPTER TWO

Gina lay in bed, the rain lashing down outside her window hardly giving her any incentive to get up. She hadn't got anywhere to go anyway. She turned over, hoping to get more sleep.

If it wasn't for the noise going on downstairs, she would have stayed there much longer than an extra few minutes. But there was no chance of that; Rachel and Claire had been bickering for fifteen minutes now. She covered her head with the duvet, praying they would stop.

'It's mine, you cow. I got it first!'

'I only want to wear it today! Then you can have it back.'

'No, I want to wear it. Mum got this one for me; you've got the blue one.'

'I want the pink one!'

'Well, you CAN'T HAVE IT!'

Gina stormed to the top of the stairs and hung her head over the banister. 'If you two don't stop screaming at each other, I'll take both T-shirts from you.'

'Chill out, Mum,' Rachel shouted up to her. 'Claire is just being a moody cow.'

'No, I'm not!'

'Yes, you are!'

'No, I'm NOT!'

'For crying out loud!' Gina dressed in whatever piece of clothing came to hand from the floor before marching down the stairs. 'Are you two six or sixteen? Why can't you ever act your age?' She looked at the clock. 'Actually, why aren't you two at school?'

'Spare period,' said Rachel, the lie rolling off her tongue with ease.

'You're only two weeks into a new term.' Gina clipped her ear as she walked past. 'More like you've skipped it again. Move your arse, the pair of you. I'm not having that school woman on my doorstep, going on at me as if I'm not capable of looking after my own kids.'

'You're not,' muttered Claire. It earned her a clip too.

'Ow! What was that for?' Claire rubbed at her head while Rachel laughed at her.

'Less of your lip, young lady.' Gina pushed past them, into the kitchen. This morning's and last night's dishes were piled precariously in the sink, congealed grease swimming in the murky water that they soaked in. Her hand moved to cover her nose. 'God, it stinks in here. Has someone killed a cat?'

'We would have killed it by now if we had one,' giggled Rachel.

Claire nudged her. 'Don't be stupid. I wouldn't do anything to hurt an animal. They're defenceless creatures.'

'That's not what you said when Loopy Leonard's dog nearly had hold of your ankles last week.'

'That was your fault. If you hadn't been a stupid cow and told me to –'

'Girls! Put a lid on it!' Gina lit up a cigarette and took a huge drag, coughing and spluttering the side effects of twenty years on the weed. 'Where's your father?' she asked once she'd caught her breath. 'Is the idle bastard in or out?'

'Left about an hour ago,' stated Rachel. 'Which you would have known if you'd bothered to get out of bed earlier.'

Both girls ran out of the room as Gina lunged towards them, her hand raised again. Their laughter followed them out of the house with a bang of the back door. Gina sighed: peace at last in the Bradley household.

She wondered what work on the side her husband was up to today as she made herself a mug of milky tea. Then, without another moment's thought, she settled down in the chaos of the living room to catch up with the shenanigans on *Jeremy Kyle*. Today's show was about a mother who'd had a family early in life and was now having a mid-life crisis by sleeping with a boy of sixteen. Gina switched it off after a few minutes. It reminded her too much of her own life to be called entertainment. She felt much worse than the fat woman with the huge boobs and mini-skirt that looked no wider than a belt, because at least she was having sex. Gina couldn't remember the last time she and Pete had got down and dirty. Was it last month, August? Was it July or June? Nope, she couldn't recall any special occasions.

She pushed a pile of magazines off the coffee table to make way for her feet. Then she put them out of sight. Even her white socks were the colour of dirty dish water. What was going on with her? She'd chosen this life so she didn't have to go to work so why the long face all the time? Just lately, she found she could raise her hand easier than a smile. Mind you, what had she got to show for her life so far? She had a wayward husband who didn't know the meaning of working legally for his money, a twenty-year-old son going the same way and sixteen-year-old twins who were regular visitors to Mitchell Housing Association to be interviewed by the local police. Gina hardly had time to live her life for the worries of the ones she'd brought into this world to fend for themselves. That woman on Jeremy Kyle had nothing on her.

She hauled herself up from the old and worn settee and went upstairs to the bathroom. The broken mirror above the sink showed a scary reflection. She ran a hand through red, greasy hair, not bothering to brush her teeth or wash her face. The clothes she'd picked up from the floor were two days old – or were they three? Gina sniffed cautiously at her armpits. She pulled away sharply - no wonder Pete wouldn't come anywhere near her with that smell!

She sat on the side of the bath while she filled it to the brim with hot water. She could do with a long soak and at least she could lie back in her muck alone for once. Only on rare occasions would the house be this quiet.

A few minutes later, submerged in the water, she tried to remember what had gone down last night to make her head ache so much. She remembered having a few cans of lager and a couple of whisky chasers but she was at a loss after that. Oh, yes, she recalled. Pete had phoned for a takeaway; that had been the smell from the kitchen and the mess down the front of her jumper.

Not for the first time, she wished she could turn back the clock and start her life again. Gina had lived in Stanley Avenue, on the bottom half of the Mitchell Estate, all her life. Her parents lived across the road; her sister Leah and her son, Samuel, lived next door but three. Even her brother had lived there until he'd given up his flat to live courtesy of Her Majesty's pleasure for the past year.

She often wondered if her parents hadn't moved onto the estate, would she have turned out this way? Would it only have taken another street, on another estate somewhere to make her life turn the happy way, rather than the path to nothing she was following now? From the moment she had seen Pete at high school, she had wanted him. Very soon, she'd had him. Very soon, she'd become pregnant by him. At fifteen, when all the other girls at school were discovering cigarettes, cheap cider and ecstasy tablets, she'd discovered the joys of sex behind the bus shelter. A quick blow job, a quick fumble and a quick fuck; that was all it had taken for Pete to belong to Gina. Yet she often wondered why he'd stuck with her. After all, she wasn't a catch. She was a plump, thirty-five-year old mum of three who didn't give a shit about herself anymore.

Gina slid down beneath the water and lay there. If she could hold her breath long enough, she could slip away without anyone noticing. Because she knew as sure as night was night and day was day that no one would miss her.

'Where do you want me to put this?' John asked as he heaved a heavy box up the steps to their front door.

'In the kitchen,' said Caren. 'It's written on the side of the box if you look.'

John lifted his arm slightly whilst keeping a grip on the box. 'Oh yeah.' He grinned. 'It's bloody heavy. What the hell's in it? A dead body?'

Caren picked up a box marked dining room and sighed - there wasn't a dining room here. Lord knows where she was going to put all of their belongings. The house was tiny compared to their old home. Tears sprang to her eyes. No, she wouldn't think about that, she chastised herself. This was their new home; it would have to do until something better came along.

Twenty-four Stanley Avenue. Of all the places she would end up, she hadn't thought it would be here. Stanley Avenue epitomised everything she had fought so hard to get away from when she was younger. Bloody typical she would end up right back where she had started.

A crash made her hurry through to the kitchen. She put her box down and ran to help John as he grappled with cups and saucers smashing to the floor.

'It wasn't my fault! The box split!' He looked on in dismay, waiting for the wrath of his wife. But Caren grinned.

'I hated that bloody tea set,' she laughed. Then she couldn't stop laughing, knowing full well that when she stopped she would start to cry again.

John put down what was left of the box and hugged his wife. 'It'll get better soon,' he said. 'You wait and see.'

Caren hugged him. Since she'd found out they were about to lose everything, there had been so many times that she'd hated him. It had nothing to do with apportioning blame. She'd been the one who had taken control. She'd been the one who had gone to Mitchell Housing Association to explain about their predicament. She'd been the one who'd phoned all their creditors, assuring future payments, even if they had to be the minimum payment for now. But then again, she'd always been the pushy one in their relationship. If it wasn't for her, she doubted John would have left the estate in the first place.

She watched him now as he bent to pick up the pieces of broken crockery. To her eye, he was still as gorgeous as he'd been in his early twenties. He was clean shaven, with a receding hairline. He wore the latest in designer clothes, fitting his T-shirt and jeans well, with pert buttocks and biceps. Her husband: John Williams. The man who went to the gym three times a week, to the barbers every three weeks and shopping for designer clothes on a regular basis. All that would have to stop now, though. Caren wondered if he'd realised that yet.

John squeezed her tightly. 'We'll make it work, Caz,' he said. 'Then we can move again, get our own place. Start the business up again. Buy even better cars. We can do it if we stick together.'

She nodded.

'I suppose there's a box for rubbish marked up, Mrs Organised?'

'Of course, what else would you expect?' Caren opened a kitchen cupboard and reeled at the smell. 'God knows who lived here before us, but I've a good mind to complain. It smells as if someone has died in here and it's bloody filthy.'

'Relax, babe,' John nudged her on his way out. 'It's just to remind us of how shit life will be on the Mitchell Estate and how we need to get out of here as soon as.'

'Which means you getting back to work as soon as,' Caren replied. 'Have you rung Daryl yet?' John's friend had promised him some labouring work for a few weeks.

'No, there's plenty of time. Let's get settled first. Then we can get on with creating a new life for us.'

Funny, thought Caren, as she watched him until he was out of sight, that's what I thought I'd started to do all those years ago.

'About bleeding time!' Barbara Lewis told her eldest daughter, when she finally answered the door after three loud knocks. 'I thought even an idle cow like you couldn't still be in bed at eleven thirty.'

'I am not an idle cow,' snapped Gina, 'and as you can see I'm up.'

Even though it was on the tip of her tongue to say something about Gina still being in her pyjamas, Barbara kept her mouth shut, knowing better than to get into a fight.

'Do you fancy coming into town with me?' she asked. 'I'll treat you to coffee and a jam doughnut.'

Gina flopped back down onto the settee where she'd been sprawling for the past two hours. 'Which is usually code for you want me to do something that *I* won't want to do,' she replied. 'Especially if you're buying cake.'

'Well, there is a party coming up and I don't fancy going on my own.' Gina's dad had died two years ago. 'I thought you might –'

'Me?' Gina snorted before lighting a cigarette. 'You have got to be joking.'

'They won't all be old fuddy-duddies!'

Gina threw her another look.

'So?' Barbara tried again.

Gina took a drag of her cigarette. 'I can't,' she said, smoke coming out of her mouth and down her nose. 'Even if I had something decent to wear, you know Pete wouldn't like it.'

'It's at the weekend – would he even be back to know?'

Gina ignored her sarcastic tone. Pete usually played cards on Saturday nights and didn't come home until the early hours. Often he didn't come home at all until the next morning. Gina wasn't stupid: she knew sometimes he was with other women but she couldn't prove it. Despite the Mitchell Estate being great for spreading rumours, she only ever got to hear who he was with if someone was out to cause trouble.

'Come into town with me anyway,' Barbara urged, not wanting to give up so easily.

Gina perished the thought. It would mean that she'd have to get dressed and washed and she didn't have it in her – not after drinking the remainder of a bottle of Jack Daniels' last night.

'Can't be bothered,' she said. 'Besides, I still feel rough after a heavy session.'

Barbara sat back and folded her arms across her thin body. 'You have a heavy session most nights, that's nothing new. I'm worried about you, you know. All that alcohol you knock back isn't healthy. I think –'

'For God's sake Mum, zip it, will you?' Gina snapped. 'You're getting to sound like a right nag.'

'And you're a right moody cow!' Barbara stood up. 'I only stopped by so that you'd make an effort once in a while to get out of the house.'

Gina pulled her feet up beside her. 'What's the point when I've got no money to buy anything?'

'I'll lend you a twenty from my pension.'

'I'll never be able to pay you back.'

'Can't you get anything off Pete?'

'No, I can't.'

'But he always seems to have spare cash.'

Gina wondered how she could stop this chat. What she and Pete did with their money – or how he came across it – was nothing to do with anyone else. And why did everyone think they knew what was best for her? Couldn't she be trusted to make her own mind up about things? Desperate to be left alone, she reached for the remote control and turned up the volume on the television. They sat in silence for a few minutes until her mum finally got the message.

'If you won't come with me, then I'll go on my own. I can't sit around on my arse all day even if you can. It's not healthy.' She stormed out of the room, slamming the door behind her.

Gina sighed with relief: peace at last. She was just about to settle in for another kip when the door opened again. Barbara was back, green eyes sparkling with excitement.

'You'll never guess who I've just seen!' she cried.

'No, but I'm sure you're going to tell me anyhow.' Gina knew it would most likely be one of her old cronies that she hadn't seen for a while.

'Caren Williams – you know, that girl from your school. You and Pete used to go out with her and her fella.' Barbara paused, one hand on her hip. 'Didn't you fall out with her over something and nothing?'

Gina said nothing. Of course she remembered Caren, but she wasn't going to register a flicker of interest. Her mum was right: she and Caren had hated each other at school.

Barbara grabbed her daughter's hands and tried to pull her to her feet but Gina resisted.

'I'm telling you, I've just seen Caren Williams,' she said. 'And get this... she's moving stuff into the empty house across the road from you.'

Gina was up from the settee in a flash.

CHAPTER THREE

'That's the van emptied, Caz,' John said, carrying in the last box of their possessions. Even though it was marked 'bathroom' in black capital letters, he slid it onto the kitchen worktop. 'It didn't take long to unpack everything, did it?'

'All the contents need to be unpacked too, you dope,' Caren told him. 'That's going to take ages. What time does the van have to be returned by?'

'Four thirty. I'll drop it off and walk back through the estate afterwards. It'll only take me half an hour.'

'No! Someone might see you!'

'So?'

'I don't want anyone to know we're living here!'

'What makes you think anyone else will be interested in our lives? We've been gone too long. People won't even remember us.'

Caren knew that wasn't true. They'd lived their lives on this estate and, even though she had saved hard to get them away, most of their school friends had remained here, not knowing any better. She didn't want to be associated with any of them ever again if she could help it, especially now.

John kissed her lightly on her cheek. 'I won't be too long.'

A minute later, he was back. 'I've picked up the wrong keys,' he said, throwing down a bunch on the table and picking up another set before leaving again.

Caren set to work cleaning inside the cupboards. She filled another bowl full of hot water and bleach, popped rubber gloves onto her hands to save her nails and got down on all fours. She opened the first of nine cupboards and started to scrub at its base.

A few minutes later, John was back again.

'What have you forgotten this time?' Caren kept her back towards him as she continued to scrub. 'Honestly, you'd –'

'Look who I bumped into outside,' he interrupted.

'Well, hello there, Caren.'

Caren took a sharp intake of breath before slowly backing out and turning to face them. No, it couldn't be...

Shit: it was.

'Pete!' She put on a false smile as she stood up. 'What are you doing in Stanley Avenue? Heard we were back and come to say hello?'

'No, I was just getting home and I spotted John pulling off in the van.'

Caren's heart sank but her smile remained firmly in place.

'Yeah,' said John with a smile that was in no way false at all. 'You'll never guess where he and Gina live? Right opposite us – number twenty-five. How cool is that? It'll be just like old times.'

Old times? Caren shuddered involuntarily. She'd worked hard to forget the old times. There had been no love lost between her and Gina at school and, even though people change, she'd heard that Gina had remained the same small-minded bitch that she'd always been. She knew that she'd had three kids in quick succession, knew that she hadn't worked a day in her life. She'd heard that Pete was known around the estate for not keeping his dick in his trousers, though looking at him now, with his clothes hanging off him, his scruffy hair and skin in need of a good wash, she wondered why any woman would take a fancy to him.

Oh, God, this was going to be a nightmare.

Turning away, she cast her mind back to when she'd last seen Gina Bradley. She'd been in Woolworths a few years ago, getting presents for Christmas. Gina had come walking – no, waddling – towards her, looking like she expected her to stop and make small talk as their eyes locked. She recalled being thankful that she'd made an effort to keep in shape over the years and took great pleasure in seeing Gina's resigned look as her eyes then swept from Caren's head to her toes and back again quickly. Caren had then walked straight past as if she didn't know her, a smile playing on her lips. She wasn't a vengeful person but it had felt so good, so liberating.

Once she heard John and Pete leave the room behind her, she let out the breath she'd been holding. Trying not to cry, she forced herself back down onto the floor and began to scrub away with vigour.

This situation was going from bad to worse. What had she done to deserve this!

Gina stood in her bedroom window, hoping that no one could see her as she watched the goings-on across the road. When Mum first told her about Caren, she'd had to see for herself. The two of them had stood at the window, gawping at the items of furniture that had come from the van. There had been some proper posh stuff, things Gina and Barbara had only ever been able to dream of owning. And although Barbara had lots of fun imagining what items were going into what rooms, every time something else came from the van, Gina's heart sank at the realisation that Caren must be loaded. But then again, she was back on the Mitchell Estate. She would have to find out why.

Since Mum had gone at about one o'clock, her trip into town forgotten, Gina had stood there but still she hadn't seen Caren. That was hours ago; her legs were aching but she didn't dare move in case she missed anything. She couldn't believe it – her arch-enemy, moving in directly opposite; their front doors practically parallel to one another. They would see each other every day. Gina quivered at the thought. Rewind the years and Caren Williams had been Caren Phillips. They'd known each other since infant school but they'd never really liked each other. Gina could still remember Caren looking down her nose at her when she'd become pregnant at fifteen. She had just left school – well, she hardly went to school really – when she gave birth to Danny. She was barely sixteen. Caren was going out with John then, boasting about how she planned to marry him and buy a house before *she* started a family.

It had been worse when she'd had the twins three years later; she and Pete married hastily when they were three months old. Gina had thought she'd have time to get her figure back after the birth but she was fat and round on the one wedding photo they had. She hated it.

Everyone thought she and Pete wouldn't last but they had proved them wrong. Sixteen years later and they were still married, although Pete had hardly been the loving, doting husband. Rumours around the estate were that he'd shag anything that moved but Gina wasn't sure if they were true or not. He'd confessed to a couple of affairs and she'd seen off the women each time with a good fist fight. Despite that, no one really knew whether or not they were happy and Gina wasn't telling.

Suddenly, she jumped back from the window as the front door opened. She watched as John jogged down the path and opened the boot of a small white car. Within seconds, he closed it again and ran back into the house. Gina had seen enough for her heart to start racing. Back when she was fourteen, she'd had an enormous crush on John and that bitch Caren had got to him first.

But why would John have looked at Gina when he could have Caren?

Caren was tall and svelte with long, blonde hair and fair skin. She was an only child – not like Gina being the eldest child of three – and had the latest trainers, the latest school bag, the latest everything. Gina always had the cheaper brands. She remembered crying for two weeks over a pair of Adidas trainers she'd coveted and being mortified when her mum came home with something similar but with two black stripes instead of the trademark three.

Gina, her sister Leah and brother, Jason, had been called names throughout their school years. It hadn't been a happy time for any of them. Scruffy Gina, she'd been known as. Along with smelly Gina, thick Gina, stupid Gina, ginger Gina. And the worst ones: slapper Gina, scrubber Gina, shagger Gina. It had been horrible getting pregnant so young, but it was her mistake and she had stood by it, even when she'd come away from school without an exam to her name. She hadn't needed qualifications anyway; she'd never worked since leaving school.

When Pete showed an interest in her, Gina had thought all her Christmases had come at once. It didn't matter that her coat was brown when everyone else's was red. It didn't matter that she had no money to go shopping for the latest clothes and make up. At fourteen, Gina fell in love. Yet as soon as John had shown an interest in Caren, Gina had wanted him too. To the point that she'd got very pissed on cider and threw herself at him. When he wouldn't kiss her, she offered to give him a blow job. But John hadn't wanted to know: he'd laughed at her, embarrassed by her actions. Besides, Caren had stolen his heart anyway. Gina had felt so humiliated seeing them together. John would always be sitting by Caren; her legs would be draped over his as she sat on his knee. Or he'd be standing behind her, arms encircling her tiny waist, pulling her in close.

She sighed heavily. Where had she gone wrong? Three kids and a useless pratt of a husband wasn't much to shout about. Back at school, she'd wanted to be a hairdresser. She had intended to go to college, get her own vehicle and go mobile. Unfortunately, she hadn't reckoned on a thin blue line changing all of that, shattering her dreams, breaking her illusions. And everything continued to go wrong from that day forward.

Was it any wonder she was trying to come up with a reason for Caren to be back on the estate? It couldn't be by choice. No one would ever come back here if they didn't have to. Something must have gone wrong in her oh-so-perfect life. Bizarrely, even that thought couldn't summon a smile.

Even though she had seen John earlier when Pete came home, Gina still couldn't drag herself away from the window. Curiosity was burning up inside her to see if Caren looked as good as she remembered. The last time she'd seen her in town, Caren had blanked her as she'd walked towards her in Woollies. Gina hadn't been bothered - there was nothing worse than seeing your rival looking a million dollars in a long, black winter coat, leather, knee-length boots, skinny jeans and a white jumper that actually looked white. Even more so when you were wearing shabby old jeans and manky trainers, with no make-up and mop hair. Caren had strode past her in a cloud of musky perfume as she'd slinked away to hide behind the greetings card stands.

That had been about three years ago. It was going to be strange to see her again after so long – and on a regular basis too. Whenever Gina needed to go to Vincent Square, Caren could be in the garden. When she went to collect her benefits, Caren could be in the post office sending parcels to friends overseas. When she went to the chemist to pick up her asthma inhaler, Caren might be there treating herself to a new lipstick or body lotion. When she went to the butchers for the cheap cuts, Caren might be buying the best cut of steak.

Gina pushed her nails into her palms. Now she would always have a reminder of how appalling she looked against Caren. Gina with the mop of ginger hair; Gina with the body of an Oompa-Lumpa - a waist measurement that was way past the healthy limit - Gina with the lines of a smoker prominent around her mouth, Gina with the clothes that looked like they came from a charity shop. Gina with the husband who didn't give enough of a shit to try to cajole her into doing something about it.

Suddenly, Caren appeared in the doorway. Gina felt tears prick her eyes: Caren hadn't changed one iota since that day in Woollies. Her skin was tanned, her nails painted. She still had the long, flowing hair but it was tied out of the way with a pink scarf that matched the shade of her lipstick precisely. She wore light-coloured tight jeans, Chelsea boots popping out from beneath them. Checked shirt sleeves were rolled up out of the way.

She watched Caren glance up and down the avenue. Her arms were folded and she seemed to be drinking in the mood of the place; it was clear that she didn't look very happy. Gina could almost see an invisible cloak of anxiety shrouding her.

For the first time that day, she smiled. If Caren Williams thought that Gina was going to welcome her into the avenue with open arms, she had another think coming. Her family had the monopoly on Stanley Avenue, and nothing ever got past them for long. She'd make it her business to have the low down on why Caren and John had come back.

And then maybe it was time to have some fun.

'How come you get to be the boss again?' Claire asked her twin sister as they walked to their usual hangout - the car park of Shop&Save across on Vincent Square. It was nearing eight o'clock; they were off to meet up with the rest of their gang. Now the nights were drawing in, there were more opportunities to cause mayhem.

Rachel peered from behind her hood, her face barely visible to the outside world. 'What do you mean?'

Claire faltered, unsure what to say now that she had voiced her feelings. 'I mean, since Stacey got sent down, you think you're in charge of the gang. Why can't it be both of us?'

Rachel grinned and threw an arm around Claire's shoulder, pulling her close. 'Don't be daft, you nutter. I don't run the gang – we do.'

'It doesn't feel like that.'

Rachel pushed her away playfully. 'We could have some real fun with them, if you like?' When Claire frowned, she continued. 'We could play one against the other; get the low down on who they like best.'

Claire looked away.

'What's wrong with that?'

'You always want to know who's the best.'

'Don't go all moody on me,' Rachel whined. She held a ten pound note at each end and wiggled it about. 'I've lifted this from Mum. Let's go and get some lager.'

As they ran across Davy Road towards the square, they made a car slow down by running in front of it, giggling and laughing. Looks wise, if it wasn't for a small scar to the right of Rachel's eye where their brother, Danny, had pushed her from the seesaw at the age of five, it was hard to tell them apart. Compared to their mother, who was five foot and a dot, they were a few inches taller. They both had short, red hair. Their trousers were always baggy, always inches too long and bunched up at the ankles. They wore no jewellery, no make up: no bling was allowed in the Mitchell Mob, except for piercings. Sometimes it was as hard to tell their gender as it was to tell them apart.

Gang wise, it was hard to distinguish them from any of the other girls. The Mitchell Mob, as they called themselves, dressed in a uniform of dark hoodies, top of the range trainers and baggy jeans or tracksuit bottoms. They all rode mountain bikes, swapped around consistently to hide their identity further. If any of them were in trouble, it was hard to prove.

As a gang, each one of them had their own identity, but to an outsider, they were a bunch of girls out to cause mayhem. Pack mentality almost always took over and any innocent bystander walking past could become their latest prey. Tonight, there were five girls waiting for them in their usual spot outside the doorway of Shop&Save. It was the perfect place for them to cause maximum trouble. They could also scrounge cigarettes and the odd can of lager from people coming out. That was, until they were moved on – they were always moved on eventually, either by the store manager or the local police. It depended on how rowdy they became.

The girls were sitting on the low railing separating the car park from the walkway. So far the promised rain for the evening had failed to materialise but that, and the added menace of darkness falling, meant that it was fairly quiet.

'What's up?' Rachel asked as she stood in front of them, her hands shoved deep in her pockets.

'Nowt really,' said Ashley Bruce. She was small and thin, with black hair cut into a severe bob, several earrings dangling from both ears. 'It's boring. There's no one about yet.'

Rachel glanced up and down Davy Road, wondering if Ashley meant victims for them to taunt or the boys. Rachel had arranged to meet Jake Tunnicliffe at quarter past eight – unless he stood her up again like last week, the bastard.

'Heard about Stacey?' Louise Woodcock chirped up from the end of the railing. Her right foot swung back and forth in a semi-circle over the crumbling surface of the path.

Rachel's green eyes narrowed at the mention of Stacey's name. Stacey Hunter was her enemy. 'What about her?' she asked.

'She gets out soon.'

'Already?' said Claire. 'I thought she had at least another three months to do.'

'Let out on good behaviour.'

'More like she's been sucking up,' Rachel said deliberately.

The other girls laughed; even so, unease at the revelation could clearly be sensed. Stacey Hunter had been sent down for nine months for getting caught after mugging a woman and leaving her with a front tooth missing. For Rachel, it had been pure poetry as her biggest threat was locked up for a while. After battling it out with Louise, she and Claire had taken over and made headway with the membership. Now, instead of five members, there were seven of them - soon to be eight, if the rumours about Charlie Morrison were true. Rachel had been working on her for a month to join the Mitchell Mob.

'I suppose she'll take over again when she's out,' Louise said with a taunt in her voice.

Rachel shook her head. 'I don't think so. This is mine and Claire's patch now. Right, girls?' She stared at each one of them; sitting together they looked like a line of blackbirds on a telephone wire.

One by one, in uncomfortable silence, they nodded agreement.

'Good.' Rachel squeezed in between Shell Walker and Hayley Jones. 'Anyone got any fags?'

'Naw,' said Hayley.

'Me neither,' said Shell.

'My old man only had two so I couldn't lift any,' said Louise.

'So whose turn is it?' As all eyes went to the ground, Rachel sighed. 'I suppose it'll have to be me then. Claire, watch my back while I get some, would you?'

Claire nodded, catching the disrespectful look that came from Louise. Even though she and Rachel had the upper hand, it made her feel uneasy. Louise had brought up Stacey getting out next month, and if it was obvious to her that she was looking forward to it more than she was letting on, it would be obvious to the others.

She ran to Rachel as she stood outside the doors of Shop&Save, hoping to blag the odd cigarette here and there until she had enough. She glanced back at the gang again, huddled together in a circle now. They looked like they were in deep discussion about something or other – or someone or other. A shiver ran through her body.

It wasn't easy being Claire Bradley when your opposite had nerves of steel.

CHAPTER FOUR

On the Sunday evening of their first weekend on Stanley Avenue, Caren was snuggled up on the sofa watching television when John appeared in the doorway. He was dressed in a white long-sleeved shirt over the top of dark jeans. Freshly showered, she could smell the tang of his aftershave from where she was sitting. All at once she felt a tingle of excitement - maybe she could entice him into having a quickie before he went out. But her smile morphed into a frown when he picked up his wallet and put it in his back pocket.

'Surely you're not off out already?' She looked at the clock: it was just past eight thirty. 'You said it would be for a quick pint.'

'I thought I'd make a night of it.' John avoided her eye as he piled loose change into his pocket. 'Haven't been out in a while and it'll be good to catch up with Pete and a few of the old crowd.'

'Nice of you to ask me along too,' she sulked, knowing full well that she wouldn't have gone regardless.

John bent down, resting his hands on her thighs. 'It's only the one night.' He stuck out his bottom lip, looking very much like a five-year-old. 'I've been a good boy lately, haven't I?'

Caren tried not to smirk. God, he smelt so good. She ran her hands up and over his back.

'Don't be too late,' she told him, not wanting to start another bickering match. They'd been doing their fair share of that since the move – silly things over something and nothing.

'I won't.' John leaned forward to kiss her.

'And don't make too much noise when you come in,' she yelled just before the door shut.

She went through to the kitchen, cursing again as she eyed the bare walls stripped and ready to be wallpapered with something more decent than the ancient woodchip that had taken an age to remove: the ghastly stuff had come off like chewing gum. Now that the units had been cleaned, they were fairly decent, despite the one drawer handle hanging on precariously, but they were nothing compared to the kitchen in their last house. Caren had been so proud to show it off to friends, host dinner parties there, drinks after work - now she wouldn't dare tell anyone her new address. Call her a snob but she'd rather let people think she'd dropped off the face of the earth than tell them she was back on the Mitchell Estate.

She reached a bottle of wine from the fridge and poured a large glass. At least they could pay for small luxuries, although she knew they wouldn't even be able to afford those if John didn't get some sort of work soon. This past week, they'd spent a lot of time doing the vast list of odd jobs needed to get the property to a decent standard. Everything else, she was sure, would mostly be completed over the next few days. At least then they could both start looking for work. And maybe John would meet new people: there was no way she was going to make tonight's meet with Pete something that happened on a regular basis. Pete would bring John down and she wasn't going to have that.

She rummaged in the cupboard for a bag of crisps, thinking that she'd get the local newspaper tomorrow evening and they could scour it together. She wasn't afraid to go out to work for someone else again. She'd cook, she'd clean, she'd shine shoes, clean up the muck from... well, maybe not that last one. Caren took a quick look at her manicured nails, splaying one hand out in front. They were her pride and joy, her nails. Personally she thought a woman wasn't dressed properly if her nails were shoddy. She wondered: maybe now it was time to get the business she'd been planning up and running.

Across at number twenty-five, Gina was flat out on the settee when John walked into her living room. She'd been watching some reality TV crap but her eyes flitted from top to toe in a second to take in his clean shoes, designer clothes and the crispness of his white shirt. Immediately, she felt her cheeks burn, the smell of his aftershave having the same effect on her as it had on Caren a few minutes earlier.

'Hi, Gina,' John said, moving aside a pile of magazines before sitting down on the armchair. He stared at the overflowing coffee table, before putting them down onto the floor.

'Hi, John.'

Pete handed John a can of lager before rushing upstairs to get changed. He'd only got in minutes earlier. It was obvious what today's cash in hand job had been: he smelt of petrol.

She swung her feet round to the floor, trying to pull in her stomach as she sat upright. 'How are you doing?' she asked, running a hand through hair she knew hadn't been washed for five days. 'Getting settled now?'

John nodded after taking a slurp of his drink. 'It's not so bad on Stanley Avenue. Caren was dreading coming back, though.'

I bet she was, the snotty cow, Gina thought but kept it to herself.

'I suppose it will take a while for you both to settle,' she said instead.

John shook his head. 'Not me. I feel like I've never been away.'

'Oh?' Gina sensed an information giveaway.

'I've always liked The Mitchell Estate. It feels like coming home again to me.' He grinned. 'It's great catching up with Pete and seeing old friends.'

Gina sat forward more, hoping to feign polite interest rather than curiosity. 'What does Caren think? I heard you had a lovely house.'

'We did. It was a corker, I have to admit. Caren is a real homemaker.'

Ouch.

'She can turn anything into a better place. I suppose in theory we can live anywhere and she'll make it into far more than it is.'

'So Caren isn't happy about the move, then?' Gina dug deeper, cursing the fact that she was talking to a man. Hadn't he got any idea what information she was after!

John took another swig of lager. 'No, she hates it right now – says something about us moving off here within twelve months but I can't see that happening.'

'Why's that?'

'Well, we're in far too much debt and –'

'Right, Johnno,' said Pete, appearing in the doorway. 'Sorry about that – didn't get in from work until late.'

Compared to John, Gina didn't even want to look at Pete in his farmer-checked-shirt that hadn't seen an iron since she'd bought it for him from the market, jeans that weren't faded for style but from age and white, dirty trainers. His hair was gelled back like a clone of Dracula.

'Work?' She huffed. 'Siphoning petrol and diesel from vehicles isn't earning a decent living like normal people do.'

'Pays for your fags, doesn't it, you moody cow.'

Pete leaned forward to take one from amongst the detritus on the coffee table but Gina slapped his hand. 'Piss off. It looks like the girls have already helped themselves, the cheeky mares. And you can get your own after that sarcastic comment, Pete Bradley.'

'Suits me.' Pete smirked as he pulled out a handful of notes, throwing a tenner into her lap. 'Here, I'm feeling generous. Buy yourself another pack.'

John laughed and stood up. 'Nothing's changed with you two, I see? Still bickering all the time.'

'She wouldn't have me any other way,' Pete replied. 'She knows where her bread is buttered.'

Gina faked a yawn. 'Oh please,' she said. 'Go now before I slice you in two with my razor sharp tongue.'

The door closed behind them a few moments later and the house felt instantly gloomy. Gina pulled her feet up onto the settee again, reached for the remote and switched the volume up on the television. God, that had been embarrassing. Trust Pete to try and make a fool of her. You'd think that over twenty years together, she'd be used to his put downs by now but still they hurt – especially when said in front of John, who she hadn't seen for so long. Who, she realised, she still had a massive crush on. But then again, that wasn't hard when you stood him next to Pete. To Gina's eyes, John had got better with age.

It just wasn't fair.

*

'It's quarter to nine. Do you think she'll show?' Claire asked her sister as they sat on the low railing outside Shop&Save with the other girls. Although it had been raining for most of that day, it had stopped now but the wind had picked up instead. Crisp packets and chocolate wrappers over by the doorway created a mini tornado. They closed their eyes momentarily as a cloud of dust flew up into the air.

'She'd better, if she knows what's good for her,' Rachel said with a scowl.

Just before nine, Charlie Morrison came running around the corner, not stopping until she was level with them. She sat down on the railing next to Claire, holding her side as she caught her breath.

'Soz I'm late,' she said eventually. 'Mum wanted me to look after my baby brother. I told her to get lost so she clouted me one. I ended up getting locked in my room.' Charlie ran a hand through short, blonde hair, messing up her carefully styled spikes. 'I waited 'til I heard her on the phone and legged it through my bedroom window, out onto the porch.'

Rachel grinned. 'Nice one. Won't she wait up for you, though?'

'Don't care – I'm always getting lamped when I get home anyway, so I might as well have some fun while I'm out.' She smiled shyly at the others, suddenly her nerve deserting her. Her gaze dropped to the floor.

It didn't go unnoticed by Rachel. She stood up and nudged her sharply. 'You still up for it?'

Charlie nodded. 'What do you want me to do?'

'Ever robbed anyone?'

'No.'

'Then that's what you can do.'

Charlie swallowed. 'Can I pick a victim?'

Rachel shook her head slowly. 'No, we'll choose.' She looked at the others. 'Won't we, girls?'

Some of the group nodded.

'Yeah, let's not make it too easy,' said Ashley. 'I remember my initiation. It was hell.'

'Only because you were such a wimp,' Claire teased, squeezing in between her and Louise on the railing.

'Me? A wimp?' Ashley faked a hurt expression. '*You*,' she pointed to Rachel, 'chose a hard knob for me and I got a good kicking.'

'We got our hands on some good booze though,' Shell sniggered, 'while you were on the floor.'

As the girls continued to cajole and laugh, Rachel watched the shop doorway to see who was coming and going. It was a good fifteen minutes before she spotted two girls, one of whom had given her lip at school, and she knew the initiation could go ahead. Time to kick ass as The Mitchell Mob.

'Charlie, get their bags and see what's in them,' she told her.

Charlie grinned when she saw who Rachel had picked out for her. She interlaced her fingers, pushed them back and stretched them out in anticipation. 'Which one shall I do first? Or shall I do them both?'

'Both!'

'Okay. Oy, you two!' Charlie shouted as she ran towards them. 'Care to join us for a moment?'

The two girls stopped in their tracks as Charlie reached them, the others not far behind.

'It's Sarah, isn't it?' Charlie spoke to the younger one. 'Sarah Syphilis.'

The girls burst into laughter and circled the sisters.

Sarah glanced at her older sister, just before her bag was whipped off her shoulder.

'Whatcha doing out here, all alone, at the shops?' asked Charlie.

'Give that back to her,' the older girl said.

Charlie grabbed the collar of her jacket and pulled her close. 'Don't push your luck, Jill Crawford, if you know what's good for you.'

'If you know what's good for you, you'll back off right now,' Jill dared to speak again. 'I'll get my brother on you and then you won't be so sure of yourself.'

Charlie slapped her hard across her cheek. 'Do you think I'm scared of a brother coming after me?' She punched Jill in the stomach, watched her face crumple a second before her knees.

While Sarah's bag was searched and the contents thrown into the road by Claire and Hayley, Charlie laid into Jill. Twice she elbowed her in the back, then she brought her fist up underneath and caught her in the chin. Jill tried to grab Charlie's hood but Charlie was too strong for her. Another punch in the stomach and she curled up in a ball, trying to fend off the remaining blows, praying that Charlie wouldn't use her feet. All the time, Sarah screamed as she watched what was happening to her sister, the rest of the girls in the gang egging Charlie on. People began to appear at the doorway of Shop&Save. Someone shouted over angrily at them.

'Punch her lights out,' said Louise, ignoring them.

'Yeah, kick her in the head so that she can hear bells ringing,' added Hayley.

'Give her one for me,' cried Claire, tossing Sarah's purse on the ground in disgust. 'There's hardly anything in here, just a few measly coins. Next time, Rachel, we need someone with a wallet.'

Rachel shot her twin a warning look. 'Don't tell me what we need to do,' she hissed. 'Or you can take down the next victim.'

'No way! It's not my turn again. I did –'

'Well, shut the fuck up then.' Rachel moved towards Jill, who by now was crawling away, and pulled her head up sharply by the hair, delighted to see fear in the girl's eyes. It was a perfect time to reiterate what they were all about.

'So, your olds – who do you tell them attacked you?' she asked.

'I – I didn't see who it was,' Jill muttered.

'And who do you tell everyone else who attacked you?'

'The Mitchell Mob,' Jill sobbed.

Rachel shoved her forward head first and Jill fell to all fours. For good measure, she kicked her up the backside. 'Now, get out of my sight, you pathetic loser.' She turned to Charlie, who had returned after chasing Sarah away, and grinned.

'You're in.'

34

CHAPTER FIVE

Caren padded across the dark red quarry tiles, being careful to avoid the chunk missing from the corner of one right in the middle of the kitchen floor, and yanked the cold water tap clockwise as much as was physically possible. The bloody thing wouldn't stop dripping. Drip, drip, drip, all day, every day since they'd moved in. She leaned on the kitchen worktop and sighed loudly.

Two weeks they'd been in this dump and, despite the jobs they'd carried out, she hadn't begun to make a dent in making it feel like home. She looked out at the tip of a rear garden: she could just about make out a pathway through the jungle of grass and overgrown hedges. A mass of green, apart from the huge pile of rubbish left by the previous tenant – she'd been onto Mitchell Housing Association and been told that she'd have to shift it herself! Compared to the house they'd left behind, this garden could have fitted onto her decking area before heading towards the well-maintained, landscaped gardens.

Even the late September day was trying to be cheery. She squinted as the autumn sun peeked out from behind a rain cloud. It was ten thirty. After coming in at 2am the night before and waking with a hangover, John had taken the car to have two new tyres because it had failed its MOT. Not able to stand another minute alone with the few remaining boxes left to unpack, she grabbed her keys and bag and headed for the door. It was too depressing to face right now; she had to get out. A trip across the shops would do her good, even if just for a bit of fresh air.

She walked down the front path and came face to face with Gina Bradley. She cursed silently underneath her breath.

Gina spotted her at the same time. Fuck! If she'd known she was going to bump into Mrs Frigging Perfect, she would have made more of an effort before she'd left the house. As it was, she was only nipping out for some fags to get out of Pete's hair. They'd been arguing for well over an hour; she'd stormed out with a slam of the back door. So, wearing antique leggings that sagged absurdly at the knees, slippers and a black T-shirt, her hair unkempt and not a flicker of age-defying make up on, she was looking dire to say the least.

She walked slowly down the path, glancing in Caren's direction but trying not to make eye contact. Damn, she looked as good as she had when she'd watched her moving in. Her hair hung straight like a velvet curtain, framing her face on either side. She wore make up to enhance her beauty, black trousers and a smart jacket that looked like it had cost a fortune. Gina could hear her heels tippy-tapping down the steps from here. Finished off with a Burberry scarf knotted around her neck, to Gina, she oozed class.

They reached the street at exactly the same time.

Caren knew it would be awkward when they first met again but she wasn't going to be the one who was discourteous. Brought up with manners, she knew it would give her the upper hand if she used them. Gina would assume she wouldn't want to bother with her. Well, she didn't, but she could at least hide it well.

'Hi, Gina,' she smiled falsely.

'Hello,' said Gina, giving her the once over in as intimidating a manner as she could muster.

A silence followed as both women stood still. Caren wondered what to say next while Gina stared at her.

'Where are you off to?' asked Gina sharply.

'To the shops. I fancied a bit of fresh air.' Another silence. 'You?'

Gina shrugged. 'Off to my mum's – you remember, she lives at number twenty-eight? My dad died but she's going strong, the old doll.'

'Oh.' Twenty-eight was next door but one. Caren hoped there wouldn't be any more of the Bradley clan in Stanley Avenue. One was more than she could bear right now.

But Gina picked up on the 'oh' like a dog with a rabbit.

'What do you mean, *oh*?'

'Nothing.' Caren took a step forward, wondering how quickly she could get away.

'I suppose this avenue is too low down for you and your precious John,' Gina spat out nastily. 'Me and my family have quite a few houses here. My sister, Leah lives at number thirty-three – not that she's home much now since she started seeing her fella. So, that's three of us. Is that enough scum for you in one place?'

Even though she'd half expected it, Caren was taken aback by Gina's hostility. 'I didn't mean anything,' she said.

'Good, because there's nothing to worry your little head about. We won't be bothering with the likes of you.'

'And what exactly is that supposed to mean?'

Gina pointed at her. 'You... you think you're so high and mighty but you're as low as the rest of us. What brought you back to the Mitchell Estate, hmm? Remember what you said? Because I do. 'I'm never coming back to this shit-hole', you said.'

'I wouldn't be back if it wasn't for...' Caren's words faltered as she realised she was about to give away more than she'd intended.

'If it wasn't for you going bankrupt?' Gina smiled, loving the look on Caren's face.

'How did you find out?' Beneath her make-up, Caren paled. She couldn't believe John had blabbed about that. How dare he tell everyone their problems!

'He told me and Pete last night, when they came home pissed.' Gina smiled even more when she saw Caren's eyes widen. 'Didn't he tell you that he stopped by our house afterwards? I was going to go to bed because it was so late but I'm glad I stayed up now. They brought back fish and chips and shared it all with me. I did loads of bread and butter and we opened some cans. You're not mad with him, are you?'

Trying to keep her emotions from spilling out, Caren shook her head. 'No, I'm not his keeper. And you know John, he can look after himself.' She made a big deal about checking her watch. 'Look, I'd better be going, I'll be late back else.'

Gina popped up a hand and waggled her fingers. 'Ta-ra for now,' she said to Caren's disappearing form. Watching her scurry away, she smiled and congratulated herself. Even looking like she did as opposed to Caren's picture of beauty, she'd managed to get the upper hand. She opened the gate to her mum's house and practically ran up the path. Suddenly the need for a cigarette had gone.

Ruth Millington turned the key in the lock of number thirty-two Stanley Avenue, pushing open the door quickly so that she could put the bags she had carried down. She stood upright and rubbed at the small of her back. God, they had been heavy. She shouldn't have tried to carry that many but she hadn't realised how far away she was here from the bus stop. Her fingers had ridges where the bags had dug into them. She clenched and unclenched them to get back their circulation.

Tears welled in her eyes as she gazed around the dismal hallway, at the yellow stripy wallpaper that was peeling off more than it was stuck onto the walls. The carpet had seen far better days, worn and grimy with some spectacular dirty marks, but it would have to stay down. Either that or they could all walk on bare floorboards. There was no money to spend on flooring.

She dragged heavy feet into the living room. It was a bright space, a large window at either end. The fireplace was made from old, cream tiles and probably worth a fortune now if it wasn't chipped in a dozen places. There was no carpet in there. Ruth looked above the windows: there were no curtain rails. There wasn't even a bulb in the electrical fitting hanging pitifully from the ceiling.

Feeling familiar panic bubbling up inside her, Ruth tried to keep it at bay. She went upstairs. Directly in front was the bathroom. Although she'd seen the property the week before, the only thing she could remember about the room was the state of the bath and the toilet. Tentatively, she pushed open the door, hoping to find that the cleaning fairies had taken pity on her, but no such luck. There was a rust mark between the hot and cold taps down the white-enamel bath where the water must have dripped for years. It swirled down into the plug hole. Ruth doubted that would come off, no matter how much bleach and elbow grease she used.

She peered into the toilet, gagging at what she saw, and knocked down the lid. The force of it slamming made it slide to the right, only one hinge keeping it in place. Ruth flushed it, wishing it would take her away into the deepest, darkest depths of nowhere. But then again, wasn't she already there?

The eerie silence suddenly became welcome as she stepped in and out of the three bedrooms. At least the boys had separate rooms, even though they were now living in Stanley Avenue. She hadn't wanted to move here but she'd had no choice. There were no more empty properties with three bedrooms. Two bedrooms would have been a challenge. Mason and Jamie would never give her a moment's peace if they'd had to share a room. And all this because that bastard Martin Wallace had decided that he needed some space. Three years she'd given him and what had he given her, apart from the odd backhander and a huge dose of depression and anxiety? Nothing. He hadn't even had the decency to help her move, and she'd had to fork out for a removal van.

Finally, she made her way back downstairs and into the kitchen. The units were made from white Formica, the cheapest you could get on a job lot, she reckoned. A front of one drawer was missing and two doors hung lopsided. She ran a hand over the grubby worktop before bursting into tears. The house would take ages to get right, especially with her arm playing up again. She pulled up her sleeve and pecked at the scab forming there. Then she dug her nails into it. It stung like hell, but she scratched until it was bleeding again. Quickly, she rolled down her sleeve before she did even more damage.

A knock came at the front door, echoing around the hallway: she could almost feel the emptiness from where she stood. Ruth wiped her eyes before moving.

'Morning love,' said a tall, thin man, carrying two small boxes. 'Where do you want these going?'

'Mason's room. Turn right at the top of the stairs, back of the house.'

The man nodded. 'Right you are. Ooh, is that the kettle I hear boiling?'

'I doubt it,' said Ruth. 'It's in one of the boxes on your van.

Couldn't carry it on the bus, could I?'

The man wouldn't be deterred. 'I tell you what,' he nodded his head towards the door. 'I'll find the kettle, you make a drink and I'll share my digestives with you. What do you say?'

Ruth nodded: anything to get him gone and on his way so she could be alone. She couldn't bear to be among cheery people at the moment, especially ones whom she was paying to do a job for her. Alone with her thoughts, her feelings, her sorrows – that's what she needed. Even if it was ten minutes before she had to fetch the boys from school; before all hell broke loose again.

'I've just bumped into that stuck up cow, Caren Williams,' Gina said to Barbara as she let herself into her mum's house and found her in the kitchen. 'She's already getting on my nerves with her high and mighty attitude.'

Barbara was sitting at the table, three curlers in the front of her grey hair, sipping at a cup of tea.

'At least she made an effort to work and move off this estate,' she replied.

'She thinks she's too good for Stanley Avenue. I'll show her if she doesn't watch with the attitude.' Gina slid her hand across towards an open packet of biscuits. Barbara slapped her fingers away. 'Ow! What was that for?'

'I'm ashamed of you, Gina. Why couldn't you be nice to Caren? She must be feeling really vulnerable right now, what with losing her house and all.'

Gina folded her arms. If she knew she'd get this much grief, she wouldn't have bothered to escape from Pete! 'Bloody hell, Mum, you've changed your tune. You said she'd had her come-uppance when she first moved in.'

'Yes, but that was before I'd seen what she's done to that house.' Barbara looked up from the magazine she was scanning. 'She's cleaned every window, all the sills, cleared the front garden of rubbish and John's cut back all the hedges. You can't walk up your pathway without getting soaked when it's been raining – and there's enough rubbish in *your* garden to have a ten foot bonfire.'

'You know we haven't got any hedge cutters,' Gina offered

lamely, already anticipating her mother's reply.

'You could borrow mine at any time – even at my age, I still use them. And stop making excuses for that lazy bastard you call a husband. Why can't he be like John?'

Why indeed, thought Gina.

'Mum, don't start all this again.' She pushed herself out of the chair and switched on the kettle.

'Hit a nerve, have I?' Barbara smirked.

'Well, you've never worked a day in your life, so I don't see how you can go on about me.'

'I didn't need to work because your Dad provided for this family. Not everyone was on the take. I had my morals.'

'Yeah, morals you forgot when you were arguing or fighting with someone from the estate. Honestly, Mum, it's like the pot calling the kettle black. You were no better than me.'

Barbara relented as she looked over at her daughter. 'I suppose you're right. But I really wish you'd make more of an effort with your life. You need to do something with your time instead of waiting for your next benefits payment to come through.'

'That's not all I live for,' Gina retorted. 'I have my family.'

Barbara frowned. 'Your bloody girls have been up to no good again, though. I heard Mrs Watson talking about them earlier.'

'You don't believe anything she says, do you?'

'They aren't exactly saints.'

'I know but they're kids. I bet me and Leah were the same when we were their age.'

Barbara smiled then. 'You were! And I had your brother too. I don't know how I coped with the lot of you.' She pointed at Gina. 'Remember that time when you were going through your punk stage and you went beating up anyone who didn't like the same music as you?'

Gina giggled. 'What about Leah with that old man she was seeing? I remember you and Dad being livid.'

'Of course we were. He was a bloody pervert, if you ask me. I mean, our Leah was fifteen and he was nearing on thirty. It should never be allowed.' Barbara reached for her daughter's hand and took it gently in her own. 'Seriously, Gina, I worry about you.

You're getting old before your time.'

Gina stared at her mother. She knew she was being compared to Caren Williams and that hurt. She made coffee and plonked the mugs down onto the table with a thud. Tears stung her eyes but she refused to let them fall.

'Hey,' Barbara squeezed her hand quickly, 'don't get upset now. You know I only want the best for you – for all of you, really.'

'Don't compare me to her, then.'

'I'm not. I couldn't possibly...' Barbara stopped, the unspoken words saying so much regardless.

'You see,' Gina pulled away her hand, 'even you think I'm a slob.'

'No, I –'

She clasped the hem of her T-shirt. 'So you think I look good in this?' Then she pointed at her head. 'You think my hair looks like I've stepped out of a salon? You think I make an effort every day?'

'No, I just think you should make more of an effort every now and again. Our Leah makes an effort and she's –'

'She's thinner than me? Is that what you were going to say?'

'I was going to say she's younger than you.'

'She doesn't have three kids or Pete for a husband,' Gina pouted. 'She's not –'

'If there's anything going, you could work the twilight shift with her.'

'I don't want to work in some stupid factory doing menial tasks, thank you very much.'

'So you'd rather be supported by that useless layabout of yours?' Barbara folded her arms. 'All those knock off jobs he does? They'll catch up with him one day, like they did with your brother.'

Gina stood up, the chair scraping across the floor beneath her. 'I'm sick of everyone thinking that my family are low life. And I can cope with all the jibes and the stares from everyone else, but to hear it from my own mother? That really stings.'

'I didn't mean –'

'Yes, you did.'

Gina turned and left the house. Would her family ever think she was good for anything?

CHAPTER SIX

As soon as John came back with their car and she'd closed the back door behind him, Caren laid into him.

'You had no right to tell them that we're bankrupt!' she shouted. 'Or anyone, come to think of it. It's our business!'

'I'm sorry! I didn't think it was such a big deal.' John pushed past her into the kitchen.

Caren prodded him forcefully in his back as he stood over the sink. 'I don't want everyone knowing that we have no money.'

John ran the tap before filling the glass with water. He took a huge gulp.

Caren prodded him in the back again. 'Are you listening to me? I didn't want anyone to know.'

'They would have found out sooner or later. You can't keep anything secret around here.'

'Not where Gina Bradley is concerned! She'll take great pleasure in blabbing her mouth off and then...' tears formed in her eyes, 'everyone will know that we're stuck here!'

John put the glass down onto the drainer. 'Do you have to keep dragging it up at every opportunity?'

'It's the truth. It's not going to get any better and I –'

'I've had enough of this. I'm going out.'

'But you've only just got in!'

'For your information, I'm going to carry on tidying up the back garden. You can help, if you like. Or is your love of gardening supposed to be a secret too?'

'I'm surprised you're not going across to the scummy side of the street. I bet you'd prefer it over there, slumming it with Gina and Pete!'

John slammed the back door on his way out. Tears pricked at her eyes again. What was happening to them? Was this house always going to bring them down? Ever since they'd got here they'd done nothing but argue. Caren needed John's support as much as he needed hers, but he didn't seem able to offer it. Why, oh why, hadn't they been quicker on the uptake of that tiny two bedroom flat she'd found, just on the outskirts of the city? If they'd seen it a couple of days earlier, they could have been in there, but someone had beaten them to it. It wouldn't have been ideal – it would have meant living in each other's pockets but it would have been in a nicer neighbourhood – far away from the Mitchell Estate.

But the real thing that annoyed her was that she'd been left with everything to sort out. She now had full control of their finances – not that they had a lot of money, but what they received from now on, what pittance was left over after all the debt payments had been made at the end of each month, was due to go into an account in her sole name. John wasn't good with money so every week she intended to draw out a set amount of cash and nothing else; once it had gone, there'd be no more until the following week. It would be like being sixteen again, when she'd made sure they'd saved every penny for a deposit towards getting off the estate. It had taken a lot of hard work to get where they were. She wasn't going to lose everything else as well as that, no matter what.

Caren couldn't bear the thought of anyone else being with John if they were to split up due to the pressure they were under. Like most couples they had their ups and downs but they got through them. Could she cope without him forever? And then to know that he'd be in the arms of someone else? She wasn't even going to think about it. She wiped away the lone tear that had fallen, sniffed and went to join John in the garden.

Feeling well and truly stressed after her disastrous morning, Gina slumped in front of the television and lit another cigarette. The house was empty now. It was eleven thirty - Pete had most probably gone to the pub, seeing as he had no work on at the moment.

Looking around the living room made her even more upset.

Faded white paintwork; the ceiling a nicotine yellow colour. Cheap wallpaper that had been up since they had moved in sixteen years ago – well, what remained of it - torn off or scuffed in so many places, drawn on when the kids were younger. The door leading to the stairs had a huge hole in the bottom of it where Danny had kicked it in temper and it hadn't been replaced because they'd have to pay for the damage. And she didn't even want to look at the state of the threadbare carpet. What colour it had started its life as she could barely remember – which added insult to injury as she'd watched the vast array of wallpaper rolls and paint tins that had gone into Caren's house over the past couple of weeks. She'd seen John a couple of times with paint splattered jeans, Caren with the same. Pete would never dream of doing any DIY, no matter how much she nagged. That's what had started the argument this morning.

She recalled the last time she'd had a go at him to do something around the house. That disagreement had turned into a full-blown row, and Pete had thrown his ready-meal across the kitchen. There were still remnants of the artificial colourings on the grout in the tiles around the sink that the housing association had fitted. Despite her best efforts at trying to get it white again, it looked like the grout had gone rusty.

Gina clenched her teeth. Was she going to be compared to Caren fucking Williams all of the time now? Even her mother thought she could do better. Idly, she switched on the television. There was a talk show on featuring a bunch of male strippers. She stared a little closer. One of the men looked a bit like John. Gina suddenly felt a rush of heat as she recalled how she was infatuated by him at school. She wished she could get his attention again.

Suddenly, she had a thought. She quickly turned to the television menu and scrolled down through it. Sure enough, there was a makeover program on. Perhaps there was a way she could improve herself. It was never too late, surely?

Engrossed in the program, she jumped when the back door slammed and Pete come rushing into the room. She grabbed for the remote but he'd already seen the television screen.

'What are you doing back?' she stammered, this time her face flushing through embarrassment.

'I need my tool bag and my steel toe caps – a job's come up. What the hell are you watching?'

'Nothing!'

'You'll never make anything of yourself sitting on the settee resting that fat arse of yours.'

Gina glowered at him. 'Thanks for the vote of confidence,' she snapped. 'And why would I make an effort for you? You don't give a shit about me anymore.'

'That's because you look like you do.' Pete searched out his boots behind the settee. They were caked in mud, which he brushed off onto the carpet. 'You need to do some exercise if you want to look good, before that arse stretches from here to Blackpool. I keep telling you not to stuff your face.'

'Shut up.' Gina turned the volume up on the television. 'You'd never notice if I did change myself. You'd be far too busy down the pub.'

Pete laughed. 'Don't be daft, woman. If you made more of an effort I wouldn't have to spend my time at the pub.' He snorted. 'You are so stupid.'

'So why do you come home to me?' Gina taunted.

'Ah, that's easy.' Pete ran his tongue across his top lip. 'You do a mean blowjob.'

Gina flung a cushion at him as he headed for the door. Pete stood in the doorway, pushing his tongue into his cheek simulating fellatio. Gina threw another cushion but he'd gone before it fell to the floor.

She turned the television back to the previous channel. The credits on the program were rolling: damn, she'd missed the end. Now she'd never see what Stephanie Lathisha from Chester had been transformed into.

She picked up one of the twin's magazines and flicked through it. Maybe there was something she could do to get Pete interested again. She was tired of solo sex and her batteries were running low on her vibrator. It was too ambitious to lose three stone in three days and the thought of exercise made her shudder. So what about a new image: clothes, shoes, underwear? But that would take money and she hadn't got any of that. Neither had she got the figure to put into it to look attractive.

She turned the page to see an article about the latest trend in hairstyles. Fingering her own hair as she looked at each one, she brought the magazine nearer to study picture two. It was a short, choppy, extremely of-the-time hairstyle. The model had the same red colour hair as she did and she didn't look much younger than Gina so she might be able to pull it off. Actually, she looked about sixteen but Gina ignored this fact.

Maybe a new hairstyle could be the start of her new image. All it took was one step, then maybe she could go on a diet and then she could pick and choose what clothes she wanted to wear.

And maybe John Williams would fancy you.

Gina shook her head to rid herself of the image that had invaded it. She and John, bodies entwined on Madame fucking Williams' settee, having sex right under her nose, as John was unable to resist the new Gina. She felt that familiar tingling between her legs as she imagined where he would kiss her, where his hands would be, how his body would feel on top of hers. That would show stuck-up Caren that she meant business.

Without further ado, she picked up her phone and rang Tracy Tanner, the local mobile hairdresser.

'I'm bunking off school this afternoon, Claire. Fancy coming into town with me?'

'Yeah, I'm sick of this course already. Shall we have lunch out?'

'Why of course.' Rachel put on a posh accent. 'I think we can run to a *Mac-o-Donald's*. What do you say?'

'Indeed, indeed.' Claire nodded. She gave a royal wave. 'And one might run to a strawberry milkshake too.'

Rachel grinned before breaking out into a run, her sister following closely behind. They charged through the school gates and out into the rabbit warren of streets that made up the Mitchell Estate. In minutes, they were on a bus heading for the shopping centre in Stockleigh.

'Mum'll kill us if anyone sees us today,' said Claire.

'Don't be so whiney,' said Rachel, stretching her legs across the seat behind Claire so that no one could sit next to her.

'I'm just saying.' Claire turned back to face her. 'She'll go mad if we're caught again.'

'We won't have to get caught then.' Rachel looked up as the bus pulled into the kerb at the next stop and a short, squat man got on. He looked to be in his late fifties.

'Ooh, here comes moaning Archie Meredith from Christopher Avenue,' said Rachel.

The girls watched as he paid his fare and marched down the aisle to a seat a few rows in front of theirs. Before he sat down, he scowled at them.

'Did you see that?' said Rachel incredulously. 'He looked at us as if we were shit.' She got to her feet. 'Come on, Claire. Let's have some fun.'

Claire slid along the seat and followed Rachel as she sat behind Archie. He was reading a newspaper.

Rachel leaned forward. 'What're you doing on the bus, Archie? Is your car knackered?'

'Mind your own business,' he grunted.

'What're you reading?' asked Claire.

'I bet he's only looking at the pictures,' nodded Rachel.

Archie glanced over his shoulder and frowned at them.

'I bet he's staring at tits on page three.'

Claire laughed loudly.

Archie ignored them and turned over the page.

'Tits. Tits. Tits.'

This time, Archie took the bait. He turned to Rachel. 'Act your age, you stupid girl!'

'Who are you calling stupid, you old fucker!' Rachel glared back at him.

'Why, you cheeky little cow! I suppose you're bunking off school because you're too stupid to see the benefit of a little education?'

As Claire giggled, Rachel glared at her.

'What are you laughing at? He's dissing us, you moron.'

'I'm not a moron!'

'You are a moron,' said Archie. 'You and your sister. And your brother and your mother and father. You're all a bunch of morons.'

'I'd watch what you're saying or else I'll –'

Archie roared with laughter.

'I'm not a moron,' Claire repeated. 'I'm sick of you making out that I'm stupid all of the time.' She got up and sat nearer to the front of the bus.

'I didn't mean anything, you stupid cow,' Rachel cried after her. 'Hey, wait for me.'

'Run along, now, little girl,' said Archie. 'Go and annoy someone else; that's all you're capable of.'

Rachel stopped and turned back to him. She leaned in close, smelling old-fashioned aftershave and a fresh scent of soap. 'I'd shut the fuck up if I were you,' she told him.

'Or else you'll what?'

Rachel smiled sweetly, leaned forward and whispered in his ear. 'I'll tell everyone I saw you fucking Melissa Knight behind the shops on more than one occasion.'

'You lying little bitch!' Archie's face began to turn the colour of a tomato. 'I've never –'

'That's not what I heard.'

'It's a lie. I'd never do anything like –'

'*I* know that,' Rachel leaned back a touch so that she could look him in the eye, 'but no one else does. And you know how quickly rumours spread on the Mitchell Estate. So I'd watch who you're calling a moron, if I were you, or I'll have that rumour doing the one hundred metres in less than ten seconds.' She stood up abruptly. 'Whoops, here's my stop.'

'Come back here, you little cow!' Archie stood up too. But Rachel was already off the bus and hoping to make amends with Claire.

'What the fuck have you done –'

Gina stopped Pete mid-sentence with a raised hand and an icy stare. 'Don't you dare say anything else,' she muttered. 'It was your fault I did it in the first place.'

'Me?' Pete stared back wide-eyed. 'What did I do?'

'You said I should make more of an effort, so I did.' Gina pointed to what hair she had left on her head. 'And this is what I ended up with.'

'I didn't tell you to shave your head!'

'I haven't shaved my head!'

'You could have fooled me. You look like a –'

Gina flounced out of the room, eager to get away from his spiteful comments. She headed for the safety of the front room, only to find the girls sitting on the settee.

'What the fuck have you done to your hair?' said Rachel, eyes as wide as her father's.

By this time, Gina was close to tears. 'Don't you have a go as well,' she snapped, storming past them to run upstairs. In her bedroom, she slammed the door shut and threw herself onto the bed. Damn that Tracy Tanner. It should have been a simple haircut to get right: a short, inverted bob with a block fringe. But Tracy couldn't get both sides to an equal length, and in a fit of frustration as she watched her hair getting shorter and shorter, Gina had snatched the scissors and snipped away angrily. Tracy could then only make a bad job of a terrible mess – short back and sides with a round face was not the trendy and sexy look she had envisaged.

What was wrong with her? Gina sobbed – couldn't she get anything right? Tracy was cheap and all she could afford. Damn her mother for getting on to her this morning. Damn Pete for catching her watching the makeover show. And damn that fucking Caren. If she hadn't moved in across the street, there wouldn't be a need to make herself feel attractive.

There was a knock on the door. 'Can we come in?' asked Claire.

'Not if you're going to take the piss.'

'We're not,' said Rachel. Both girls sat down on the bed beside their mother.

Gina sat up so they could check out her hair. Immediately she saw the look in their eyes, she began to cry again. 'You see?' she sobbed. 'I look like a bloke.'

Neither of them said that she didn't but Claire gave her a hug. 'You might have known, asking Tracy to do it. I heard she got a slapping last month when she butchered Mandy Flannigan's hair. Didn't you hear about it?'

Gina shook her head.

'She wanted to go blonde. Even I know you can't put a blonde hair dye straight onto dark hair. She ended up green, it was awful. Tracy got a bloody nose for it – and Mandy paid over a hundred quid to put it right and made Tracy cough up for it. I'm surprised she hasn't stopped; I'd never use her.'

'Thanks for telling me now,' sniffed Gina.

Claire raced through to the bathroom and came back with a handful of toilet roll. She gave it to Gina before sitting down again.

'Maybe we could help you do something with it?' she proposed.

Gina huffed as she wiped her face. 'What on earth could you do with this? I'll have to wear a hat for months until it's grown back.'

'That's a great idea.' Rachel nudged her and grinned. 'How about I lift you a pink baseball cap when we next go into the town?'

'You'll do no such thing,' Gina admonished. 'If you get caught again, you'll end up in real trouble; not just from me and your father.'

'Mum, I was kidding, right?'

'It doesn't look that bad,' added Claire. 'And you can pretty it up with a hair band or some sparkly clips.'

'And it'll grow again,' said Rachel.

Gina gave them a weak smile. It would get better in time – or by downing a bottle of whisky in the interim.

'I think I need a drink.' Gina looked at them both before shuffling to sit at the edge of the bed. 'If you can sneak the bottle past your dad, I'll let you off about why you weren't at school this afternoon.'

Claire and Rachel shared a look: how did she know?

'I saw you running for the bus.'

'I'll get the bottle.' Rachel got up quickly, followed by her sister, just as eager not to be told off.

With a huge sigh, Gina dared to face the mirror. She stared at herself for a moment before starting to tug at the short strands. They were far too short for the shape of her face: she did look like a tomato, an overripe one at that. Tracy had cut a fringe into the so-called style and her ears were on show. She tried to smile and look on the bright side; at least she could wear earrings now.

But the smile faded as quickly as it had arrived. All she'd wanted to do was to look a little smarter, make an effort for a change but she'd got it wrong again. Maybe it wasn't worth the effort anyway, she mused. Maybe she *was* destined to be fat and ugly with a man's hairstyle for the rest of her days. Maybe in a cruel twist of fate her hair would never grow again and she'd have to change her name to Gerry.

'Here.' Rachel passed Claire a small bottle.

Claire sniffed. 'Mum's whisky! How did you manage that?' she asked before taking a sip.

'It was easy; I took it into our room before giving it to her.' Rachel snatched the bottle back from Claire. 'She won't notice that some of it's missing.'

The girls were on their way to the shops to meet up with the rest of the gang. Rachel was looking forward to it immensely. Tonight they had another initiation test. Leanne Bailey wanted to join the Mitchell Mob and Rachel had lined her up with something special, providing her timing went to plan.

'I bet Mum's still pissed off,' said Claire. 'Her hair looks a mess, doesn't it?'

Rachel nodded, throwing the now empty bottle over the hedge of a garden they were walking past. 'She should be taught a lesson, that Tracy. Maybe there's something we can do to get her back.'

'Like what?'

'I'm not sure; we'll have to think about it. But first, some fun.' Rachel turned to Claire. 'Let's do over Archie Meredith.'

Claire stopped. 'No, Rach, you can't do anything to him. We'll be in big trouble if we –'

Rachel sighed. 'You're whining again, Claire.'

'No, I'm not, I'm just saying –'

'We won't be doing anything – Leanne will – so chill out!'

'What will she have to do?'

'That depends. If Archie comes to the shops like he usually does, then she can wreck his car.'

Despite her misgivings, Claire felt her stomach flip over.

'If he doesn't come to the shops, then we're gonna go to his house.'

'And do what?'

'We're gonna throw a brick through his window.'

'Now who's being stupid,' said Claire.

'What do you mean?'

'All Mitchell Housing Association's properties have UPVC windows.'

Rachel sighed impatiently. 'So?'

'So, they're all fitted with double-glazing. The brick might break one glass pane but it probably won't go through two.'

'How do you know?'

'Danny told me. Completely fooled him once; he thought it would go right through. Problem was, he was trying to smash his way out of the factory he was nicking from so he got caught by the pigs.'

Rachel snarled before walking on. 'I didn't know that!'

'But at least you know now! And it'll stop us looking like idiots.' Claire ran to catch her up.

They were nearing the shops now. Rachel could see the gang up ahead waiting for them to arrive. It was going dark; even so the car park on the square was fully lit. CCTV cameras were in operation but there were certain places that they couldn't reach. Many a time, Rachel and Claire had been questioned about some crime or other that they'd been seen nearby, before or after. They were the queens of keeping quiet and, so far, age had been on their side. Claire had been concerned about this once they'd turned sixteen but Rachel said they would continue to get away with things if they kept their mouths shut. No one would crack the Bradley girls, she was fond of saying.

Just like clockwork, Archie Meredith turned up as he did every night at nine. He parked his car, scowled at them all as he walked past, and headed into Shop&Save. The moment he was out of sight, Rachel pulled up her hood and nudged Leanne.

'Now!' she cried.

Leanne picked up a large brick from the side of the car park and ran over to Archie's car. First, she smashed it into the right headlight and then the left. Next she twisted back both of the windscreen wipers. Then she took out her front door key and ran it along the whole length of the nearside, across the boot lid and right along the passenger side. When she saw another car pulling in, she legged it back to the gang who then split up in a regimented manner. Louise went with Rachel and Claire and ran across Davy Road, down the steps into Roland Avenue. Leanne, Shell and Hayley headed for the site where the White Lion pub had been until it was burned down the previous year. Charlie and Ashley stayed near the shops as advised.

'I wish we'd stayed at the shops now,' sighed Rachel as she bent over to catch her breath. 'It would have been fun to watch Archie when he sees his car trashed.'

After twenty minutes, they sauntered back. Archie was standing by his car, a policeman taking down his details.

'What's up, Archie?' Rachel shouted as she walked past them. 'Someone do you over?'

'Mind your own business!' Archie shouted back.

'Looks like you've upset someone. I wonder who that could be.'

Archie frowned then his face began to contort. 'Why, you little bitch! It was you!' He turned to the policeman standing next to him. 'It was her and that bloody gang of girls she hangs around with.'

'Why would you think that?' PC Mark Smith asked as he took down the names of the girls he could see.

'She,' he pointed to Rachel, 'had a go at me on the bus this morning. Said she'd seen me somewhere I wasn't... with –'

'You want to watch yourself, Archie,' Rachel said as she drew level with him. 'Rumours have a nasty way of flaring up on this estate.'

'I never –' Archie moved forward but Mark put out his arm to stop him. He stared at the three girls. 'Move along now. I'll be over to talk to you soon anyway.'

'Why?' asked Rachel. 'We weren't even here!'

'That's what I aim to find out. Because I saw you here no less than half an hour ago when I drove past.'

'So?'

'So... I'll be over in a minute.'

Rachel strutted off to join the others. As she got to them, she turned and gave Archie Meredith the bird.

'You should have seen his face when he saw what had happened,' Charlie laughed.

'I don't want to know about it,' snapped Rachel.

Claire turned to her with a frown. 'What's up with you?'

'Nothing!'

Rachel perched on the railing and glared at PC Smith. Tonight hadn't gone to plan because of him. Why did he have to turn up so quickly? Most of the time, people complained about the lack of policing. Oh, he just happened to drive past half an hour ago? Yeah, right. And now she'd missed her fun with Archie. She'd wanted to laugh and laugh in his stupid podgy face and let him know who had done the damage and him to be unable to prove it. Now, because the law had turned up quickly for a change, she hadn't been able to do that. And it irked her.

'I did what you said, Rach,' said Leanne. 'Am I part of the gang now?'

Rachel glared at her, until Leanne lowered her eyes. 'There won't be a fucking gang if we don't get a little more savvy.'

'What do you mean?' said Claire, the only one confident enough to stand up to her.

'I mean him.' Rachel pointed over to Mark. 'I'm sick of everyone thinking that we're just a girl gang. He's laughing at us and I don't like it. The sooner people on this estate realise they can't mess with the Mitchell Mob,' she added, 'the better. And that includes the coppers.'

CHAPTER SEVEN

Josie had been about to visit one of her friendlier tenants, Cathy Mason, who lived in Christopher Avenue when Archie Meredith shouted her over.

'It's not on,' he said as she sat on his settee, taking coffee with him and his wife. 'It's going to cost me a fortune to put my car right. In fact, I can't afford to do it all in one go. The paintwork will have to stay damaged.'

'There isn't any evidence to say exactly who it was,' Josie told him, although it pained her to say. 'The CCTV cameras barely picked the girls up anyway. They've been questioned but you know as well as I do, they all say they didn't do it and they are so hard to tell apart. I'm really sorry.'

'They're a bunch of animals!'

'The only thing I can do is see if I can get more of a police presence over there,' she said. 'I doubt it with resources how they are, and I know it won't help you now, but –'

'But they're never there, are they?' Archie folded his arms across his protruding belly. 'I know they're needed elsewhere, I'm not complaining in that sense, but there aren't enough coppers to go round this godforsaken place because it's getting worse.'

'I wish we could move,' Mary Meredith said quietly.

Josie looked across at her. Mary was in her mid-fifties. She could tell from looking at her that she had been a beautiful woman in her earlier years. She'd put a bit of weight on due to being struck down with multiple sclerosis several years ago and was now confined to a wheelchair. But she still took pride in her appearance; her clothes were clean, her hair washed and styled.

Josie knew both of their children: Mark who was now twenty-seven and Amanda who was nearing thirty, if she remembered correctly. They had never been in trouble with the police and always kept themselves to themselves. Mark had family of his own now and, although Amanda had moved off the estate, she came to help out with Mary every other day.

There was no mistaking the tears glistening in Mary's eyes. Seeing them made Josie well up too.

'I wish I could help you,' she said to both of them. 'But you know as well as I do that there's nothing I *can* do.'

'You could talk to their parents,' suggested Archie. 'Before I get myself into trouble down the pub when I lamp Pete Bradley.' Archie squeezed his index finger and his thumb together. 'I was that close to it on Sunday night. But knowing my luck, I'd get locked up for it.' He smiled affectionately. 'And who would look after my Mary, then?'

Mary smiled too, but the tears were still there. Josie's heart went out to them. They were a lovely couple. Archie had worked all his life, and provided for them both when Mary had been taken ill. Despite her best intentions not to, Josie relented.

'Let me have a word with Mrs Bradley and see if we can ease things for a while. Sometimes she keeps them away from the square. I'll talk to –'

Archie shook his head. 'Thanks, Josie. I know your hands are tied, and I know you mean well, but it won't work. They'll only move on and cause trouble elsewhere. Trouble breeds trouble. They're better on the square, where people can see them, I suppose.'

Josie knew what he meant. How could she give them peace when a man built like Archie Meredith didn't feel safe going to fetch his wife a bottle of cough medicine from the shops after dark? Archie wasn't very tall but what he lacked in height, he gave back in muscle. His job as a roofer kept him fit. To know that he was wary of the estate after dark gave Josie the creeps in itself.

But what could she possibly do for them?

'Let me talk to Mrs Bradley first,' she tried again. 'I'll check in at the police post and see if they have anything to link the girls to the crime. But you know as well as I do that those bloody girls are too clever to get caught out.'

Archie smiled a little. 'You're one of the good people, Josie.'

*

'OY!' a voice bellowed from behind as Josie got out of her car in Stanley Avenue thirty minutes later. She locked the door before turning around. When she saw who it was, she cursed under her breath.

'Yes, you,' cried Barbara as she drew level with her. 'I hope you're not off to moan at our Gina again.'

'What I say to Gina is confidential, Mrs Lewis.' Josie turned and began to walk away. But Barbara followed her.

'She's my daughter, you cheeky cow. She tells me everything.'

I doubt that very much, Josie thought. She continued up the pathway towards Gina's front door as quickly as possible.

'She'll have done nothing wrong,' Barbara continued, marching behind her. 'She's always in trouble for something someone else has done. If it isn't the twins, it's Danny. If it isn't Danny, it's that useless layabout of a husband. Why can't you give the poor girl a break?'

'Mrs Lewis,' Josie turned on her heels so abruptly that she narrowly missed knocking Barbara to the floor, 'why don't you let me do my job? I'm sure Gina will tell you all about it once I'm gone.'

Barbara marched back to her own house as Josie knocked on the Bradleys' front door. Cathy hadn't been in after she'd visited Archie Meredith - what she'd give for another sit down at a respectable tenant's home rather than being about to enter the lion's den!

She'd almost given up when the front door opened.

'What do *you* want now?' Gina cried. 'My family haven't done anything wrong as far as I am aware.'

'Can I come in and chat for a moment?' Josie said. It wasn't a question, more of a statement.

'I'm not interested in anything you have to say.'

'Can I come in or are we going to tell the whole of Stanley Avenue what's going on?'

Gina let out a huge sigh and walked into the house, leaving the door open for Josie to follow. As usual, she manoeuvred herself past boxes stacked in the hallway: four of bottled lager, one pack of

32 toilet rolls, several boxes of crisps, and a fair number of cigarettes.

'These things are a hazard in here,' said Josie as she squeezed through into the living room. 'I've told you before to move them. If you ever have a fire, you'll be –'

'If I ever have a fire I bet you'll be the first to say it was an insurance scam!' Gina retorted angrily. She flopped down onto the settee, lit another cigarette, threw her lighter down onto the coffee table and took a long, unhealthy drag. 'And you should be doing something about that Reynolds' family. Their music was blaring into the early hours again last weekend.'

'I've come to chat to you, not take a complaint from you.'

'So it's all right for them to be ant-social, but not my family?'

Ignoring her, Josie sat on the armchair, first moving the pile of washing to one side.

'Are the girls at school?' she asked.

'Of course they are.' Gina folded her arms.

'Were they over on Vincent Square on Tuesday evening?'

Gina cast her mind back to Tuesday. Ah, yes, the hair disaster day. Well, she'd be damned if she could remember anything after finishing off the whisky before starting on the lager – apart from the hangover the following day.

'I'm not sure,' she replied.

'Mr Meredith from Christopher Avenue had his car trashed. Your girls were seen near to, as well as –'

'You see, you're blaming my girls already!' She moved in closer to Josie.

'No, I only want to talk,' said Josie. 'Things do seem to be getting out of hand with Rachel and Claire. And I'm not just talking about the damage to the car. There have been some really nasty catfights lately.'

'That sounds more like it.'

Unexpectedly, Josie noticed a tear in Gina's eye. She supposed it must get to her every now and then. How could it not do?

'All I'm really bothered about is what it might lead to,' she spoke softer now. 'I'm sure you remember when Stacey Hunter ended up in juvenile detention and –'

'My girls won't end up *there*!'

'If you let me finish, I was going to say since she's gone, Rachel and Claire seem hell-bent on taking her place at the head of this stupid gang they've created. I heard they've been getting the other girls in their group to do initiation tests.'

'That's my girls.' Gina couldn't help but smile.

Josie ignored her sarcasm. 'I'm actually more concerned about what will happen when Stacey gets out.'

Gina frowned. 'What do you mean?'

'Don't you think there's going to be trouble if she doesn't get her place back at the helm? I doubt that Rachel and Claire will back down, so there may be what we'd call a turf war.'

'A turf war? This isn't exactly the east end of London!'

'You know what I mean. Stacey Hunter is a nasty piece of work. Having a step father like Lenny Pickton means she's grown up in a world of violence. She thought nothing of the attack she carried out that got her locked up in the first instance. If Rachel and Claire don't watch their step, who knows how far things might escalate?'

'My girls can hold their own.'

'But what if they can't?' Josie paused. 'It isn't Rachel that I'd be worried about as much as Claire. She doesn't seem as strong as her sister and if Stacey wants to make trouble when she comes out, you know she will. She won't be bothered about going down again and she won't be bothered about taking your girls with her.'

Gina finally caught on to Josie's meaning. Christ, she didn't want to lose the girls too, despite how much grief they caused her. She sat back with a sigh of resignation.

'What can I do?' she said. 'Neither of them listens to me anymore.'

'Can't you try and talk to them?' Josie urged. 'I know it was a bad turn of phrase when I said a turf war but it's highly likely if Stacey hears they're trying to rule her out as coming back as their leader. I'm not sure the police will be able to stop them. They're like animals when they get going.'

Gina frowned – that was her daughters she was referring to. But she realised that Josie meant no harm.

'I'll see what I can do,' she told her.

'Maybe Mr Bradley could have a word?'

'Pete?' Gina snorted as she reached for another cigarette. 'He's bloody hopeless. I'll try and talk to them.'

Josie stood up. She looked at Gina with a heavy heart. Even though her family troubles were of her own making, she couldn't help feeling sorry for her at times. No one would take any notice of Gina: Josie had seen it so many times on the estate. Her brood were too strong-willed. But she had to admire her for wanting to try. And she hoped that Rachel and Claire Bradley would take note of the bollocking their mother was about to dish out.

'Will you two keep the din down in there?' Ruth shouted through to the living room, almost making as much noise as Mason and Jamie combined. The screeching was getting on her nerves. They'd been playing soldier games for near on an hour now. She wished they would settle down and watch a DVD but there was no television set up yet. As it was, she only had the portable television that she'd had for years now. Although she'd paid towards the widescreen television at Martin's house, there was no mention of it coming with her when he'd chucked them out.

How could he have been so cruel, after all that time? She'd spent three years with him, and for what? So he could sling her out on the streets at the first opportunity that some new skirt came along. It had been that Tracy Tanner's doing, she knew it. As well as being a mobile hairdresser, Tracy worked a couple of nights down at The Butcher's Arms. She'd only been in there on one occasion with him – babysitters were hard to come by when you didn't have any friends – but she'd noticed immediately the effect that Martin had on Tracy. Martin was tall, not too scrawny, with a lush of black hair and denim blue eyes. They were the first thing to attract Ruth when she'd met him at the job centre.

He'd been seeing Tracy for over a year on the side when she'd found out they were an item. England had been playing and Martin had gone to The Butcher's Arms to watch the match. He'd only been gone an hour when Jamie had been taken ill. She'd rushed around to a neighbour's and asked them to keep an eye on both boys until she had fetched Martin. She'd run most of the way to the pub, arriving breathless and red-faced.

But she'd been even more red-faced when she'd spotted him in the corner with Tracy Tanner. At first, she hadn't been able to tell who the woman was because Martin's tongue was down her throat. As she'd stood over them while they continued, Tracy had opened her eyes eventually and pulled away. The look Martin gave her when he turned around was one she would never forget. He sneered; then he laughed. Then he turned back to kiss Tracy Tanner. Ruth had run out of the pub.

Two days later, while Jamie was recovering from what turned out to be no more than a nasty virus, Martin dropped his bombshell. He wanted them out and he wanted them out as soon as possible. He was moving Tracy Tanner in. Ruth hadn't got a leg to stand on: the property was rented in Martin's sole name. He was the one who was in the wrong, yet she lost her home and what she looked on as her security.

'Mum, can I have some chocolate?' Mason asked as he ran up to her.

'There isn't any left,' said Ruth, as she tidied the work surface. 'You and Jamie had the last of it yesterday.'

Mason kicked the kitchen cupboard, the bang reverberating around the room. 'Why can't you go out and fetch some more?'

'I'm busy.'

Mason raised his voice. 'You're a stupid mum.'

Ruth sighed. 'Don't start all that again. What have I told you about calling people stupid?'

'You are. Stupid, stupid, STUPID!'

'Not now, Mason, please!'

'Stupid, stupid, STUPID.'

Ruth raced towards him, narrowly missing him as he ran through the door. She could hear his laughter as he tore up the stairs to join his brother. Why did she have to have two boys? All she'd ever wanted was a girl that she could dress up; that she could take shopping; that she could help do her hair. God had been cruel to her in so many ways. Not only had he taken their father away far too early, but he'd then turned her little horrors into eight and ten-year-old fully blown nightmares.

The house now quiet, for a moment at least, she settled down to wash the kitchen flooring. It looked like it had been there long before either Jamie or Mason had been born. She scrubbed frantically at the black scrape marks until her arms ached, but they wouldn't budge.

She sat on her haunches while she caught her breath, wiping her brow with the back of her hand. 'Ow!' She pulled back her arm. Her wrist was covered in a bandage: there was blood seeping through at the edges. The cut on her arm was her latest torture. If she didn't watch what she was doing, it would become infected and she'd have to seek medical attention and then all the questioning would begin again.

Ruth pulled up her sleeve, ignoring all the scars that ran across her arm. Scratches, wounds of yesteryear, some deep, some faint, some scabbing over nicely. But it was the one on her wrist that was giving her problems. It hadn't stopped throbbing for days. In frustration, she unravelled the bandage. As the wound came closer to being unveiled, she winced. The gauze had stuck to the congealed blood. She pulled at it gently, millimetre by millimetre, wincing again with every move. Then the mess was revealed in all its glory – or should that be gory.

Ruth felt the tears building up: how could she do this to herself? She was such an expert on cutting now, how could she have gone that deep? She wasn't even giving the wound time to heal over before she started at it again.

But she knew why – feeling that hurt took the pain of her everyday life away. While she was cutting, hurting herself, no one else could. The pain was part of her, yet she felt detached as she pushed a craft knife into the open wound night after night and sliced away a little more. She glanced down at it, the blood steadily increasing from where she'd pulled away the gauze. Then, hearing banging footsteps down the stairs, she quickly covered it up.

'Mum!' Jamie bounded in this time. 'Mason's hit me.'

'No I haven't!' Mason came in behind him. 'I never touched the little squirt.'

'Yes, you did!'

'No, I didn't!'

'Yes, you did!'

'Shut up, the pair of you!' cried Ruth. 'If you can't play nicely together, I'll split you up.'

Jamie started to cry. It was then that she noticed the red mark on his cheek. She pulled him close, bent down to his level and then addressed his brother.

'For God's sake, Mason,' she started.

'I didn't hit him hard.' Mason walked past her to the sink. 'He's a wimp.'

'You'd be a wimp if I hit you like that.' Ruth wiped away Jamie's tears as the red patch turned to scarlet.

'You wouldn't dare.' Mason glared at her. 'You're a wimp too.'

'Why, you little...' Ruth stood up straight again, grabbed Mason roughly by the neck of his jumper and turned him back to face her. She bunched her hand into a fist, raised it high and...

She stopped it in mid-air. Seeing the fear in his eyes had pierced her heart.

'Don't you touch me!' he shouted.

Ruth put her fist down and let go of his jumper. She didn't know who was shaking the most.

'Say sorry to your brother,' she said quietly.

'Sorry,' said Mason.

Ruth turned back to Jamie, only to catch him pulling faces behind her back. The little bastard!

'Get out of my sight,' she said. 'Both of you. NOW!'

Jamie turned and ran. Mason followed quickly behind him. When he got to the door, he turned back.

'I hate you,' he said.

Ruth started to cry. She sat down in the middle of the kitchen floor and put her head in her hands. This was hopeless: it was too much for her to cope on her own. She pulled at her hair sharply. 'Bad mother; bad mother; bad mother,' she repeated over and over.

It wasn't fear that had stopped her from lashing out at Jamie. It was the fact that she knew once she started, she wouldn't have been able to stop.

CHAPTER EIGHT

Caren awoke the next morning when she felt an arm encircle her waist and pull her across the bed. She found herself spooned into John and she closed her eyes to snuggle down again.

'What time is it?' she whispered as his hand sidled up and down the outside of her thigh, then changed to his fingertips.

'Early but I'm horny,' he whispered back.

Caren shivered as she felt his breath on her neck. He moved her hair and kissed her bare shoulder. Sleepily, she sighed and let him. His hands moved lower and around to her breasts, he stroked a nipple through her vest. Then his hand found its way inside the top.

Caren took it, parted her legs and pressed it to her. She could sense John smiling as his fingers slipped inside her. She gasped and opened her legs a little wider. The sound of her breathing invaded the room as he moved over her, getting her wet and excited in moments. Eventually, she turned towards him and he kissed her with fervour. She manoeuvred her body beneath his and ran her hands over his back as he continued, down over his naked buttocks which she pulled in closer to her. His kisses were sharper now, deeper, his tongue exploring her mouth. And then he was gone.

He circled her breast with the tip of his tongue, his hand in between her legs again. Caren grasped his hair as he bit down hard on one nipple before running his tongue over her chest to find the other one. Once that was standing erect, he moved further down her body, massaging her, teasing her, tantalising her. As the unmistakeable waves of passion engulfed her, she arched her back, moaning slightly.

John looked up at her as he took her over the edge, waited for her to subside enough for him to push himself gently inside her. They kissed a long time before gaining an easy rhythm and moving together as one. Slowly, slowly. Faster, faster. Caren grabbed John's buttocks as he thrust deeper and deeper into her.

Then they were still.

John lay above her as his breathing returned to normal. Then he kissed her lightly on the nose, pulled her near again and snuggled into her.

Caren entwined her legs with his, sighing with content as a smile played on her lips

God, that was good.

Gina was woken by a loud bang as the back door slammed yet again. She glanced at the clock on her bedside table. It was quarter to nine: most probably it was the twins going out, hopefully on their way to school.

Pete rolled over beside her and she pushed him away. 'Move, you moron,' she said. 'I'll be on the floor in a minute.'

She lay still as she waited for him to settle again. But then the snoring began.

Gina nudged him sharply. 'Shut the fuck up, will you? I can't hear myself think.'

'We're in bed, what's there to think about?' Pete mumbled. 'Mind you, what else is there to do in here but sleep?'

'Don't be so disgusting,' Gina snapped. 'It's all sex with you.'

'I can't remember getting jiggy with you in ages.' Pete grinned. 'We could always squeeze in a session now, if you're up to it?'

She was about to protest when she wondered what the new, improved Gina would do. Even though her hair had turned out to be a disaster, she still wanted to be different; live her life a little more.

'Okay then.' She cuddled up to him but moved away as quickly. 'God, booze breath.' She flapped her hand in front of her mouth. 'You'll have to brush your teeth first.'

'Aw, come on, Gene,' Pete protested. 'You don't have to have fresh breath to do what I want you to do.'

Gina sighed as Pete rolled over on his back. He placed his hand on the bulge that had appeared in his pants. 'Come on, girl. Do us proud. You know you want to.'

'You'd better return the favour, Pete,' she said as she disappeared beneath the covers. She nearly gagged as she got to his pants. God, the man was filthy. 'You need a bath too,' she told him but it came out as a muffle.

'Can't hear you,' said Pete, reaching inside for his cock and flashing it out. It hit her in the face.

'Oy! You'll give me a black eye if you're not careful. Now lay back and be quiet.'

While she took him in her mouth and concentrated on the task in hand, she imagined that John was lying beneath her. She heard Pete gasp – no, it was John that gasped, stupid, she scolded herself.

Pete began to tense his legs and thrust upwards, taking her out of her daydream.

'Fuck, Gina, that's good,' he said.

Gina wished that he'd shut up. How could she imagine it was John she was giving pleasure to if this idiot wouldn't be quiet! She moved up and down faster, faster, moving her hand to the base of the penis and up and down the shaft. Finally, she heard an almighty groan and his body went rigid with pleasure. Gina sighed: thank God for that – mission accomplished for another month. Now it was her turn.

She emerged from underneath the covers, slipped out of her T-shirt and wriggled her knickers down. Turning towards him, she leaned on one elbow. 'Right, me now,' she said expectantly.

But Pete jumped out of bed. He grabbed the pants from off the floor and sniffed them before pulling them on again.

'I have to be out for nine,' he replied, reaching for the jeans that he'd left on the floor the night before. 'I said I'd meet Barry over on the square. We're doing a job today.'

Gina picked up his pillow and threw it at him as he headed out of the door. 'You self-centred git!' she cried. Then she pummelled her feet on the mattress.

John wouldn't have left her feeling frustrated like that. John would have made sure her horny mood was taken advantage of.

Damn Pete, the selfish bastard.

With resignation, she took her vibrator from the drawer.

After tea that evening, Gina made her way upstairs to have that talk with the twins. The girls shared the large bedroom at the back of the house. Gina had tried to give them their own bedrooms from an early age, changing the parlour room downstairs into a bedroom for Danny. It wasn't ideal; they really needed somewhere to eat but as they couldn't afford a proper dining table, they always ended up squeezed into the kitchen anyway.

When they were ten, she'd tried to install in them a sense of individuality, but it had become quite clear that they didn't want to be separated, not even at night time. When she'd check on them before going to bed herself, she'd go into Rachel's room and find Claire snuggled up beside her. Or she'd go into Claire's room and find Rachel sleeping top to toe. So it had made more sense to take back the parlour room, move them in together and let Danny have his old room back.

She knocked on the door. 'Girls, I need to talk to you,' she said, marching in and turning down the music blaring from the tinny CD player they shared.

Rachel was lying on her bed, reading a magazine. Claire was sitting next to her.

'Don't you ever knock?' Rachel sighed.

'I have knocked,' Gina told them. 'I've also had a visit from Josie Mellor yesterday.'

'Whatever she says, we haven't done,' said Claire. 'She's always blaming us for everything.'

'That's because you're usually in the thick of things.'

Both girls spoke in unison. 'No, we're not.'

Gina sat down on the edge of Claire's bed. 'It's what I want to talk to you about. I need ammunition for when she next comes round asking all sorts of questions. I need to know that you haven't been involved in any of the incidents she mentioned.'

'We don't know anything about Archie Meredith's car getting bashed up,' said Rachel.

'How did you know I was going to ask about that?'

'I – I just know that you'll blame us for it anyway. You never stick up for us.'

'I do!' said Gina. 'I get a roasting for it most of the time, too.'

Claire put down her magazine. 'What do you really want, Mum?'

'What I *don't* want is you two going the same way as your brother.'

'Huh, like we'd ever.'

Rachel nodded in agreement with her sister. 'We're far better at getting away with things.'

'That's not what I mean! Danny chanced his luck and he got caught last year.'

'Yeah, well, Danny's a knob,' said Rachel. She lay back on the bed and sighed. 'And an idiot. I mean, he got away with that murder charge when Miles' factory got done over and then he gets caught nicking stuff from Halford's. What a comedown he had.'

Claire laughed and turned to Mum. 'We won't get caught. We're far too clever.'

'You mean getting other girls to do your dirty work for you?'

Both girls glared at her then.

'You think I don't know what's been going on?'

'Nothing's been going on,' snapped Rachel.

'So when Stacey's out, she won't be bothered by the fact that you seem to have taken over as gang leaders?'

Rachel sat upright. Claire nervously looked her way.

'You have no idea how hard it is to survive on this estate, Mum,' said Rachel.

'*Survive*?' Gina tried in vain to keep the incredulous tone from her voice. 'We don't live in the ghetto.'

'Dur,' said Claire. 'Take a look out of the window. Yes we do.'

'You've been watching too much television.' Gina shook her head in exasperation. 'I know living on the Mitchell Estate isn't exactly a barrel of laughs, but there are worse places.'

'Where?'

Gina stood up and raised her hands in the air in surrender. 'I give up with you two,' she said. 'Do what you want. But I'm warning you both,' she pointed at Rachel,' you, madam, in particular, be very careful what you do. These things have a habit of coming back and biting you. Don't say you haven't been warned.'

As soon as Gina left the room, Claire turned to Rachel. 'Stacey will want to take over, won't she?'

'Well, we're not going to let her.'

Claire looked away. Quite frankly, the thought of Stacey getting out next week was enough to start her worrying about it already.

Rachel shot forward, grabbed Claire's chin and yanked her neck round so that she was facing her.

'We're not going to let her take over, *are we*?' she repeated, staring at her intently.

'No – no,' Claire managed to say.

Rachel pushed her sister away. 'Good.'

Claire went to sit on her own bed. She hated it when Rachel got all mouthy with her. And why did she have to cause trouble all of the time?

'We need to come up with a plan,' Rachel told her, the leg perched on her knee swinging violently from side to side. 'Stacey won't be content with second in command.'

'I thought I was second in command.'

Rachel ignored her. 'If she wants to get back on top, she'll have me to put down first. I'm not letting go of the lead, no way.'

'I thought I was second in command,' reiterated Claire.

'Shut the fuck up. I'm thinking.'

'I've been thinking,' Caren said to John as they ate their lunch together the following week. 'I'm going to start working for myself.'

John looked up from his pasta dish with a frown before shoving in another forkful.

Caren held up a hand and waggled her fingers at him. He looked blankly at her.

'Nails, dur! I'm going to set myself up mobile. It might not bring much in but it'll be a start. And it'll get me out of the house.'

'Great.' John continued to eat.

'So that only leaves you to fix yourself up now,' she added.

Yeah, Pete's been telling me about –'

'You're not doing his type of work!'

'What do you mean by that?'

Caren put down her fork. 'I know what he gets up to. He's never earned a decent day's pay in his life.'

'He gets by all right. Him and Gina –'

'It's nothing legal! He's a bad influence and knowing you, you'll get sucked into his way of life. Before you know it, you'll be doing time for some petty crime or another.'

'It's easy money. Besides, I've been too busy to start making contacts.'

'You already have contacts! Some of *them* might have work for you.' Caren stood up. 'It's only pride that stops you. You need to stop being so picky.'

'So picky?'

'Yes.' Caren moved to the sink and shoved the plate into the washing up bowl. 'There's work to be had out there with people you already know. Jesus, go and beg if you have to but we need to –'

'You think it's so easy, don't you?' John said quietly.

Caren turned to him. 'Of course it isn't easy, but you have to do it. I'm willing to give it a go too.'

John huffed. 'Anyone can paint nails for the scabby bitches on this estate. You'll make a frigging fortune. None of them ever get their hands dirty.'

John stood up quickly, his chair scraping across the tiles. Not bothering to put it back under the table, he marched towards the door.

Caren threw down the dish cloth. 'Where are you running off to now?'

'Away from you and your nagging. Maybe my best will never be good enough for you,' John continued. 'Maybe I'd be better off on my own.'

'So you can shirk all your responsibilities?'

'Like I said, I'm doing my best!'

Caren burst into tears. 'I hate living like this,' she cried. 'We don't have any money in the bank to call our own – we can hardly afford to pay the bills. And if we weren't living in this hell hole, we wouldn't be bickering all the time.'

John stared at her for a moment before walking across and taking her into his arms.

'What are we going to do?' she sobbed, his hands soothing her as he rubbed her back. 'I don't want to fight all the time but I feel so vulnerable living here.'

'It won't be for long.' John tilted her chin up. 'I'll make more of an effort, I promise. If you want to move off here straight away, I'll start looking for somewhere to live too.'

'One step at a time,' Caren sniffed. She smiled through her tears. 'I don't want us to break up over this. We've come so far through the years. We can't quit now.'

John continued to stare at her. 'Who said anything about quitting?' He kissed her lightly on the tip of her nose.

'I'm bored,' Claire said to Rachel as the girls congregated outside Shop&Save that evening. 'Who can we irritate?'

Rachel took a noisy slurp from her can of lager before replying. 'I can't be bothered tonight.'

'Aw, come on.' Leanne circled round on her bike in front of them. 'I fancy some fun too.'

'Shut up, Leanne,' said Rachel.

'What's with you, you moody cow?' Leanne snapped back. 'Anyone would think you were worried about something.'

Rachel glared at her. 'I said shut it.'

Leanne shrugged and continued to circle them on her bike.

'Ohmigod,' squealed Charlie. 'Looks who's here.'

Rachel glanced in the direction that Charlie was running to see Stacey Hunter walking towards them.

'Fuck.' Claire's hands gripped the railing they were perched on, twisting and turning quickly.

It didn't go unnoticed by Rachel. 'Quit looking scared of her,' she retorted.

'I *am* scared of her,' whispered Claire.

Rachel shook her head. 'You'd better not be.'

The rest of the girls crowded around Stacey as she drew near to the car park. She was a tall girl, with deep-set eyes and a small nose. Brown hair was cut so close to her head that it was hard to tell her gender. Her face was void of any colour, several earrings dangling from an ear. A small tattoo on the back of her right hand spelt out the word 'sinner.'

She approached Rachel with assurance. 'Hi,' she said.

'Hi yourself.'

'How're tricks?'

'So, so.'

Stacey thrust her hands deep into her pockets and pulled out a packet of cigarettes. 'Anyone want one?'

Suddenly she was the star attraction.

'God, yeah. I could murder a fag,' said Leanne.

'Me too,' Louise pulled one out. 'Ta.'

Stacey handed them out before addressing the twins.

'Claire?' she offered the packet to her.

Claire shrugged, unsure what to do. She looked at Rachel, who with a slight nod of her head, indicated that it was all right for her to take one.

Stacey shoved the packet into Rachel's chest. 'Do you want one?'

Rachel purposely took two. She placed one behind her ear and the other one went in her mouth. Charlie lit it for her and she took a drag before looking up again.

Stacey and Rachel stared at each other like a pair of gunslingers ready to duel. The atmosphere turned to one of mixed tensions. Some of the girls couldn't wait for the showdown: some of them were worried of its outcome. All of them were wondering who to pledge allegiance to once things started to get rough.

It was Stacey who finally broke the silence as she spotted a navy blue BMW driving towards them.

'Here's my ride. Thanks for watching over my patch,' she told Rachel, 'and my girls, but now I'm out, I've come to claim back my turf.'

Rachel glared at her. 'Over my dead body,' she replied.

Stacey nodded her head slowly. 'I'm sure that can be arranged.'

Rachel only had time to fume as Stacey ran towards the car.

From where she sat, she could see the driver was Sam Harvey, a well-known trouble maker from the estate. Stacey slid into the passenger seat and he sped off quickly.

Rachel walked off then, kicking over an advertising board outside Shop&Save as she drew level with it.

'What's up with you?' Louise shouted after her. 'You're not losing your bottle, are you?'

Rachel stopped in her tracks and turned back. 'No, I'm not losing my fucking bottle! For your information, I think we need to move on to bigger things – not just nicking stuff from easy targets. It's a joke. I want everyone to be afraid of the Mitchell Mob; I want everyone talking about us. And for that we need to go up a gear.'

'What do you mean?' Louise was the first to challenge. 'We cause enough mayhem already.'

'If I get into any more trouble, my olds will ground me,' Charlie spoke out.

'Me too,' said Ashley. 'I got a backhander after we did Meredith's car. My olds knew I'd been involved even though I denied it.'

'Sounds like some of us are getting cold feet about belonging to the Mitchell Mob.' Rachel folded her arms in defiance.

'I don't want to get locked up like Stacey,' said Louise.

'You have to take chances in this game to survive, so if we get sent down, we get sent down,' reiterated Rachel.

Had Rachel noticed the wary looks travelling between the girls, she might have chosen her words better. Instead, to hide how nervous she felt, she went in guns blazing, pointing at them.

'You lot need to decide your loyalties. I'm not giving in to the likes of Stacey Hunter so things will get tough for a while. She might think she's hard but I'd smash her face in any day. And none of you need to make me into an enemy, or I'll start on you too.'

She paused but no one spoke out. Great, just how she liked it; they were quaking in their trainers.

So there was absolutely no need for anyone to know that she was too.

CHAPTER NINE

As Caren tackled a pile of ironing, she thought more about the idea she'd had about going mobile to do nails. When she'd spoken to John about it, he'd said to hold fire and to see what came up for him. But that had been over a week ago and he still hadn't sorted anything out – although she knew something was going on. She'd hardly seen him for the past couple of days. Every time she asked him what he'd been up to, he'd tap his finger to his nose and smile. She wondered if he was doing a trial for a company, see if he was what they were after.

'Hey, gorgeous,' he said when he came in twenty minutes later. He wrapped an arm around her waist and kissed her on the cheek. 'You okay?'

'Yes, you?'

'I am indeed.' John threw a wad of notes down onto the ironing board.

Caren stared at them, then at him. She put down the iron. 'Where did you get that from?'

'I've been working.'

Caren smiled, noticing that his jeans and boots were covered in white powder. 'I knew you were up to something.' She pointed to a chair. 'Sit down and you can tell me all about it. I'll make coffee.'

'It was only for a couple of days.'

'But it's a start, isn't it? Was it a trial for someone?'

'Not exactly.' John sat down. 'I've been working with Pete. A mate of his needed some plastering doing. I've been labouring for him.'

Caren's smile dropped away.

'You wanted money, didn't you?'

'Yes, but –'

John sighed. 'Then get into the real world. Jobs don't come

along ten a penny. So I thought I might as well get some money coming in while I try to find something permanent.'

'You said you wouldn't get involved with his dirty deals!'

John sniggered. 'Plastering is hardly a dirty deal.'

'You know what I mean.'

'I'm trying my best, Caz!'

'No, you're not. Working cash in hand isn't what we do.'

'It'll put food on the table.'

'Yes, I know, but –'

'I thought it would make you happy.'

'Well, it won't. I know it's only a plastering job now, but what next? Pete's a taker. He'll use anyone he can to make a quick buck.' She pointed to the money. 'How much do you think he got, if he gave you a hundred?'

'He got the same.'

'Did you see him pocket his share?'

'No, but he wouldn't –'

'I wouldn't put anything past him. He's a loser, John, and hanging round with him, no matter what your best intentions are, will do you more harm than good.'

'Okay, little miss fix-it. You tell me how to get a job.'

'Get out of Pete's pocket and start acting like a –'

'For fuck's sake!' John grabbed the money from the ironing board. 'I'll take this, shall I? I might as well gamble it away because it won't be good enough for you.'

'That's not going to solve –'

'You've got to face up to things. We've been here for over a month now. I've not had a sniff of a job so I've done what I thought was best.'

Caren stopped then. There was nothing she could say to that.

John's brow furrowed. 'I'm not sure if I'll ever be good enough for you.' He threw the money down onto the floor and left with the slam of the door.

Caren flinched. Stupid, stupid, stupid! Why had she pushed him into an argument again? She knew he had their best intentions at heart but what she didn't want was him getting used to the amount of money he could get on the side while claiming benefits. There was always someone in the papers who thought they'd get away with it but, inevitably, they got caught out. And that was beside the point: they were not, and never would be, benefit cheats.

Upstairs, she heard John in the bedroom; at least he hadn't gone out. She knew he'd calm down by the time he emerged from the shower. That was one good thing about him; he could never stay angry for long.

God, how she detested Pete Bradley. He would be their downfall if she let him.

Caren sighed. Yet another day in paradise.

As soon as Rachel and Claire turned the corner into Davy Road that night, they saw Stacey. She was talking to Hayley and Shell, huddled up in discussion. None of them noticed as they approached.

Rachel had seen this coming but she didn't think Stacey would act so quickly. First, she'd caught her talking to Louise a couple of nights ago. Louise had run over to Rachel as soon as she'd spotted her and when questioned had said Stacey was after the tenner she owed her before she got sent down. Now, here she was again, determined to get her gang back. Rachel pulled up the hood of her jacket. Well, one way or another, she was going to find out how determined she was. Even though she was wary, she'd have to show her who was boss.

'What the fuck do you want?' Rachel asked as she drew level with them.

'Nothing.'

'Back off my girls, then.'

'They're not your girls.'

'No?'

'No.'

Rachel turned to Hayley and then Shell. 'Maybe you two need to think about loyalties,' she snapped.

Shell dropped her eyes immediately but Hayley stared at Rachel for a while. At last, with a quick glance at Stacey, she too looked away.

Claire, hanging round in the background like a spare part, finally moved forward.

'Right, that's sorted,' she threw into the tense atmosphere. 'Now, let's get some fags. I'm dying for a drag.' As Rachel and Stacey strutted their stuff like two peacocks, she grabbed hold of Hayley's arm and dragged her nearer to the entrance of Shop&Save. 'Come on, you're better at scrounging than me.'

Eventually, Stacey moved away.

'Bye, bye,' Rachel shouted after her. 'See you again soon – I don't think.'

Stacey turned back. 'You won't win, redhead,' she spoke coolly before continuing.

'Want to take a bet on it?'

'No point when the odds are stacked against you.'

Once Stacey was in the distance, Rachel turned to Shell and punched her on the upper arm.

'Ow!' Shell cried out.

'Show me up again and you'll get a lot more of that.'

Ruth woke up with another headache. Was it any wonder with the vodka she'd knocked back last night? She tried to focus on the bedroom, still not familiar enough to feel at home in. The nights were drawing in now – soon the clocks would be going back and the dark would descend in more ways than one. Ruth hated winter. In summer, it was much easier to rid herself of a bad mood if the sun was shining and she could sit in the garden. In winter, when it was cold and raining and windy and icy, it took all of her strength not to pull the duvet over her head and stay there all day.

'Mum, there's no bread left!' Jamie shouted up the stairs.

Ruth sighed: couldn't that boy do anything quietly? She dragged herself downstairs to face the day.

'You'll have to have cereal for your breakfast,' she told Jamie as she joined him in the kitchen. She opened the fridge to pull out the milk. Damn, there wasn't a lot of milk either. She'd have to call in at the shops on her way back from school.

'But I want toast!'

'You can't have any.'

Jamie threw down the empty bread packet and stamped on it. Without a second thought, Ruth leaned forward and slapped him around the face.

'Shut up with the moaning,' she told him. 'You'll have what you're given. Now, go and see where your brother is.'

Ruth ran a hand through her hair and began to pull at it. Then she heard the scream. She looked at Jamie in confusion. He was sobbing, and holding his face. For a moment, she froze. Then she rushed over, pulling him into her arms quickly.

'I'm so sorry,' she whispered. 'I didn't mean to hurt you.'

It was the truth: in actual fact, she couldn't remember *hitting* him. But as she saw a red mark appearing on his cheek, she hugged him again. What had made her do that? She was tired, of course. She hadn't had more than a couple of hours sleep the night before. Trying to drown her sorrows with the vodka, she'd ended up wide awake and weepy. But usually tiredness didn't make her lash out like that, especially not at one of the boys.

'What's up?' A sleepy Mason appeared in the doorway, rubbing at his eyes.

'M-mum hit me,' Jamie said through his sobs.

Ruth looked at Mason. 'I didn't mean to. I –'

Mason ran at his mother, his fists grabbing handfuls of her hair.

'Don't hurt my brother!' he screamed.

'Ow! Mason, let go!'

But Mason held on, long enough for Jamie to run past his mum and out of the room.

'I hate you! I hate you! I hate you!' shouted Mason.

With every word, he pulled her hair a little harder. Ruth forced one of his hands away and then the other. In moments, she had the better of him.

'Let me go, you little bastard!' she yelled in his face. 'I've had enough of you and Jamie. You think I like looking after you two every day of my life? You think it's easy to do this, when you two misbehave like you do? You should show some respect. I'm your mother!'

Breathing heavily, Ruth only came to her senses when she heard the rush of his bladder releasing itself. She looked down.

'Oh, Mason, I'm sorry.'

Ruth looked at him, a snivelling wreck who had pissed his pants and was now too afraid to speak. Over in the doorway, his brother watched on in horror, the mark on his cheek reddening with every second that passed. What was she going to do about her temper?

Ruth stood up and turned away from them before they could see her crying. 'I think you'd better get ready for school,' she said. 'We need to leave in half an hour.'

Ruth worried about her behaviour as she took the boys to school. What on earth had gone on this morning? It was one thing to get drunk and have a go at bringing pain to herself. But she had never lashed out at her children in temper. Not like that. And it scared her to think what she might be capable of. She decided to check up with Doctor Morgan, see if any of her tablets needed changing.

After calling in at the surgery to make an appointment, she stopped off at the shops to pick up some chocolate before heading back to the house. But halfway along Stanley Avenue, her morning got decidedly worse.

'Ruth? Ruth Millington?'

She turned to see who had shouted, her shoulders sinking immediately. 'Hi, Gina,' she replied.

Gina opened her gate and walked over. 'I thought it was you,' she said. 'I heard you'd moved into number thirty-two.'

Ruth nodded but Gina didn't give her time to speak.

'It looks a right dump. How are you going to cope with that on your own?' Gina folded her arms across her coffee-stained T-shirt and smirked. 'You are on your own now, aren't you?'

'No, I have my children with me.'

Gina smirked. 'You know that's not what I meant. Your fella's been shagging around, hasn't he?'

Ruth turned to walk away. 'That's none of your business.'

'That's where you're wrong. Everything on this avenue is my business. I make it that way, so you'd better get used to it.'

Ruth closed her eyes for a moment as she tried to blot out Gina's words. A ranting neighbour, one she'd known vaguely at school and disliked, having a go at her in the middle of the street was the last thing she needed right now. She took a step away.

'Hey!' Gina grabbed her by the arm. 'Don't walk away from me when I'm talking to you.'

'I'm sorry, Gina, I'm tired. Why don't we catch up later?'

'You think I want to catch up with you?' Gina moved closer. 'I don't think so. I'm just letting you know the rules that you have to abide by so that you can survive on Stanley Avenue; so that you settle in okay and don't give me any trouble.'

Ruth sighed. 'What are you after? Because if you're after a fight, I don't have it in me.'

'Oh, chill woman. I'm not out for your blood yet. But I will be if you step a foot wrong – or take a shine to my Pete. I know that your husband died but mine is off limits, do you hear?'

At the mention of Glenn's name, Ruth felt like she'd had a knife thrust into her heart and twisted savagely. Her eyes filled with tears as his face flashed before them.

'Involved in a car accident, wasn't he?' Gina added. 'I heard he was drunk when he –'

'You heard wrong,' Ruth interrupted. 'Another driver hit him head on. He – he died instantly. It wasn't his fault.'

Gina raised her eyebrows. 'You'll tell me anything. I suppose you'll tell me next that your Martin wasn't getting his end away with Tracy Tanner.'

Ruth couldn't cope with any more verbal abuse. She began to walk away quickly. But Gina followed her.

'I know your sort, Ruth Millington – if that's still your name. You've lost your husband and you couldn't keep the next fella in check. So just you keep your hands off mine.'

Ruth walked faster.

'If I hear that you've as much as looked at my Pete, I'll knock your fucking head off. Do you hear me? Oy!'

Ruth was at her garden gate now. She ran the last few steps to get away from the screeching behind her. Once inside the house, she drew the bolt across the front door and sat behind it, trying to calm her breathing before she had a panic attack.

The letter box clattered open.

'You're only a few doors away from me,' Gina yelled through it.

'I can find you anytime, remember that.'

Ruth jumped as the letterbox snapped shut again. She ran through to the kitchen and slammed the door. Her back to it, she slid to the floor and sobbed.

Although they should have been at school that morning, it was ten thirty and Rachel and Claire were still lying in bed. Claire was reading the latest edition of *Heat* Magazine. Rachel was messing about on her mobile phone. Suddenly, it beeped as a text message came in.

'*Not meeting u 2nite. Hanging round with Stacey. Shell is 2. No hard feelings? Hayls.*'

Rachel bit down hard on her bottom lip. Those cows! She knew they were up to something the other night. She should have punched Stacey Hunter when she had the chance.

She thought back to the other members in the gang, wondering who she could keep on side for the longest, Louise or Charlie? Louise had been with Stacey from the beginning. Now that Hayley and Shell had jumped ship, it would seem safer for her to gravitate towards Stacey too. And Stacey had been making headway to get Charlie to join her before she got sent down.

Suddenly, Rachel saw her little empire falling down before her. She glanced across at her sister, knowing she'd be no use if it came to a full blown war. She'd have to do some planning; see if she could get Hayley and Shell back on side, because if she didn't, she and Claire would end up as sitting ducks. Despite the big attitude she portrayed when they were out with the gang, it was only an act. She knew Stacey would come out on top.

In frustration, she threw her phone onto the bed. 'Fucking bitches!' she hissed.

'What's up?' asked Claire.

'Hayley and Shell have gone back to Stacey.'

Claire gasped. 'But, I thought they were with us!'

'So did I.'

'What shall we do?'

'We'll have to get them back.'

'How?'

Rachel sighed. 'I don't fucking know. What do you think?'

Claire shrugged. 'Why can't we go back to how it was before?'

'What do you mean?'

'When we were all together, it used to be a laugh and I reckon –'

'Are you saying that I'm a shit leader?' Rachel picked up a slipper and threw it at her.

Claire dodged it. 'No, I'm –'

'You'd better not be. You're my sister; you're supposed to stick up for me, think my ideas are good; fight the fight with me.'

'I know that, but –' Claire ducked as another slipper flew past her head. 'Back off, will you and let me speak!'

'Fuck off.' Rachel pulled the duvet over her head.

'Why is it that you always have your say but you won't listen to me?'

The duvet flipped up again. 'Because you talk so much shit.'

'I only talk as much shit as you do.'

'Shut up.'

'I'm just saying that if you don't want to be leader any more, it's a perfect time to say. Stacey would take us back right now, but if we start messing around with the others, then we'll be the ones hunted down.'

'And you think that bothers me?'

'It bothers me!' Claire paused. 'And if you must know you've become really nasty and I'm not sure it suits you.'

'Ha, that's a laugh, coming from you. We've always been known for being nasty.'

'We've been known for causing trouble, and wrecking things and nicking things, but not beating people up.'

'Well, you're part of this so you'll have to do what I say.'

Claire sighed. It was her turn to pull the duvet over her head. She knew Rachel wasn't listening.

But she had tried.

CHAPTER TEN

Ruth reached for her wine glass again, sighing when she saw it was empty. She staggered through to the kitchen to fill it up, only to find the bottle empty too. She couldn't afford to drink wine but after the day she'd had, it had gone into her shopping basket as if it were an everyday essential. Three for a tenner that she hadn't really got: one of them must work out as free, surely? So, in theory, she was really only about to start on her first bottle, not the second.

It was nine thirty on a very murky, very lonely, Tuesday evening. Ruth opened the bottle and took it back into the living room. She poured a glassful and drank it immediately. She wanted to be drunk, over the edge; pass out paralytic as soon as possible. She couldn't take the pain caused by the images flashing through her mind since she'd bumped into Gina that morning.

Tears pricked her eyes as she thought of Glen. They had been married for seven years when he'd been killed. He'd been an electrician for one of the major electricity suppliers. The money was good, giving them a lifestyle far better than any tenant of Stanley Avenue could expect. But good money also meant overtime and being on call. That night, Glenn had been called out to fix a broken power line. Afterwards, he rang to say he'd be home soon and to get the kettle on because he was chilled to the bone. The winter temperatures had dropped to minus five. Ruth told him she'd be ready with hot chocolate and cheese on toast.

But Glenn never made it back. He'd been driving the work's van; another driver in a truck coming towards him had lost it on a bend, slid straight into him, pushing him over the side of a bank. According to the police, the van had rolled over a couple of times but Glenn wouldn't have known about it as a bump to his head seemed to have killed him outright.

Going to the front door and finding two policemen with bad news had been the worst thing that had ever happened in her life. At twenty-eight, her world and her future had been crushed. Everything she knew had been taken from her; and she had two small boys to look after.

After the funeral, over the next few months she spiralled further and further into depression. As the money stopped coming in, the mortgage went into arrears, the bills started to pile up, and eventually the house was repossessed. She and the boys went to stay with her parents. During this time, Ruth struggled to get on with the day-to-day mundane things and it was only a matter of time before she cracked. Luckily, her parents took control of caring for Mason and Jamie. Ruth couldn't look after herself: there was no way she could see to two demanding boys as well. But slowly, she began to cope again. Eventually, she moved into a flat – the boys moving in with her on a permanent basis a month later – and she began to enjoy spending time getting to know them again. Being a mother was an important job, one she'd loved before she lost Glenn, her soul mate.

Oh, Glenn. She picked up the photo frame she'd been hugging to herself for most of the day and then took another swig of her wine before trying to focus on the room. She'd made it as homely as possible with what she had but still it looked sparse. It looked, and felt, like a house not a home. And that was her fault because she'd gone and lost the only man who had shown an interest in her since Glenn had died.

Ruth had started to self-harm about six months after she'd moved in with Martin. She could remember the day quite clearly: it had been the first time he'd hit her. He came home from the pub to find his dinner in the oven, shrivelled up because he was late, but he lashed out at her when she'd moaned at him. A crack across the mouth and a face-full of mashed potatoes had made her run to her room. She began to pick at a scar that she'd got from a burn on the oven door. Bit by bit, she picked at it until the half inch scar became a two inch mass of pus and blood. She ended up going to the doctors and he gave her some antibiotic cream. She remembered clearly the sting of the cream, putting it on every hour rather than the intended twice a day. Hurting herself blocked the pain she was feeling. For those few minutes, the anguish she felt took away everything else. The pain sometimes became so intense that she cried, but she didn't stop. It was meant to try and wipe out her abysmal existence; it was her punishment. She couldn't cope with Mason; she couldn't cope with Jamie; she couldn't cope with herself. Hell, she couldn't even cope with life.

She took another gulp of the wine, the urge to self-harm becoming stronger with each passing minute. She slapped at her face, trying to ease the throbbing inside her head. She needed to hurt herself: she knew it would make her feel better. Stuff the do-gooders who thought it was a terrible thing to do. Stuff the people who stared at her arms as they caught a glimpse every now and then.

She picked at the most recent scar on her arm. It hadn't had time to heal yet: she doubted it ever would at this rate. She dug her nails in, then picked, picked, picked until she saw the blood ooze out. There was blood underneath her fingernails: it satisfied her somewhat. But it wasn't enough. She fetched her craft knife.

'Mum, don't do that.'

Ruth looked up a few minutes later, trying to focus on the figure standing in front of her. Was it Mason or was it Jamie? And what the fuck were they doing out of bed?

'Mason?'

'Put down that thing. I hate it when you do that.'

'Do what?'

Mason pointed. 'That.'

Ruth looked down at her hand. She'd bought the knife from a craft shop in the town; it had been a godsend, perfect for the job at hand. As she looked at it more clearly, yet again it was covered in blood. She smiled; it made her feel so good.

'Oh, that,' she said, putting it down on the table. 'It's nothing. I've just found it down the side of the cooker. It must have been left behind by the people who lived here before.'

'I know what you do.' Mason stepped towards her. 'I know you cut yourself. I've seen you lots of times. Why do you do that, Mum? Why do –'

Ruth grabbed Mason's arm, pulled him nearer. She didn't notice him grimace from the stench of her breath.

'You've been spying on me, you little bastard!'

'No, Mum. I –'

'Have you told anyone?'

'No! You're hurting me!'

'You'd better not say anything to anyone. ANYONE, do you hear?'

'I haven't.' Mason was crying now.

Ruth pulled him nearer still; she was having trouble focusing on him. Why wouldn't he stay in one place?

'If you do tell someone, they'll put you and your brother into care. You'll end up in a children's home, with lots of other naughty kids and you and your brother will be split up. Because it's your fault that I do this. You and your brother. You won't behave yourself. You're always up to mischief. Always doing something that you shouldn't. There's no way anyone would want the two of you, anyway. You're nothing but a bloody liability.'

Mason stood still now, tears pouring down his face. 'I – I only wanted a drink of water,' he whispered.

It was enough to bring Ruth out of her trance. She pushed him away from her. 'Go on then and be quick about it.'

Mason did as he was told and was gone in seconds. Ruth grabbed for the craft knife, picking it up by the blade and relishing the feel of it pressing into the skin on her fingers. Stuff them, she thought as she settled back into the settee. Stuff Mason, and Jamie. And Martin. And that fucking Gina Bradley.

As she drew the craft knife across the inside of her arm, for a second as she saw the red line getting thicker and thicker, she felt that little bit better.

While Ruth watched the blood drip out of the cut and onto her T-shirt, Gina was trying to focus on the cards fanned out in her hand. She peered at them with resignation. They weren't good enough to win. She contemplated whether to call it a day or have another lager.

Pete put his cards down onto the table one by one, a

triumphant grin on his face. He reached for the pile of coins on the table in front of him, but John placed a hand over his.

'Not so quick, my friend.' John spread out his cards. 'Look at 'em and weep, my son,' he grinned, pulling the money towards him. 'I win again.'

'You lucky git,' Pete cried as he shuffled the cards again. He looked at Gina. 'Another game?'

Gina shook her head. 'You've had all my fag money so far.'

There was a knock at the front door. All three of them looked up in surprise. It was way past midnight.

Gina got to her feet just as another knock rang out, this time much louder. 'All right, all right, I'm coming.'

'Where is he?' Caren pushed past her and into the house.

'Well, hello, to you too,' Gina smiled lazily. Oh, she was going to enjoy this.

'Jeez, what a mess,' Caren muttered quietly as she walked through the living room and into the kitchen.

'Oy, I heard that, you cheeky cow.' Gina followed close behind her.

'Caren!' John smiled at her before returning to look at the cards in his hand.

Caren stood over them, folding her arms. 'John, it's gone midnight again. How long are you going to be this time?'

'As long as it takes to win this fat fucker's money.'

'Less of the fat, you cheeky bugger,' Pete laughed. He flicked his eyes up to Caren and then back to his cards. 'He won't be long now, so hurry back home, little wifey.'

John fanned his hand out on the table. 'Beat that, loser.'

Pete looked back at his own cards before admitting defeat. He threw them down. 'You are one hell of a lucky bastard.'

'He won't be, by the time I've finished with him.' Caren waved a hand in front of John's face. 'Remember me? I'm standing by your side.'

'Chill out,' said Gina, sitting back down at the table. 'We're playing for ten pence pieces, not ten pound notes. He won't bankrupt you again, if that's what's worrying you.'

'I knew you shouldn't have opened your mouth,' Caren hissed.

Looking awkward, John shrugged the comment off. 'I'm having a night out with friends. A few beers and a laugh, that's all.'

'Have you no sense of pride?' Caren lowered her head to his level. 'Why would you ever call these two friends?'

'Hey!' snapped Gina.

'All I'm saying is you've got to get up early in the morning –'

John sniggered. 'What do I have to get up for? All you do is nag, nag, nag.'

Caren baulked. 'This isn't the time to get into a full-blown row.'

'No, I suppose not.' John sighed. 'You'll more than likely keep that for tomorrow.'

Gina sat grinning as she watched the exchange with intrigue. A plan began to form in her mind, just exactly how she could get one up on Caren after all.

Silence engulfed the room as Caren stood fuming. When John didn't look up for a few seconds, she snapped. 'Fine, have it your way. But if you're not home in fifteen minutes, the bolts will be across and you'll have to sleep here.'

John looked up in alarm but Caren was already heading out of the room. He went to shout after her but noticing Pete staring at him, shrugged and grabbed the cards. He began to shuffle out a new game, hardly jumping at all as the front door slammed moments later.

'Another beer, boys?' Gina rushed over to the fridge.

'Now, you see?' Pete slapped her bottom as she went past. 'That's how a woman should treat you – with respect.'

John said nothing. He picked up his hand and gave it the once over. Typical; his luck had changed.

As Gina removed the bottle tops, leaving the one that dropped to the floor, she turned back to the table and noticed the scowl on John's face. Bleeding hell, she hadn't realised how hen-pecked he was. Maybe she should try and persuade them to do this more often. Then, if she could get Caren to lock him out again, maybe she could take advantage of the situation. She smiled deviously. Caren had handed her husband over on a huge serving platter. Pretty soon, he'd be hers for the taking.

CHAPTER ELEVEN

Caren was in the kitchen when John came downstairs the next morning. It was nine thirty: she'd been up since six.

'Can I come in?' he asked, holding his hands up in surrender.

'If you must.'

He tried to touch her arm as she moved past him but she slapped it out of the way. Noisily, she piled the dishes in the sink, glad that the radio was on to avoid the inevitable silence.

'I'm sorry, I was out of order. I had too much to drink. I'm a total idiot.'

'You missed off selfish bastard.' Caren wiped at her hands with the tea towel. 'And don't forget the I'm with my mates again so fuck off wifey bastard. You made me look like a right nag.'

'I didn't mean to.'

'You could have fooled me. Gina was relishing every second of it. I wish I'd leaned over and wiped that smug look off her face.'

John smirked: he knew that was never going to happen. Caren's tongue was lethal but a fighter she wasn't.

'I am sorry,' he said again. 'Sometimes I want to forget things for a while. And where better to forget normality than across the road. It really is a weird place: all those boxes of stuff everywhere. And clothes piled high; magazines and mugs and... I couldn't wait to get out, if I'm honest.'

'I can't understand why you have to forget things by going over there. I mean, why can't you sit with me in the evening?'

'After the mood you'd been in all day?' John scoffed.

Caren sighed. He was right: she'd been in a foul temper yesterday. She hadn't got a particular reason to feel angry, but she'd been really crabby with him. In fact, she recalled, ashamed at herself now, she'd wanted to pick a fight with him because she was so fed up. No wonder he'd slammed out to get some peace.

'How about I make it up to you this evening?' she offered. 'I'll cook up something special and we can check out the television, watch a film.' She grinned. 'I'll even let you choose.'

'I thought you'd be really mad.'

'I am really mad, but I don't want to fight. So...' she reached for his hand and placed it on her breast. 'A film and good food – unless you can think of anything else you might like to do?'

Rachel put a finger to her lips and turned to look at Claire. 'Over there.' She pointed into the distance. By the side of Shop&Save car park sat two girls, their backs towards them.

'Ready?' she whispered to Claire.

'Ready.'

It had taken five nights of stalking, coming out early to check on their prey, before they'd managed to get Hayley and Shell alone without Stacey Hunter. They knew Stacey wouldn't be far behind but she didn't need to be in this fight. This was payback for the two of them running to Stacey the minute their backs were turned.

They weaved in between the parked cars and across to where they were sitting. Before they could react, Rachel and Claire grabbed a girl apiece around the neck, pulled them backwards and down onto the gravel. Rachel tackled Hayley, the stronger one of the two. She sat astride her and punched her in the face. Hayley struggled to gain ground but it was a no-win situation. All she could do was buck her legs to see if she could knock Rachel off balance.

Claire, however, had failed to keep Shell down on the ground. As Shell landed a punch to the side of her head, she rushed at her, fists and feet flying at the same time.

Rachel aimed another fist at Hayley's face and struck her in the mouth. She noticed a splattering of blood across her knuckles and looked up. Hayley's top lip had split. Knowing she had the upper hand, Rachel took a moment to catch her breath. Then she punched her one last time before getting up to help out her sister.

Claire was pulling Shell around by the hood of her jacket, trying to knock her to the ground again. Rachel grabbed Shell's hair as she swung past her and thumped her in the face. Shell dropped to her knees in an instant. Rachel drew back her foot to kick her but Claire put a hand on her arm.

'NO!'

Rachel turned with a glint in her eye that Claire had learned to recognise as the danger zone.

Ignoring it, Rachel kicked Shell in the stomach.

Claire pushed Rachel to one side. 'Back off, Rach!'

'Move out of my way.'

'No. There are people everywhere!'

Rachel looked around her. A group of lads at the far end of the car park stood watching. A man and his dog walking past stopped to wonder what was going on. An elderly couple hurried to the safety of their car.

Claire held her breath, knowing enough to recognize the situation was hardly under control. She'd been there so many times before, thinking that Rachel had calmed down only for her to turn back and kick the unsuspecting victim and continue with the fight. But the lull in action was long enough for Shell to pull herself up, and stagger off with Hayley.

Rachel stared after them but didn't move to follow. Claire let out her breath again. She clenched and unclenched her hands, felt the ache. Her left eye was swelling by the second; Shell had caught her good and proper. She glanced in their direction but they'd already disappeared out of sight. No doubt one of them would be on the phone to Stacey, telling of how the Bradley twins had caught them off guard. She wondered how long it would be before someone jumped the two of them. She sure as hell wasn't looking forward to it. But for now, it was over.

Rachel, suddenly more calm and collected than she'd been in a long time, felt that feeling of superiority wash over her. 'What the fuck are you lot staring at?' she shouted to the lads who were still watching. They all turned away. One thing she knew, not a one of them would dare speak out, talk about the incident. They were too scared of what she'd do to them. She pulled her sister close and they walked off together.

'So what shall we do now?' she asked her.

'I might go home and get cleaned up. Mum'll kill me if she sees me like this.'

Rachel shrugged, knowing when she was beat. As they walked off, she felt that familiar stirring inside. The fight of their lives was brewing: she knew this was the beginning. It was going to be tough, for Claire especially, but right now, all she could think about was that she was ready.

Bring it on.

The following afternoon, Ruth sat at the kitchen table. The darkness was falling. Although she could feel and see the warning signs, she knew there wasn't anything she could do to stop it. Being with Martin meant she'd had to hide it, control it; keep it well hidden. But since she'd moved to Stanley Avenue without him, it had begun to control her again. She knew it was going to consume her completely soon.

It was half past two: another half hour and she'd have to make the trek to fetch the boys from school. Well now, wouldn't that be exciting? Yeah, a real bundle of laughs. Mason had hardly said a word to her since her outburst the other night, no matter how much she'd smiled, cajoled, apologised and pleaded with him. Jamie hadn't been too bad; he was too young to understand why his mum was happy one minute and screaming at him the next. In his own little world, he was just glad when she was happy.

But Mason ignoring her made Ruth realise how terrible it must be for them. She ran a hand through unwashed hair. What must they think of her – a drunken mother who cut herself, screamed at them all the time when all they were doing was enjoying their childhood? Would they compare her to the mothers of the kids at school? The perfect mothers with their perfect lives, their perfect homes, their perfect husbands.

Glenn, Glenn, Glenn. That stupid cow Gina had brought him hurtling to the front of her mind again. She tapped a foot on the floor persistently. What would he think of her now? Would Glenn hang his head in shame? Would he grab her by the shoulders and shake her? Would he talk some sense into her or would he realise that it was too late? All she wanted was to feel his arms around her, be drawn into his embrace and held there. It was the only place she'd ever felt safe. Without that, there was nowhere to hide.

She reached for the small plastic bottle in front of her as the oppressive silence began to draw her in. Her hand clasped around it tightly. Next to it was the rest of the vodka that she'd started the previous night. She pulled that nearer too.

It would be so easy. A pill: a swig of vodka. Another pill: another swill of vodka. How long would it take? She peered at the clock: twenty to three. Who would care enough to see why she hadn't turned up to collect Mason and Jamie? Who else knew of her existence? She thought of her mum, alone since her dad died two years ago. They'd fallen out over something so stupid, so trivial that she couldn't remember what. It was probably about Martin, it usually was.

The knock on the front door made her visibly jump. She turned her head slightly. Through the open kitchen door, she could see through to the hallway. It was her way back into the real world.

She stayed sitting at the table.

Another knock: she ignored that too, watching as a white card came through the letter box and fluttered to the floor moments later. There wasn't another knock after that. But, for now, the spell had been broken. Ruth hid the bottle and the pills, wiped a cloth quickly around her face and reached for her keys. She picked the card up on her way out. It was from the housing officer, that bloody Josie Mellor again.

Ruth threw it in the wheelie bin as she left the house.

Josie had her suspicions that Ruth was at home that afternoon. But, then again, it was near time for the school run. Maybe if she'd got there a little sooner as planned, she would have caught her. But she'd been dragged into another discussion about Susan Harrison in Derek Place, the state of her welfare as well as her two kids and the property. She'd tried to get in there too, on several occasions, but each time had been, well, shooed away, to put it politely.

With a sense of dread, she walked up the path towards Gina Bradley's front door. She rapped on it sharply. As usual, Gina opened it in her own time.

'For fuck's sake, not you again,' she cried.

'Yes, it's me –'

'What have they done this time?' Gina didn't wait for an answer. She went back into the living room.

'Do you know anything about the fight on the square the other night?' Josie asked as she followed behind.

'Nope.' Gina sat down and pressed play on the TV remote control.

Josie perched on the armchair and sighed - the place was a tip as usual. 'Gina, I don't know how many times I'm going to sit here and warn you about the girls' behaviour.'

'Then don't.'

'You're happy if they end up in a detention centre?'

'It would get them off my back.' Gina glared at Josie. 'And it would get you off my back too.'

Josie leaned forward and pressed the mute button on the remote control.

'Hey!' Gina protested, raising her hands in the air. 'You can't do that!'

'I need you to listen to me. The CCTV camera clearly shows the fight but not which two girls dragged the others to the floor. However, there were lots of people around to witness the event.'

'And?'

'And the police are going to be talking to them.'

'And these witnesses are going to make statements, are they?'

Josie sighed. 'I'm not sure, but –'

'Thought as much.'

'The police can charge without witness statements now there is evidence on film.'

'If they can distinguish one girl from another, like you say.' Gina closed her eyes and pinched the top of her nose. 'I do my best. What more do you want from me?'

Josie's silence spoke volumes. She knew she wouldn't get through to Gina, nor her layabout husband, but she couldn't let go. If she could make Gina see sense, if she could change her attitude, then maybe it would rub off on the girls. Even if Gina got to one of them, they were so close they could both change. She decided to switch tactics.

'Have you ever thought about coming along to any of the sessions at The Workshop or the community house?'

Gina snorted. 'And join your goody-goody tribe? I don't think so.'

'Why not? I reckon it'd be good for you to get out and do something different.'

'Happy doing what I do, thanks.'

'Are you really?'

Gina shrugged.

'But don't you ever get bored?'

'There's plenty to watch on the telly.'

'Well, maybe if you got involved in The Workshop sessions, then the girls might come along too. I'm always crying out for volunteers and someone like you, who knows the estate, might –'

Gina laughed then. 'You have no idea.'

'Well, I –'

'You don't have kids, do you?'

'Not yet,' she replied.

'Leaving it a little late, aren't we?'

'That's none of your business.'

'And what me and my girls do is none of your business either.'

Josie sighed in frustration. 'Clearly it's not worth me visiting to see if I can help out.'

'Clearly.' Gina was already reaching for the remote control.

'Okay, have it your way. No doubt the next people to call will be the police and they won't take any crap from you. You've had your chance to get involved and start acting as you should. I can't do any more for you if –'

'See yourself out, will you?' Gina interrupted.

'Fine,' snapped Josie. 'But don't say that I didn't try.'

Once Josie had gone, her words hanging heavy in the air, Gina felt tears prick her eyes. She knew Josie was only trying to help but what the hell did she know about her life really? She folded her arms and put her feet up on the coffee table, flicking through the TV channels again. The program she was watching before she was so rudely interrupted had finished.

Damn that woman! How come every time Josie Mellor came knocking, the minute she left she'd start getting all weepy? So what if her girls were the scum of the estate – how was that her fault? Weren't all teens hard to control? Every time she picked up a newspaper, there was always some story or another to be read about it. What made her girls so different? And this was the Mitchell Estate – did Josie really expect anything to change?

She knew she sounded defeatist but living this life for so long had taken its toll on her. She would never have any faith, any belief that her life could change for the better. It would only get worse, year after year after year.

She glanced at the clock to find it was nearly tea time. Her stomach felt like her throat had been cut. What did she fancy? A nice fresh chicken salad with crusty bread? A nice bowl of homemade soup? She stretched her arms above her head, her tears long ago banished. Stuff it: she'd never change. It wasn't in her to lose weight and look all girlie. Better to welcome her inner fat demon with open arms and go down to the chippy later on.

CHAPTER TWELVE

After their triumph two nights earlier, Rachel and Claire were on a high. Shell and Hayley had kept well away from them and the rest of the gang. The other members had been in awe of what they'd done. Rachel still felt that her rightful place was at the head of the gang. She was top dog.

So when the counter attack came, they were completely caught off guard. It happened when they turned the corner of Stanley Avenue onto Davy Road. Feeling safe in their own territory, they hadn't expected anyone to assault them there. Fists went flying, feet kicked out. Claire took a punch to the nose and dropped to her knees. Rachel was dragged to the floor by two girls: it was hard to tell who, their hoods tied up by their chins. She took punch after punch, two onto one overpowering her.

Claire jumped at the nearest girl. She pawed at the hood, finally managing to pull it back. Wondering which bitch she'd got hold of out of Hayley and Shell, she was shocked at who she revealed.

'Charlie!'

'You traitor!' Rachel punched the side of her head.

Charlie staggered back. As a natural lull came, the two of them stood side by side, wondering who the hell was hidden by the other hood. When Leanne revealed herself, Rachel gasped.

'You!' Claire launched herself at her. But Rachel stood in front of her to block her way.

'Leave it!' she said.

'But they can't get –'

'I said leave it!'

Claire stood glaring at them. She finally calmed down enough for Rachel to let go of her.

'Why?' she turned to Charlie. She'd thought Charlie was a true friend. How could she have done that to them?

'It's our initiation test,' said Charlie.

Rachel understood then. 'You've gone back to Stacey, haven't you?'

'I was never with her in the first place.'

'But you're with her now?'

Charlie nodded.

'And you?' Rachel looked at Leanne.

She nodded too.

'Which means the gangs are equal now.'

'Which is exactly what Stacey intended,' said Leanne. 'She wants us all back, in one gang, or...'

'Or?' said Rachel.

Leanne shrugged. 'Surely you can work that one out for yourself. Come on, Charlie. We're finished here.'

With all the noise as the girls let themselves in through the back door, Gina jumped clean out of the forty winks she was having between episodes of Coronation Street. She rushed through to the kitchen to see what all the commotion was.

'I'll kill her,' Rachel said, reaching for a tea towel. 'I'll fucking kill her! Charlie, of all people!'

'What the hell's going on?' Gina demanded.

Rachel kept her back towards Gina as she ran the tap and wet the towel underneath it. Claire looked down to the floor. She knew it had been a bad idea to come home but Rachel's top lip had split. There was blood all down her jumper.

'Rachel?' said Gina.

'It's nothing,' she said.

Gina marched over and tilted Rachel's chin up to the light. 'You've been fighting again.' She sighed. 'Will you two ever learn!'

'It wasn't our fault,' Claire protested, folding her arms. 'We didn't start it.'

Gina raised her eyebrows. 'No, but I bet you started the fight that got you this beating.'

Rachel held the cloth to her mouth. 'It wasn't us!'

'It doesn't matter.' Gina pointed to the table. 'Sit, both of you.' No one moved. 'I said SIT!'

The two girls flounced across the room and sat down. Claire pushed aside the dirty tea plates that wouldn't be washed until they were needed again. She sniffed: her nose was beginning to swell already.

Gina sat down across from them. 'What's going on with you two?' she asked. 'All of a sudden you've grown into monsters. More than that, you're acting like animals. Not much better than a pack of wild dogs.' She pointed at Rachel, holding the towel to her mouth. 'It's horrible to see you looking like this, but what's worse, is how you got like that. Fighting in the street – where were you exactly?'

'At the bottom of the avenue. The bitches were waiting for us when we turned into Davy Road.'

'Have you any idea how nasty that looks – to see girls fighting?'

'It's common, Mum,' said Rachel. 'You need to get with the times.'

'I don't give a shit if it's common! All I know is that it's disgusting and you need to pack it in. Christ, you leave school in a few months: who's going to employ you if you continue to act like children?'

'Like anyone will employ us anyway.' Claire sniggered. 'Just think, Mum, come summer time, we'll be here and under your feet.'

Gina stared at Claire, trying not to give her inner thoughts away. That wasn't something she'd ever look forward to but she knew it would probably be the reality of the situation. Both girls spent more time away from school than in lessons so she knew they most probably wouldn't make the grades for their exams – that is if she could get them to turn up to take any.

'But don't you have any ambitions? Anything you want to do when you leave school?'

'The only ambition I have right now is to ram my fist into Stacey Hunter's face.'

'Rachel!'

'She's dead when I get hold of her. I'm going to rip every hair from her head if she starts after mine. But not before I've thrown a few punches at her and –'

'If you don't shut up with the big talk, I'll reach over there and give you a crack myself!'

Rachel stood up so quickly that her chair fell to the floor. 'I've had enough of this. I'm off out.'

'No, you're not.' Gina looked at each one of them in turn. 'You two are grounded.'

'That's not fair,' Claire protested.

'Until you can go out without causing trouble, I think –'

'But we didn't start anything!'

'They'll get back at you though and... have you any idea what can happen in the heat of the moment? It could all end in tears.'

'The only tears will be coming from Stacey when I punch her lights out,' declared Rachel. She moved towards the door.

Gina followed her, pulling her back before she made it outside. 'Where do you think you're going?'

'Out!'

'And I've just told you that you're grounded, for the rest of the week.'

'Let go of me,' said Rachel.

'Come on, Rach.' Claire stood up. 'Let's go listen to some music.'

But Rachel was intent on staring her mother down. 'Let go of me,' she repeated.

When Gina didn't relinquish her grip, she saw Rachel's free hand curl up into a fist and aim it at her face. In the nick of time, she blocked it with her forearm and then slapped Rachel across the face.

Rachel's eyes widened and filled with tears.

Gina moved her head closer. 'Don't you dare, do you hear me? Don't you fucking DARE! I may be smaller than you, I may be older than you, but I am your mother and you will respect me for that. When I say you're grounded, I mean it. Now get up to your room, and I don't want to see you,' she turned to Claire, who was looking visibly shocked, 'either of you, until tomorrow morning. Is that clear?'

Hearing their footsteps thundering up the stairs, Gina sat down at the table again and reached for a cigarette. She finally controlled her shaking hands enough to light it. The nicotine hit calmed her down momentarily. She ran a hand through her hair: it was like watching Danny growing up all over again, but this time she had two of them. She inhaled again and again as panic struck her. Would she be able to stay in control when they got that little bit older?

It was ten to nine: where was Pete? She hadn't seen him since that morning when he'd gone out to sign on for his benefits. Damn the man for not being around to help her deal with this. She didn't dare risk nipping around to her mum's to talk about what had happened; she knew the minute she disappeared, they'd be out again, seeking revenge on Stacey. It was bound to happen; she wasn't stupid enough to think otherwise. But for now, the hope was to calm down the situation. If Rachel and Claire went after Stacey, one of them could end up getting seriously hurt.

Gina sighed into the empty room. She took a last couple of drags from her cigarette before putting it out. Then she dropped to her knees on the kitchen floor, opened the door to the sink unit and fumbled about at the back of it. Hidden behind numerous cleaning materials that went untouched, she found half a bottle of vodka. Not bothering with a glass, she twisted off the cap and knocked back a considerable amount in one swig. Damn, that tasted good.

She wiped her mouth with the back of her sleeve. Then she waddled through into the living room with the rest of the vodka. She flopped onto the settee and reached for the remote control.

Damn those bloody girls.

'What's *wrong* with you?' Claire asked Rachel as they went into their room. 'Have you gone totally barmy?'

Rachel flung herself down onto her bed. 'Leave me alone.'

'But you were going to hit Mum!'

'So?'

Claire gasped. 'So you should never hit your olds. I know she can be a pain at times, and an idle cow, but she's our Mum.'

Rachel buried her head in her pillow and pummelled the mattress either side. 'Argh!'

Claire sat down beside her. 'You were way out of order.'

'It's that bitch's fault, that Stacey Hunter. She started all of this.'

'Maybe but you don't have to be so nasty to Mum. She's on our side; she just doesn't want us to get involved in any more trouble.'

'You're only saying that because you're scared of what Stacey might do.'

'No, I'm not!'

'Yes, you are. You're scared of your own fucking shadow.'

Claire got up and left the room then. There was no talking to Rachel when she was in this sort of mood; she'd have to wait for her to calm down. Instead, she went to the bathroom to inspect the damage done by Leanne. In the cracked mirror above the sink, she saw what a mess she looked. She pressed a hand to the swelling on her nose and winced. Charlie had thrown a really good punch: she'd never gone down so quickly before. She peered a little closer: there was a tiny cut at the side and one eye had started to discolour. She was going to have a right shiner tomorrow. Still, it meant legitimate time off school. They weren't allowed to go in looking like they'd done ten rounds in a boxing ring. Besides if she did, it would probably be her who got detention for fighting, even though she hadn't been the instigator.

She cleaned herself up and went back to their room. Rachel was lying on her side, her face towards the wall. As she lay back on her own bed, Claire listened intently but she couldn't hear anything. She knew Rachel wasn't asleep but she didn't seem to be crying either.

'Rach?'

Nothing.

'Rach?' A little louder but nothing again.

Sighing, she grabbed a magazine from the floor and lost herself in a world of celebrity.

Rachel wasn't sleeping. She'd turned her back as soon as she heard Claire come out of the bathroom because she didn't want her to see that she'd been crying. But even though she'd been expecting something to happen, she'd had enough tonight.

Although she'd known that Stacey wouldn't take things lying

down and she'd been ready for a fight, she thought it would happen across on the square. Both she and Claire had been unprepared. They weren't even on their bikes, or else they wouldn't have been caught.

But the way she was feeling was more to do with hitting out at her mum. She felt guilty. Claire was right; she shouldn't have lashed out at her. Even though she always gave her lip, respect was respect. There were some things you didn't do on the Mitchell Estate. Hitting your olds was one of them.

Was she out of control, like Mum said? Was she going to end up going off her head like Stacey Hunter? She looked over at Claire. Her head was in a magazine, her right foot tapping away. She turned on her side to face her.

'You have to stick with me on this,' she said.

'Meaning?'

'Meaning that I'm going to stay top dog. I just need to get rid of Stacey.'

Claire closed the magazine, threw it onto the floor and lay on her side, facing her sister. 'How?'

'I'm not sure. I'll have to think about it. Have you got any ideas?'

Claire thought for a moment, then shook her head. 'I'll have a think too. But you'd better make sure that whatever it is, you take Stacey out or she'll be the one that's always top dog.'

'You don't think we can do it?'

Claire shrugged. 'I'm not sure it's worth bothering about, if I'm honest.'

Rachel raised herself to one elbow. 'But we –'

'I'm not saying that I won't help you. I'm just saying that we could go back to how it was.'

'No.'

'But it used to be a laugh!'

'I said no, all right!'

'Okay, okay, calm down.'

'I need to know that you'll be with me.'

'Of course I'll be with you, but –'

'Good. We'll sort her out and then we'll take control again. It'll be a doddle, you'll see. Once we take Stacey down, the rest will follow. It'll –'

'What do you mean, once we take Stacey down?' Claire interrupted.

'It's the only way. They got us tonight, they think we'll retaliate. So instead we go for Stacey. She'll never suss that out, until it's too late.'

'But we can't fight her. Well, I can't anyway. She'll beat me to a frigging pulp.'

Rachel frowned. 'We can do it together!'

'But that's not fair!'

'Was it fair what they did to us tonight?'

'It was only because we did it to Hayls and Shell.'

'But we're known for doing everything together. If we attack Stacey so that she knows we mean business, she'll be shit scared of us catching her again, she'll back off and –'

'– and then you'll be top dog,' Claire said.

'Exactly.'

Claire looked away. Everything was always about Rachel. It was Rachel who wanted to get back at Stacey. She'd come out head of the gang; Claire, however, having done some of the dirty work with her, would then have to play second fiddle. It wasn't fair. That's why she liked Stacey being in charge. For her, it meant not being undermined by her dominant twin.

Rachel glared at her. 'You're not going to help me?'

'Sure I'll help you. I'm just not sure that I should.'

'Because you are my sister; that should be enough.'

'You're my sister, too, but you never listen to me.'

'Yes, but I look out for you.'

Claire said nothing. There wasn't any point.

Across the street, Caren shuddered as she opened the back door and took out the rubbish. She lifted the lid of the bin and jumped as she heard a noise behind her. The only light coming from the kitchen window, she peered into the darkness.

'Hello?' she ventured.

'Why, hello, gorgeous.'

Caren sighed as Pete came out of the shadows.

'John's inside,' she told him.

'It's not John I've come to see. It's you.' He grabbed her upper arm, roughly jerking her towards him. 'What the fuck are you playing at?'

'I don't know what you're –'

'You told John to keep away from me, didn't you?'

'Let go of me!' Caren tried to shake off his grip as he pushed her up against the wall of the house. He pressed against her, his leg between her thighs forcing her feet to widen. Then he grabbed her chin.

Caren's breath began to come in rasps. She banged her foot on the wall, hoping to alert John. But she knew he'd be watching the television: she'd only gone in the kitchen to make a cup of tea before the late evening news began.

'I could have you,' Pete said.

Caren froze.

'Right here; no one would see us. I'm sure we could be quiet.'

'Leave me alone.' Her arms stuck down by her sides, she felt her knees beginning to give way. Pete moved his face towards her. Caren squirmed as he kissed her. She clenched her teeth when she felt his tongue against them.

He pressed roughly on her breast. 'Don't be a prick tease, now. I know you want me. I can tell every time I see you.' He reached for her hand and placed it on his crotch.

Oh, God, she could feel his hardness.

'See what you do to me.'

Caren whimpered in fright. 'John will be out in a minute,' she whispered.

Pete kissed her again. This time she moved her head to the side. He thrust his tongue into her ear. Then he grabbed her chin again.

'If John wants to see his mates, catch up on old times and play a few card games, you won't stop him. Do you hear?'

Caren nodded.

'And I don't want John to know about this, or else there'll be more where that came from. As you can see, there's always a time when I can get you alone.'

She nodded again, this time fervently.

'Good girl.' Pete kissed her one last time before moving away.

CHAPTER THIRTEEN

Caren sat in the living room, trying not to spill the tea she was attempting to drink. Instead of leaving after he'd groped her, Pete walked into their house as if nothing had happened and invited John out for a late drink. Caren faked a smile and told John to go out. Even though he looked on in surprise, he jumped to his feet and ran upstairs to get changed, leaving Pete in the living room with her. A frosty silence lingered in the air as they watched the news. Pete kept glancing across at her but her eyes stayed firmly on the television screen.

It was a long ten minutes before John appeared again. She sent him on his way with a kiss. As soon as the front door closed behind them, she rushed upstairs and took a shower. She scrubbed her skin until it felt raw, shaking as she recalled what Pete had done, what he'd said, what he'd touched.

Sitting on the settee afterwards, she realised that what had happened could easily happen again. Pete lived right across the road. If he wanted to, he could watch the house, see when John disappeared and come hurtling across. She'd have to lock the doors all the time from now on ;there was no way she could leave them open, in case he showed up unannounced again.

She wondered – had he been waiting for her or had it just been good timing on his part? Had he been watching for her routine? She thought about telling John but immediately dismissed the idea. What if Pete denied it – what would she do then? Who would John believe? She'd like to think it was her, but after their recent arguments about the time he was spending over there, John would have his doubts. Who wouldn't?

Caren began to cry again. She was in a no win situation. Damn that man and his family. What chance did she have of keeping John on the straight and narrow now?

*

Further down Stanley Avenue, Ruth was trying to get her boys to go to bed. She hadn't realised the time after falling asleep on the sofa. After having a glass or two of wine, she felt exhausted, drained, a dark mood coming down quickly but she couldn't be bothered to move.

'Come on you two,' she said. 'You've school in the morning.'

'Don't want to go to school,' Mason said, banging his feet against the wall as he lay on his back in the armchair.

'You have to go to school.'

'No, we don't. We can stay at home and look after you.'

Ruth smiled absent-mindedly. 'That's nice.'

'We need to look after you because you're mad.' Mason made a circling motion by his temple. 'You're a mad mum. You're a mad mum.'

'You're a mad mum!' Jamie joined in, banging his toy car in time to his syllables.

Ruth closed her eyes and pinched the bridge of her nose. 'Bed, you two. Now!'

'No,' said Jamie.

Ruth stood up quickly. 'How many more times do I have to tell you?' She pointed to the door. 'Bed, now!'

They scurried away quickly.

Ruth sat down again. Once they were asleep, she could break out the bottle of Bacardi she'd bought. Get pissed on her own, fall asleep here on the sofa and end the day as she'd begun it. Jeez, her life was so exciting.

The noise of the boys stomping around upstairs soon escalated. Jamie started to scream. Ruth pressed mute on the remote control.

'Pack it in, you two!' she shouted up to them. But the noise continued.

'Mum!' screamed Jamie, rushing into her. 'Mason is hitting me!'

Ruth ignored him. 'La la la.' She turned the sound up on the television, notch by notch by notch, until the sound distorted. Stuff them, she thought. She too could play stupid games.

Suddenly, there was a bang on the wall beside her. Ruth jumped out of her trance and switched the volume down.

'Are you fucking mad?' a voice shouted from next door. 'Pack it in or I'll put your windows through.'

Ruth switched the sound off completely. Jamie's screams had turned to sobs now but she didn't comfort him. They'd sort themselves out: they always did.

In the kitchen, she reached for the Bacardi. Not bothering with a glass, she twisted off the top and swigged it neat from the bottle. Faster, faster, the liquid poured down her throat, spilling over her lips, down her neck in her hurry to get it all in there.

Block out the pain.

Block out the hurt.

Block out the darkness.

She stared at the bottle before throwing it at the wall. As it smashed, she screamed. It was much louder than Jamie.

As soon as Gina's back was turned the following evening, Claire and Rachel sneaked out of the house. They were on the prowl for Stacey. When she wasn't across on Vincent Square, they waited outside her house until she came out.

'Hunter!' Rachel shouted when she spotted her. 'A word.'

Stacey tutted loudly. 'What do you two want?'

'You.' Rachel punched her in the face before she had time to do anything about it. But it didn't have the desired effect: Stacey stayed on her feet.

'Is that all you've got, bitch?' She taunted. 'Or do I have to fight you both?'

Rachel punched her again. Claire rushed at her.

Stacey fell to one knee but stood upright again immediately. She screamed as her fists flew out in every direction.

'Oy! What's going on out here?' A man in his thirties appeared behind his garden gate next door. He pointed down the street. 'Fuck off out of here, Stacey. You wake my kids up and you'll know it.'

Rachel took the opportunity to catch her breath, holding on to her ribs where Stacey had caught her a blow. This wasn't going to plan. They were supposed to take her down, kick the shit out of her and then drag her over to the shops where the rest of the girls would probably be waiting for her by then.

Except Stacey wouldn't *go* down. Even with the two of them, she stood her ground. Blood trickled from her nose but she had her fists up, ready to hit out again at any moment.

'I said fucking move!' The man opened his gate and ran towards them, a piece of wood in his hands raised in the air.

All three of them ran. At the end of the street, Rachel and Claire headed toward the Square. Stacey doubled back and ran down the steps and along Peter's Walk.

'You fucking coward!' Rachel shouted after her.

'That was close,' said Claire.'

'I know; he was a nutter waving that wood around like that.'

'I didn't mean him.' Claire turned to her. 'We were lucky to get away then, Rach. Stacey took us both on and she was winning! If he hadn't come out, she'd have hurt one of us and then have started on the other. *She's* the nutter.'

Rachel knew she was right. They'd have to think of another plan – and quickly. Other than that, Stacey would win the battle.

'Let's get over to the Square,' she said, 'and put our side of the story out first.'

'Which is?'

'We were winning, right?'

While her twins were out fighting again, Gina lay soaking in the bath. A glass of wine balancing on the ledge, she ran a cheap razor over her legs. She found it tough going to get rid of the pale hairs growing there; they hadn't seen a blade in ages. The water was turning positively murkier as she dipped the razor in and left the scum behind.

'Shit!' She cried out as the blade nicked her again. She wiped away the blood as it emerged. At this rate, she'd need to cover up her legs and, for once, that wasn't on the agenda. Tonight she'd be wearing easy clothes for easy access, because tonight she was going to have John Williams. She was going to sleep with him right underneath the nose of that snotty bitch he called his wife.

She rubbed a hand over her right breast. Just thinking about what she was going to do was turning her on. Her hand moved lower as she imagined more of what they would be doing. John would take her in his arms and pull her onto his lap. She'd feel his hardness beneath her, rub herself up against him while they kissed. Long smoochy kisses that she and Pete had given up years ago. Then she'd move his hands to her breasts and he'd knead them while she climbed on top of him. He'd kiss her while he moved her up and down, up and down, up and down. The image in her mind became tuned into her body and as she felt the ripples of pleasure engulf her, she said his name aloud.

Afterwards, she lay in the cooling bath water and smiled. She knew John wanted her. She'd seen the looks he'd been throwing her; sly, secretive looks that only she would have noticed. Pete was going out with John again so, once they'd come in from the pub, she would keep them drinking. She'd have to be careful though – she didn't want him to suffer from brewer's droop – but she needed to get them drunk enough so that he'd fall asleep on the sofa and Pete would head off for bed. It was a perfect plan, really.

She reached for the shampoo, rubbed a dollop in her hair, and ducked beneath the water. Had she seen the scum forming, she might have thought twice about it.

But things didn't go to plan for Gina. Pete and John arrived back just after midnight and had wanted a fry-up. Although Claire had gone to bed, Rachel was up and sitting on the settee chatting to John as he gobbled down a bacon buttie.

Pete slapped Gina's bottom as she came back into the room with a sandwich for herself. 'Great grub,' he spoke with his mouthful. He laughed and looked across at John. 'I suppose she's useful for something.'

'Hey, do you mind!' Gina glared at him before knocking Rachel's feet off the coffee table. Then she squeezed herself into the space between her and John.

'Jeez, Mum,' Rachel complained. 'You're too fat to sit on here.'

'Oy!' Gina felt her skin burning up. But when John joined in with the laughter, she smiled then, glancing surreptitiously at him.

She knew it was an act to keep everyone from guessing what he really thought.

'You like me just the way I am, John, don't you?' she couldn't help asking.

'Erm, yeah, course I do,' said John.

Pete and Rachel burst into raucous laughter.

Pete checked his watch, stood up and stretched. 'I'm off to bed now my belly's full. I need to be up early in the morning. Got some work on at the builder's yard. You up for it, John?'

John sighed. Even knowing Caren would give him hell didn't stop him nodding. They needed the money.

'Need to be gone by eight.'

John looked aghast. 'Eight? I'd better be off.' He stood up but had to steady himself on the arm of the settee. 'Bloody hell, Bradley. How many have we had?'

Pete sniggered. 'Dunno, I lost count.'

Rachel stretched her arms above her head. 'I'm off too. Do you need a hand upstairs, Dad?'

'Cheeky cow.' Pete grinned. Then he looked at John. 'Why don't you crash down there tonight? You look a bit green.'

'I'll be fine in a minute.' John held his head in his hands like it was going to fall off.

'Sit there for a while. Gina'll look after you, won't you, bird?'

'Sure.' Gina tried to sound nonchalant. This was turning out to be perfect after all: John faking his head hurting was genius.

John stood up once the other two had gone. 'I need some water.'

Gina followed him through to the kitchen.

John steadied himself on a cupboard door as he looked for a glass. He staggered back before opening another one.

'Here, use this.' Gina handed him a mug.

He belched noisily and grinned like a naughty schoolboy. 'Ta.'

The sound of water gushing rang in her ears. It spurted everywhere as John tried to put the mug underneath the tap. 'Fuck!'

Gina turned it off quickly. John looked down at his soaked T-shirt. He laughed; she began to laugh with him. Daringly, she took hold of the hem and shrugged the garment up and over his head. John laughed some more. Gina was a little put out then: he was more wasted than Pete. And the only way she could get to kiss him was if he leaned down. Five foot nothing against nearly six foot didn't quite work out. Still, an opportunity was an opportunity.

She reached for his belt buckle, undoing it quickly. 'I think these need to come down too,' she said, ignoring the fact that John's eyes were closing and he was leaning on the worktop as if his legs were going to give way.

She slipped her hand in and around him. Leaning forward as she began to stroke him to life, she dared to kiss his chest. Gentle butterfly kisses.

John gave out a groan. At long last, he began to come to life. Gina glanced up and saw him throw back his head. She laughed inwardly: at least he could get it hard enough after all that booze.

'Oh, that's good, Caz,' he said.

And the magic was spoilt.

Gina's shoulders drooped and she stepped away from him. 'I'm not Caren,' she snapped.

John's eyes opened. For a moment, he looked dazed as he struggled to figure out his whereabouts. Then he saw Gina.

'You have got to be joking!'

'It's no joke.'

John went to speak again but he couldn't find the words. Gina smiled as he left in a hurry. She had him exactly where she wanted him. Although she recognised the shock on his face, she knew it was good for him. He'd sleep with her soon, she was certain of it.

CHAPTER FOURTEEN

The next morning, Ruth awoke from her nap as the door knocker banged down heavily. She checked the time: ten fifteen. After taking the boys to school, she'd slept on the settee, last night's hangover taking its toll. She sat up but didn't go to the door; she wasn't in the mood for visitors – and it would more than likely be that Josie Mellor again. She'd tried to get in twice more since the last time she'd left a card. At this rate, Ruth would have a full deck soon.

'Ruthie?' A voice came through the letterbox. 'Ruthie, it's me.'

Martin!

Ruth staggered to her feet and rushed to the door. 'Martin!' She flung her arms around his neck. 'Oh, it's so good to see you.'

'Good to see you too. Can I come in?'

'Yes, I'll make coffee.'

'Great, although I'd prefer something stronger.'

She smiled at him. It was then that she saw what he had with him.

Martin stepped into the hall, chucking down the black bag full of his belongings. He shrugged off his holdall, leaving that to fall too. 'I've got nowhere to go, babe. It's only for a few days.'

Ruth frowned. 'You can't stay here. It's not –'

'Relax, I'll be as quiet as a mouse. No one will know that I'm here.'

'But –'

Martin leaned forward and put a finger over her lips. 'Put the kettle on, there's a good girl.'

As bold as brass, he took the stairs two at a time and disappeared. Ruth sighed and made her way through to the kitchen. By the time she'd boiled the kettle, Martin literally had his feet underneath the table.

'What happened?' she asked him.

'Got evicted. Couldn't manage without you.'

'What are you going to do?'

'Stay here for a couple of nights until I get settled somewhere else.'

'You'll have to leave then.'

Martin sighed. 'Chill out, Ruth. I won't be here for long.'

'And you'll have to sleep on the sofa.'

'Don't be daft. I'll shack up with you until I find another bed.'

'You'll do no such bloody thing!'

Martin reached across for her hand, giving it a firm squeeze. 'You've become quite the brave lady since we split up.'

Ruth pulled her hand away. She stared at him, wariness clear in her eyes. Martin hadn't even tidied up his hair that morning. His clothes looked as though he'd been wearing them for a couple of days, his facial hair saying the same thing. In his heyday, he'd been a looker. Now, nearing forty, his dark hair was receding rapidly, his teeth decaying slowly. Prominent crow's feet were visible even when he didn't smile; eyes beady like an owl.

Martin reached for her other hand. This one, she didn't move away. She knew she wasn't strong enough to fight him right now. And maybe he'd stop her from self-harming, or from hurting one of the boys. Suddenly, she could see the positive to having him back for a while – providing he hadn't bought Tracy Tanner along with him.

She smiled. 'Something stronger now?'

Once she'd settled Martin in, Ruth realised she'd have to go to the shops. She needed food: she couldn't remember the last time she'd cooked something that hadn't come from a packet. Martin had given her twenty pounds – it wouldn't go far after she'd bought him the cigarettes and lager he'd asked for as well, but it would get them something decent to eat.

Deep in thought, she hadn't been prepared to bump into Gina.

'Oy! You!' Gina screeched as she spotted her. 'I want a word with you.'

Ruth put her head down and continued, walking past another neighbour in their garden.

But Gina wasn't going to be ignored. She let the gate bang shut as she rushed over to face her. 'You want to watch your step, ignoring me like that.' She grabbed Ruth's arm. 'I might lose my temper.'

'What do you want?' Ruth asked.

'My mum said she saw you hit your little lad last week.'

'I – I – we all do it,' she replied. 'He was obviously being naughty.'

'But he's too little to stick up for himself. You shouldn't hit him.'

'I didn't hit him hard,' Ruth decided to say, unsure of exactly what Gina had seen her doing.

'It doesn't matter. You shouldn't –'

'Surely your children had a smack when they were naughty.'

'This isn't about me.' Gina folded her arms. 'This is about you.'

'Haven't you got anything better to do than have a go at people?' someone shouted from behind them.

Gina swivelled on the spot and came face to face with Caren. 'Mind your own business,' she snapped. 'This has nothing to do with you.'

'Do you get a kick out of bullying people?'

'I'm not a bully.'

'Yes, you are.'

Gina took a step nearer to Caren. 'Say anything else and I'll ram my fist into your face.'

Caren sighed. 'That's you all over, isn't it? You *and* your family. Threatening behaviour is the coward's way out.'

'Quit while you're ahead,' she warned.

'Or what? If you hit me, beat me to a pulp even, I'll be here tomorrow. If you hit me again, I'll still be around.' She took a step nearer to Gina, hoping to intimidate her with height as well as words. 'I knew you were a nasty piece of work when we were at school, and that I could understand because we were sixteen and didn't really know any better. But we're in our thirties now; you should try growing up a little.'

Gina felt her skin reddening and she raised her fist. 'Bitch!'

As the two women glared at each other, Ruth took the opportunity to continue on her journey. When Gina noticed, she shouted to her. 'Don't think I've forgotten about you. You might have got away this time, but you'll keep.'

Caren sighed. 'For God's sake, will you listen to yourself? You sound like one of those wayward daughters of yours – they're always fighting from what I hear around the estate.'

'Leave my daughters out of this!'

'Well, it's obvious where they get their traits from. You're hardly a role model – nor that husband of yours.'

Gina narrowed her eyes. 'You ought to get your own house in order first before you start knocking mine. You and John aren't so perfect.'

'Are we going to do tit for tat over each other's family now?' Caren folded her arms and leaned on the garden wall. 'Come on, then. Bring it on.'

'I'm not bringing my family into this discussion.'

'Why not? You're happy to slag off everyone else – like Ruth who's doing her best – but no one can say anything about you. Doesn't seem fair to me, that.'

'If you want to bring families into it, you haven't slept with my husband so I think I win that round.'

Caren faked raucous laughter. 'Like I'd want to do that.'

'For all your cleverness, you are a little thick at times. You don't understand, do you?'

'Understand what?'

'Listen to what I said.' Gina proceeded to pronounce her words like she was speaking to a toddler. 'You may not have slept with my husband but I have yours.'

Gina had Caren's full attention then – and a fair few neighbours who had come out to see what was going on too.

'Tuesday night, pub night,' she continued. 'John came home with Pete. I cooked them a fry up. Pete was smashed and went off to his bed. And your fella and me got down and dirty on the kitchen floor.'

Caren's eyes widened in disbelief. 'You're having a laugh. No one in their right mind would crawl around on your kitchen floor;

they don't know what they'd catch. Can you see the pattern on your tiles anymore?'

Gina played her trump card. 'When did he have his appendix out? That scar on his groin looks fairly old to me.'

Caren visibly paled. How would she know about John's scar? Her mind told her it was something as simple as it being discussed in a conversation: her heart had them shagging away on the kitchen floor.

Suddenly she lurched forward, hand raised high in readiness to slap Gina good and hard. But Gina blocked her. She grabbed her wrist and held on to it tightly.

'Tut tut. Fighting isn't the answer to everything, Mrs Williams.'

'You're lying!' said Caren.

Gina shook her head. 'No, I'm not.'

'You are! You must be. He wouldn't... he wouldn't –'

'Ask him.' Gina knew she was in the prime position. Caren wouldn't ask him: John would deny it anyway. But it would put doubt into her mind and her cosy life.

'Ask him,' she repeated.

Once in the safety of her home, Caren stood in the middle of the living room and gulped back tears. Don't let her get to you, she told herself. She's lying: John wouldn't do that. She searched out her mobile and rung him.

'Is it true?' she snapped.

'Is what true?'

'You and Gina Bradley?'

A pause.

'I can't talk to you now.' Another pause. 'Not here.'

'Why? Is that stupid fucker Pete there with you?'

'Yeah, can we do this later? I'm in the middle of plastering a wall and I need to –'

Caren disconnected the call.

No.

No!

She thought back to last week, when Pete had taken John out after he'd molested her in the garden. Were he and Gina in this together somehow? She knew it sounded irrational but surely there couldn't be any truth in it?

Calming down quickly, Caren wiped at her cheeks where a few tears had fallen. That was it: Pete and Gina were doing their best to get back at her. John wouldn't sleep with Gina. Moving here had tested them to the limits over the past few weeks but, apart from Pete's visit, everything had been okay for a few days. Yes, she knew John was working on the side, but the cash was good, and it wouldn't be forever. He had an interview for a job next week. If he got that, all their prayers would be answered and Pete would be out of their hair, unable to lead John astray – at least in theory anyway.

No, she would ignore them; their sort hated that.

Her mobile phone beeped the arrival of a text message. It was from John.

Its not wot u think. I was drunk, she tricked me.

Caren stared at the tiny display screen. She sat up abruptly and read it again.

Its not wot u think. I was drunk, she tricked me.

She frowned.

Its not wot u think. I was drunk, she tricked me.

She gasped. Gina was telling the truth.

Gina lit a cigarette as soon as she set foot in her kitchen. She sat at the table, busily puffing away, pleased with her little outburst – for all of a few minutes before doubt began to creep in.

What would happen if Caren said anything to John? Gina would have to deny it, even though half the neighbours had heard her say it. One of them was bound to say something to Pete down at The Butcher's Arms. Nothing stayed a secret on Stanley Avenue. She should know; she was usually the one spreading the rumours. Then again, maybe people would hold their tongue. The Bradley family were not to be messed with. Everyone knew that.

Gina sighed loudly. Sometimes she could be so stupid. Pete would kill her if he thought for a moment it was true – he could stop John from coming over and where would that leave her? And if Caren did start a row with John, Gina would have some lying to do. She'd have to think about it this afternoon, get her story right or she could end up with more than a red face. More likely she'd get a backhander from Pete.

But the one thing that riled her most was that she should have saved the information for later. Once he'd slept with her a couple of times, the story would have been more convincing, more hurtful too. It would have wiped that smug look off Caren's face. Everyone would know that Miss Fucking Perfect couldn't keep her man satisfied.

Gina sighed again and took another drag of her cigarette, a long drag that made her cough loudly. Now he'd never sleep with her and she'd come so close.

From the minute she'd scuttled off down Stanley Avenue with Gina Bradley screeching obscenities after her, Ruth had dreaded returning home. With every footstep back, she became more and more agitated, feeling the stickiness on her recently heeled scar oozing blood as she dug her nails in over and over.

She practically sprinted past Gina's house, expecting another torrent of abuse. But all was quiet, on both sides of the road. Wondering if the woman from number twenty-four had given Gina Bradley more than she'd bargained for, she relaxed a little.

Martin was lying on the settee in the living room watching the television when she put down her shopping on the kitchen table.

'Make us a brew, would you?' he shouted through to her. 'I'm parched.'

And I'm knackered after lugging your lager home, thought Ruth. Still, it would be good to have someone around to talk to; someone to belong to. There had been no mention of an apology, why he'd done what he'd done. Neither had there been any explanation about Tracy Tanner. She wondered who had finished the affair: it was obvious that something had happened.

'Where's that tea?' Martin shouted through.

'Coming up.' Ruth frowned. How had she thought she could do this? Now she had three of them to cater for and she didn't feel capable of looking after herself.

The kettle switched off. Ruth popped tea bags into two mugs

and continued to put the shopping away.

'Where are you getting the tea from? China?' Martin appeared in the doorway.

'It's nearly ready.' Ruth opened the fridge. 'Just getting the milk.'

He leered at her. 'Bloody hell, Ruth, you've got a right pair when you bend down.'

Ruth peered down at her chest. The neckline of her jumper wasn't showing that much.

Martin came behind and put an arm around her waist. He pressed himself to her. 'Can you feel that? You've made me hard already.' He kissed her neck. 'Might as well not waste it.'

Ruth squirmed. 'Don't do that, Martin. Not now.' He caught her by the wrist. 'Ow!' She grimaced.

'I'll make the other arm hurt too unless you let me fuck you.'

Ruth swallowed. 'I don't want –'

Martin swept a hand over the kitchen table. Mats and coasters crashed to the floor. He bent her forwards and shoved his hand up her skirt.

'You're having it, whether you like it or not,' he told her.

Ruth knew it was easier to get it over with. She heard him open his zip and then he pushed himself inside her. She groaned in pain.

He pushed in further, holding onto her shoulders. 'I know you like it rough, don't you?' He thrust into her.

Ruth held on to the table as he did it again and again. The table screeched across the tiles; still he held onto her, thrusting, swearing, thrusting, swearing.

Then it was over. Martin pulled out of her and tucked himself up. She felt his sperm running down her leg and stopped herself from gagging as she held onto the table, this time for support. Her legs didn't feel able to sustain her weight.

Martin grabbed her injured wrist and twirled her round to face him. She flinched as he squeezed it harder, intent on hurting her.

'I will have you whenever I want you,' he said, an inch away from her face. 'Got that?'

It took all of her strength to nod back at him.

'Good. Now, where's my tea?'

Ruth watched in a daze as Martin squeezed the teabag, threw it into the kitchen sink and added a dollop of milk to the drink. Then he winked at her before taking a noisy slurp.

Once he'd left the kitchen, Ruth closed the door. Then she rushed to the sink and threw up all over the teabag. The bastard! How could he force himself into her like that? Already she could feel the hurt he'd caused between her legs.

Holding onto the worktop, she managed to calm her breathing, stop herself from going into full panic mode. Her arm was burning. Instinctively, she began to pick at the scab a little more.

How had she forgotten how cruel he could be?

The minute she spotted John coming home in their car, Caren was out and down the path without another thought. She flung the overnight bag she'd packed with his clothes at his feet.

'Have you any idea how humiliating it is to know that not only have you been messing about across the road from where we –'

'I haven't!'

'– but you've been messing about with that – that thing!'

'It wasn't like that, I swear!'

'I hate you!' she spoke through gritted teeth. 'It's bad enough that we have to live here but then you go and do *that?*'

'I'm sorry!'

'You will be. You can sleep on *her* settee tonight; you're not coming in here.'

'But I don't –'

'Having a row in the street is getting quite your thing, isn't it, Caren?' Gina came up behind them.

'Fuck off, Gina.'

'Ooh, charming. Did you know you had such a foul mouth of a wife, John?'

John turned to her. 'You heard her, fuck off. You've caused enough trouble as it is, with all your lies.'

'I'm not lying. Can't you remember? You weren't that drunk now; you managed to get it hard enough.'

'Why, you little –' said Caren.

John held onto her as she tried to get past him.

Gina laughed. Pete hadn't come home yet, which gave her time to do this and then deny any of it once he was. She looked up the avenue. Mrs Porter was on the doorstep of number seventeen. Julie Elliot was standing with Sheila Ravenscroft; they were both staring their way. She looked the other way to see her Mum hanging out of the upstairs window.

'You can always come and stay at our house if she's throwing you out,' she mocked.

'Back off,' said John. 'I've had enough of you insinuating –'

'No,' Caren interrupted. 'She's right. Why *don't* you stay over there? It's where you belong, with the scum.'

'Who are you calling scum!'

John stared at Caren in disbelief. 'You can't possibly expect me to do that!'

Caren glared at him. 'I mean exactly that. You want her, you can stay with her.'

John turned to Gina. 'Now look what you've done.' He looked back to see Caren storming up the path and into the house with the slam of a door.

'She'll come round.' Gina held out a hand to him.

John took a step towards her and grabbed her roughly by the arm. 'You're such a poisonous cow. Just leave us alone.'

Gina was taken aback by his malice. 'But I thought you wanted to –'

'I don't want to do *anything* with you. Not now, not ever. You've caused enough trouble.'

They both saw Pete's car turn into the avenue.

John raced across to his house. 'Caren!' He banged on the front door. 'Caren! Let me in!'

Gina moved to her side of the road as Pete drew up.

'What's going on?' he questioned, wiping his nose on his sleeve.

'Caren and John were arguing,' said Gina. 'It was nothing really.'

'Bloody hell,' Pete grinned at her. 'They'll be rivalling us for the most rowing couple.'

Gina looked across the road again. Getting no joy from the front of the house, John had gone round to the back. She'd seen him sneak out of sight when Pete had pulled up.

'Come on, Gina,' Pete said. 'I'm starving. What's for tea?'

Gina sighed and turned towards her house. That had hardly gone to plan either.

CHAPTER FIFTEEN

The next morning, Ruth was struggling to bump her wheelie bin down the path to the pavement when she heard someone shout her name. She looked up to see Pete Bradley coming towards her. Great, what did he want – to start off where his horrible wife had finished?

'Here, let me help,' he said. He took the bin from her, bumped it down the last two steps and wheeled it in front of the garden hedge. Then he turned to her with a friendly smile. 'How are you doing, Ruth?'

'Fine thanks.' Her eyes narrowed.

'I saw Martin here yesterday. Is he on the scene again?'

Oh, here we go, thought Ruth; he must have some beef with Martin.

'He's staying for a few days, yes.' Ruth glanced shiftily upwards to her bedroom window. Martin was still in bed. Luckily, last night he'd gone out and hadn't come back until after midnight so he'd crashed out as soon as his head hit the pillow.

'Is it what you want?' asked Pete, leaning in towards her, touching her arm gently. 'I could move him on, if you like? Make sure he doesn't come bothering you again.'

'He doesn't bother me.' Her look of panic obviously gave Pete something to latch on to.

'Does he look after you?'

'Yes, but he isn't staying for good.'

'That's what they all say, isn't it? When they take advantage of a beautiful woman.'

Ruth pulled her dressing gown around her tightly. She looked up the avenue, hoping that no one could see them; even though it was only just after seven some people in Stanley Avenue actually got up for work. But she was more interested in whether Gina

Bradley was watching them. If she was, she would be in trouble.

'You're a pretty woman, Ruth. I could make life easy for you. Would you like that?'

Ruth nodded before she had time to think about the implications. She knew Martin wouldn't have any intentions of moving on. He'd want to slot himself back into her life as if the hurtful mess with Tracy Tanner had never happened. Then she shook her head.

Pete raised his eyebrows. 'Oh, I don't mean anything like bump him off. I mean warn him to move on and keep away from you.'

'He's very good with my kids,' Ruth came to Martin's defence.

'But is he good with you?'

Ruth lowered her eyes for a moment, feeling her skin flushing. How come Pete Bradley was being all nice to her?

'I haven't got a hidden agenda, if that's what you're thinking,' he added. 'I've just been watching you lately, and you don't seem happy.'

Ruth laughed inwardly. Well, that was the understatement of the month!

Pete moved closer. 'I could make things happen.'

All of a sudden panic took over and Ruth stepped back. 'I – I have to go in,' she said. 'In case he wakes up and notices I've gone.'

Pete stood at the end of the path as she scuttled inside. Ruth paused at the back door to look again: he was still there. She smiled at him.

Pete's smile widened: perfect.

Later that morning, a sheepish looking John came downstairs. Caren was in the living room. Last night had been dreadful for her. After locking him out, she soon realised he'd have nowhere to go but across the road. She'd waited for him to knock again later in the evening, knowing this time she would let him come in and explain himself. When he hadn't, she'd gone to bed but as she'd looked through their bedroom window, she'd noticed the interior light on inside their car. Moments later, she'd knocked on the window and told him to come inside. It was only the middle of October but it was still cold to sleep out. Once he'd come in, however, she'd gone to bed without talking to him – lying awake most of the night because of it.

'Are you going to give me time to explain what happened yet?' he asked.

Caren tried to play it cool. 'Fire away, but it had better be good.'

John sat down opposite her in the armchair. 'I know she must have told you we'd slept together but we hadn't.'

'The bitch broadcast it to everyone!'

'She did try it on but I was wasted. I couldn't stand up never mind get it up.'

'How eloquently put,' Caren uttered.

John gave an embarrassed giggle. 'I suppose I could have put it a better way.' He moved to sit next to her then, taking both her hands in his own. 'What I'm trying to say is that I'm really sorry. She tried it on, that's all. I pushed her away and she didn't like it.'

Caren stared over his shoulder rather than look at him directly. Of course she'd known that John wouldn't sleep with Gina. But she'd wanted him to realise that she wouldn't be standing for this nonsense of him going out with Pete whenever he fancied.

John tilted up Caren's chin. 'Did you honestly think I'd sleep with *her* when I can spend time with you?

'But you don't want to spend time with me anymore.' Caren looked pained as she said it. 'You want to be with them and get drunk every night.'

'He knows I'm struggling to get a job so he helps me out. I feel obliged to go out with him. He overpowers me.'

Caren frowned. That wouldn't be hard. John had always been a pushover.

'I'm not sure,' she admitted truthfully. 'It's making me doubt whether we can survive this – this mess.'

'We're made of stronger stuff than that, Caz.'

Caren shook her head. 'It won't work – not with them over the road, sticking their nose in at every opportunity to ruin things for us. And if –'

'As if they could ever do that.'

Caren realised how lucky he'd been to interrupt her then. She was about to tell him what happened with Pete.

'They've made a good job of it so far,' she said instead.

'Pete can be very persuasive.'

Caren struggled to keep her face straight. 'He's controlling you, can't you see that? Not only is Gina stirring trouble between us but so is Pete.'

'No, he isn't. He found me work.'

'You can find your own work!'

'It's not that easy.'

'But you've stopped trying. Since you can get cash in hand doing odd jobs – which quite frankly goes beyond my understanding as Pete Bradley is bone idle – you think you've found your feet. You need to take responsibility, John.' Caren stood up. 'And until you do, we can't move forward.'

Just after eleven thirty that evening, head full of beer and fuzzy thoughts, Martin staggered across the square in the direction of Stanley Avenue. He laughed to himself: it had been so easy to get Tracy Tanner on side again tonight. Maybe he could get away with seeing her *and* Ruth for the time being. Ruth was stupid enough to think that he wouldn't do it twice across her; silly bitch.

Without warning, someone grabbed him from behind and slammed him up against the wall between the post office and the bookies. He felt a fist in his stomach and doubled over.

'What the fuck is wrong with you?' Martin clutched his stomach as he looked up at Pete Bradley. 'Did I spill a drink over you or something? If I did, sorry mate, I'm lashed.'

'This has got nothing to do with the pub.' Pete thumped him in the stomach again. 'Keep away from Ruth Millington.'

'Ruth – my Ruth? What do you want with her?'

'She's not your Ruth and she never will be. I've had enough of you scrounging off her. You'd better back off.'

Pete brought his hand up to strike Martin again. Martin blocked his arm and threw a punch of his own, but he missed completely, twirling round in a circle. As he staggered around, Pete hit him another time. He fell to the floor as another fist found his stomach.

In the quiet of the night, Pete spoke again. 'I want you out of her house and I don't want you bothering her again. Do you hear?'

'I've probably got no fucking hearing left,' muttered Martin, spitting blood onto the pavement.

'There'll be plenty more of that if I see you there in the morning.'

Ruth woke up to the sound of the bedroom door slamming open and bouncing off the wall behind it. She squinted when Martin turned on the light. Then she saw what a mess he was.

'Ohmigod – what happened to you?'

Martin ignored her and opened the wardrobe. He began to throw his clothes on the bed, hangers clattering against each other.

Ruth scooted nearer to him. 'Martin, what's going on?'

'You're poison, do you know that?' he spat nastily at her before pulling out his holdall from the side of the drawers. 'I've only been here a night and look what's happened to me.'

Ruth spied Mason in the doorway, behind him stood his brother. 'You two – shoo!' She pointed at them.

'Yeah, piss off back to your beds,' Martin yelled at them.

Jamie ran off immediately but Mason stood his ground. Martin pushed a few T-shirts into his holdall.

'Where are you going?' asked Ruth.

'As far away from you as possible. I don't want to spend another minute in your company.' He located a pair of trainers and crammed them into the holdall too.

'But you're hurt! And you're covered in blood.' Ruth pulled off the duvet and rushed to the door. 'Let me get you a towel.'

'No, I'm leaving right now.'

Ruth pushed Mason out of the doorway, shut the door and threw herself up against it. 'You're not going anywhere,' she cried. 'I won't let you.'

'You don't have a choice.' Martin fastened the zip on the holdall and slung it over his shoulder, wincing at the pain in his stomach. 'Move out of my way.'

'No.'

'I said move.'

Ruth shook her head. 'NO!'

Martin raised his hand to strike her but stopped. If he made a mark on her, Pete would come after him again.

'Move!' He pushed her to one side.

Before Ruth had chance to stop him, he was halfway down the stairs.

She ran after him. 'Martin! Don't go! Please, don't go. Wait for me!'

But it was too late. By the time she got to the front door, Martin had already disappeared down the path. She ran to the pavement and saw him in the distance.

'Martin!' she shouted after him. 'Martin!'

She burst into tears. Why did he have to go now? She wanted him to stay; *needed* him to stay. Without him there, the darkness would descend even more.

She went back into the house a few minutes later to find Mason sitting on the bottom stair.

'Why has Martin gone, Mum?'

But Ruth ignored him and went upstairs. Then she threw herself onto her bed and cried.

The next morning, once she'd taken the boys to school, Ruth climbed back into bed. But at quarter past eleven, she heard someone knocking at the front door. She dragged weary limbs to the window and peeped out. She groaned: Pete Bradley.

He knocked again. She sighed, knowing he wouldn't go away until he'd seen her.

'Hiya,' he said as she opened the front door. 'Christ, you look terrible. Are you okay?'

'I'm fine,' Ruth lied. 'I'm just coming down with a cold. What can I do for you?'

'Nice to see you too,' Pete grinned.

Ruth gave a faint smile. 'I'm sorry. Not with it this morning.'

'Can I come in?'

Ruth paused.

'You can tell me what's wrong,' Pete encouraged. 'I won't say anything.'

Ruth held the door open for him. They went through to the

living room.

'Martin left last night,' she said when it was evident Pete wasn't going to speak until she told him what was wrong.

'But he'll come back, right? I mean, he'd only just arrived!'

Ruth shook her head. 'He was acting all weird, said he wished he'd never come back – and he'd been beaten up.'

'Beaten up? Did he say who by?'

'He hardly said a word actually. He just took his stuff and went. He didn't even stay long enough to clean himself up.'

'Something must have freaked him, because if I was your man, I wouldn't leave you.'

Ruth remembered their earlier conversation. 'This wasn't anything to do with you, was it?'

'Of course not!' Pete feigned shock.

'But you said you could make him leave!'

'You never said you wanted me to.' Pete looked around. 'Neat place you have here – much better than the doss-hole I live in. Three women in our house and none of them will lift a finger.'

Ruth smiled a little. She had always been house proud. When she was with Glenn, they'd had the best house in the street.

Pete was in front of her now. He touched her hair gently. 'I can call again, if you like?'

'I – I don't think that's a good idea.'

'Why not?'

'I'm sure Gina would have something to say about it regardless. She has a go at me practically every time I leave the house as it is. I don't want to antagonise her any more than is necessary. She'll flatten me.'

'I'll tell her to lay off.'

'And she will?' Ruth's tone was doubting.

'She'll do exactly what I tell her to do.' Pete looked pleased with himself. 'So, that's that, then. I'll pop round every couple of days and see how you're doing.'

After he'd gone, Ruth sat down and rested her head in her hands. She didn't really want Pete coming around whenever he pleased. She didn't like him that much, felt intimidated by him, but what could she do? Maybe he'd lose interest in her after a week or so and move on to someone not so close to home.

God, what a situation to be in! As quick as she'd lost one man, another came to take his place. And this one was Gina Bradley's hubby. Could things get any worse?

But for now, she'd have to play the game. After all, she was in no fit state to do anything else.

Two nights later, Claire fancied some chocolate but Rachel didn't want to nip to Shop&Save with her. It hadn't quite been dark so she'd run all the way there and back. As she got into Stanley Avenue, she slowed down to a trot.

'All alone for a change?' Stacey said, jumping from the shadows. Before Claire could react, she punched her in the side of her face.

Claire took another punch before she managed to throw one of her own. It missed its aim, catching Stacey on the shoulder.

Stacey took another shot at her, causing her to stagger back against the wall. Then she pulled out a knife. Claire saw the glint of metal. Fuck! Stacey and fist fighting was more than she could take. But Stacey with a knife: she wouldn't stand a chance.

'Leave me alone,' she said, hoping to sound more confident than she felt.

'Tell that bitch of a sister to back off or else one of you will get it.'

Claire felt the sting of the blade cutting the delicate layers as Stacey brought the knife up to her cheek, pressing it against her skin.

'This is just a warning,' said Stacey, 'because if she doesn't back down, I'm going to come after you until she does.'

Claire squeezed her eyes shut, praying she wouldn't draw the blade across her face and scar her forever.

But she didn't. A car door slamming and an engine starting up brought her to her senses. She stared at Claire when she dared to open her eyes.

'If I have to warn you again, next time I won't stop before I mark you permanently.'

Before Claire could answer, Stacey punched her in the stomach.

'Tell her,' she said.

Claire doubled over. By the time she looked up again, Stacey was gone. She gathered her senses and ran; Christ, Mum would kill her for getting into this state again.

Rachel was lying on her bed when she heard the pebble strike the glass outside. She went to the window to see who it was, hoping that it wasn't any of the Mitchell Mob as she didn't feel like going out that night.

She was confused when she peered down and saw her sister. 'What are you doing?'

'I'm in a mess,' Claire whispered loudly. 'Stacey got to me. You'll have to get me past Mum.'

'Hang on a moment. I'm coming down.'

Rachel closed the window and crept downstairs. She squeezed herself past the stuff in the hallway, let her sister in and then popped her head around the living room door. Gina was curled up asleep on the settee. Her dad hadn't come in yet. Quickly, she sneaked through, grabbed a glass and painkillers, and rushed back upstairs.

Claire was sitting on her bed, a mirror in her hand, examining the damage.

'She had a knife, Rach. Ohmigod, she had a fucking knife on me!' She started to cry.

Rachel rushed over to her, comforting her while she sobbed. What the hell was going on? This was getting beyond a joke now; they couldn't compete against weapons and she wouldn't use a knife to hurt anyone, unless in self-defence.

There was no option to back off now. Even if Stacey reverted to gang leader, she would never let them be members anymore. Rachel needed the backing of the others, as well as Claire, to stand her ground.

But she was more annoyed with herself. Why the hell hadn't she gone to the square with Claire? This had happened because she'd been in a mood and couldn't be bothered to go out. Stupid, selfish cow.

'I'm sorry,' she said, handing her sister the glass of water and painkillers. 'Here, take these.'

Claire burst into tears. 'What are we going to do, Rach?' she asked again. 'We're in big trouble.'

Rachel tilted Claire's face up to look at the damage Stacey had inflicted. Claire's nose was swollen, again. Her cheek was cut, it hadn't been done to cause any lasting damage, but her right eye was swelling too, bruising already appearing.

'Smile,' she told Claire.

'Fuck off,' she replied. 'There's nowt to smile about.'

'I want to check your teeth are okay.'

'Oh.' Claire smiled, wincing at the pain it caused.

'Nothing out of place there,' Rachel confirmed.

Claire looked in the mirror. 'Shit, I look a right mess again. Mum's going to mad when she sees me.'

Ruth sat on the settee with her head in her hands. She'd sent the boys to bed an hour earlier, having had enough of them playing up by seven thirty, but she could hear them banging away upstairs as they ran from room to room.

Why did they always act up for her? When she'd lived with Martin, they'd been sent to bed at eight and not a peep would be heard from them. Maybe he had persuasion tactics that she didn't know about, like the bogey man in the wardrobe or underneath the bed.

Martin arriving and leaving within the blink of an eye had really unnerved Ruth. She couldn't understand why he'd left so quickly. And why had he said that she was poison? At the back of her mind, she knew it must have something to do with Pete. Martin wasn't the sort of man to look a gift horse in the mouth when it came to free food and lodgings, and sex on demand whenever he felt like it. And despite the way he'd treated her in the past, Ruth had enjoyed having someone around before he'd thrown her out: someone that she could talk to, look after, see to their requirements. For the first time in a while, she'd felt needed and not just as a mother. She dismissed his rough handling of her: sex was always for his satisfaction; he had no intentions of pleasing her. But just the closeness, the feeling of a man inside her, joined with her, made her feel wanted.

'Mum, can I have a drink?' Jamie popped his head around the living room door.

'If you're quick.' Ruth didn't look up. Emotionally drained from crying all day, she wished she could go to bed and sleep forever. Maybe it would be better if she never woke up, she surmised. The boys would have to go into care but surely that would be better than living with a lunatic for a mother. One minute she was acting the way she should: the next she'd be screaming at them, trying to stop from lashing out at them. The way she felt wasn't their fault but sometimes she couldn't help it. It was those times that scared her the most.

Suddenly, she heard muted laughter and then coughing coming from the kitchen. She pulled herself up from the settee to investigate. Opening the kitchen door, she saw Mason holding up a glass of wine to Jamie's lips.

'What the hell are you two doing?' She swiped the glass from Mason's hand, catching Jamie as she did so. The glass shattered as it hit the floor.

'We only wanted to taste it!' Mason protested.

'It's not for kids.' Ruth grabbed him by the arm. 'Have you any idea how dangerous that could be, you stupid idiot?'

'But you drink it all the time!'

'I'm an adult!'

'He only had a little bit! Ow, Mum! You're hurting!'

Ruth pushed him away roughly. 'Get to your room, NOW!'

Mason shot out of the door. Jamie ran behind him but Ruth stopped him. 'Whoa, little soldier. You're going nowhere.'

'Leave me alone,' Jamie wailed.

She reached for the bottle. There didn't seem to be too much gone from it; they had more than likely just had a taster. But she couldn't be sure. She filled a large glass with water and held it to his lips.

'Drink,' she ordered. 'And you piss the bed tonight and there'll be trouble.'

'No.'

'I said, DRINK!'

Jamie knocked her hand away, water spilling onto Ruth's feet.

'Why, you little –'

Jamie took the opportunity to run.

Ruth sprinted up the stairs after him, one time touching his heel. Jamie ran into Mason's room and slammed the door shut. Ruth pushed down the handle but they held it steadfast on the other side.

'Get away from the door,' she screamed. She tried the handle again but it wouldn't go down enough for her to get in. She banged on the door for a while before dropping to her knees.

Ohmigod, what was happening to her, she asked herself, as the fog began to lift and she started to come to her senses.

Why did she turn into a monster when she was with them? Martin had been right. She was poison and she hadn't even had a drink tonight. She'd wanted to wait until later. What little wine she had wouldn't last her long.

She wasn't fit to be a mother, was she?

She never would be, would she?

As she sat crying, all of a sudden, it came to her what she had to do.

CHAPTER SIXTEEN

Gina woke up the next morning on the settee. She sat up slowly,
stretching her arms above her head and moving her neck from
side to side. It was eight fifteen and the third time that week she
hadn't made it to bed after having a drink. It wasn't good for her
bones. She wondered what had woken her. Then she heard
movement in the kitchen.

'You're up early,' she said to one of the girls, unsure which twin
it was until they turned towards her.

'Couldn't sleep,' a voice said.

Gina sat down at the table, reached for her cigarettes and lit one
up. 'Make us a brew, will you?' she said.

Another mug was placed beside the two already there, a teabag
shoved into it and a spoon of sugar added.

'What's up?'

'Nothing.'

'For God's sake, will you turn around so I know who I'm talking
too?'

Claire turned around.

Gina jumped out of her chair and across to her. 'What
happened?'

'It's nothing, Mum. It'll heal.'

'Who did this to you? Was it Stacey Hunter?'

'I was in the wrong place at the wrong time, that's all.'

'I bloody knew it. Why didn't you keep away from her, like I
told you?'

'I did! She jumped me.'

Gina saw red. This had got to stop.

'I've had enough of this,' she said. 'I'm going round to see
Maggie Hunter.'

'No, Mum.' Claire's head turned abruptly. 'Me and Rach will

sort it all out.'

'You'll do no such thing. I'll give her mother what for, letting her daughter attack one of mine.'

'Mum, please!' Claire pushed a mug of tea over to her before picking up the other two. 'We can handle it ourselves.'

'Claire!'

Knowing she wasn't going to listen, Gina let Claire scoot off back to her room, She sipped at her tea and wondered what she had done to get a pasting like that; was it over some lad or another or were she and Rachel still playing this leader of the pack thing? She knew she could sort out Stacey's mother if it became necessary. Gina might only be five foot two, but she'd been told she packed a mean punch, especially if her girls were in trouble.

'Do you think this will be okay?'

Caren looked up to see John taking out a jacket from the wardrobe. She watched as he slid it on, fitting into it easily even though it was a few years old.

'I don't see why not,' she replied. 'It'll save buying something new, which we can't afford to do anyway. Here.' She handed him a couple of ties.

'Does anyone bother with these anymore?'

'Maybe not but I think first impressions count.'

John placed one over each shoulder. 'Any preference?' he asked.

She pointed to the blue one with a faint check. 'This one,' she said. 'Do you need a new white shirt? I can get you one from Tesco, if you like.'

'Tesco?'

'You can get anything from there nowadays – good quality too.'

John was in the wardrobe again, pulling another shirt from a coat hanger. 'I reckon this one will be okay.'

Caren sat down on the bed with a thump. This was John's first interview in years, having worked for himself for so long. She wondered if he'd cope with the pressure. The job was only for a service advisor on the parts counter of the local Landrover dealer but she knew it was what he needed. And what *they* needed to get themselves back on track – and away from that nasty Bradley family.

Since the episode with Gina, things had settled down again. John had spent more time with her. They'd talked about their future: their worries. She'd told him how scared she was at the thought of being stuck in Stanley Avenue forever. He'd told her that he felt inferior because he couldn't provide for her; didn't feel like a man she'd want around her anymore. It had done them both good to get their feelings out in the open. And then yesterday, he'd come home with a huge grin, telling her he'd got a job interview.

John twirled round to face her, the shirt underneath the jacket. 'What do you think? Will I pass?'

Caren smiled, feeling her insides responding. Wow, she'd forgotten how good he looked in a suit.

'I think you scrub up pretty well, Mr Williams.' She gave him a hug, relishing the feel of his arms as he pulled her near. 'What I actually mean by that is I'd far rather see you with no clothes on at all.'

She began unfastening the buttons on his shirt.

Ruth hadn't slept much the night before. The idea had come to her in a flash; she'd thought about nothing else since, so much so that she'd started to pace the room in the early hours of the morning. It was the perfect opportunity, the only opportunity really. Should she do it? Would it be the right thing to do? It would certainly be better for the boys.

Then doubt crept in. She knew what she had to do but would she be strong enough to do it? What right did she have to inflict such pain? To walk away from her troubles – pass them on to someone else.

But it would be much better for them all in the long term. For Mason and Jamie, and for her. This way, she wouldn't be able to harm them.

She was in the kitchen bright and early the next day. Mason and Jamie came downstairs, wary after the antics the night before. As she saw them creeping in sheepishly, she realised she was making the right choice. She gave them breakfast, keeping a cheery attitude that must have confused them after last night's tricks. Then when they had finished their cereal, she sat down with them.

'How would you like to go on an adventure today, boys?' she asked, trying to muster enthusiasm into her tone.

'No school?'

'No school.'

Mason and Jamie looked at each other wide-eyed.

'Cool!' said Jamie.

'Where are we going?' asked Mason suspiciously.

'It's a surprise. I've packed you some clothes and I want you to pick a few of your favourite toys – not the big ones, mind – and I'll put them in your bags too.'

'Are we staying out all night?' Jamie wiggled his bottom about in the chair. 'Can we go to a safari park? I want to see some lions. And wolves. And an – an elephant!'

'We won't be going to a safari park!' Mason's tone was scathing at his brother's ignorance. 'We'll be going to stay with Martin.'

'No, we're not going to see Martin.' Ruth gathered together the breakfast dishes. 'Today we're going somewhere else. And we need to be ready in twenty minutes. Can you do that?'

Jamie and Mason rushed upstairs. She sighed, trying to keep in her frustration: why were they so bloody noisy all the time? Still, it would be much quieter later when they weren't around to bug her anymore. She squirted some washing-up liquid into the bowl and ran the hot water tap. Then she threw in the dishes, leaving them to soak. She needed to get herself ready quickly; she didn't want her heart to get the chance to rule her head.

Less than an hour later, they were in the town centre. Ruth had taken them into the market to get a bag of pic'n'mix sweets and a comic apiece to keep them quiet. Then she walked into the Social Services offices, sat the boys down on the settee inside the window and went to speak to the lady on reception. The office was busy, but she bided her time in the small queue. As she reached the head of it, the woman gave her an unexpected smile.

'Can I help you,' she asked, whipping away her long blonde fringe to reveal friendly eyes.

'I need someone to take care of my boys,' said Ruth.

'In what way exactly?' The woman popped a form onto the counter. 'Can you fill your details in here?'

'No, you don't understand. I'm leaving my boys here with you. The oldest is Mason and he's ten. The younger one is eight and he's called Jamie.' The woman reached for the phone and dialled an extension number as Ruth started to cry. 'Please,' she sobbed, aware that people were beginning to stare. 'Please don't split them up. They don't deserve that. It's my fault, you see. I can't be their mother. I can't look after them. So you must do it for me.' Then she turned away.

'Wait!' the woman shouted as people started to stare. 'Please! You can't just leave them here!'

'What's up, Mum?' Mason asked as she came back to them.

Ruth knelt down and pulled him into her arms. She beckoned to Jamie and hugged him too. 'I want you to be good boys now,' she said. 'Can you do that for me?'

'Why, where are you going?' asked Jamie.

'I – I won't be a minute,' she said. 'I need to pop out for something. Wait here, will you?' She turned to Mason and touched his face lightly. 'Look after your brother, Mason. You're strong enough to do that. I'm not. Always keep him safe and...' she swallowed her anguish and kept her tears inside, 'look after him. Please.'

'Mum, what are you doing?' Sensing something was wrong, Mason clung to her. She pushed him away gently but firmly.

'I love you both,' she whispered. Then she walked away.

'Mum!'

'Where is she going, Mase?' asked a bewildered Jamie. He ran to her.

Ruth hugged him fiercely. 'I'll be back in a moment. Go and sit with your brother.'

She was stopped at the door by a man with a child in a pushchair. 'You won't be back,' he said. 'You can't leave them here. They're too young to understand.'

'I can't...' Ruth fought to control a scream building up inside. She turned to look at them one more time. 'I just can't anymore.'

Before anyone could stop her, she ran out of the building and disappeared into the shoppers on the high street. She didn't stop, she didn't look back for fear of returning. Instead, she walked until she could see no more for tears and sat down. She ended up in the bus station; sat there for over an hour before climbing on a bus and heading back to Stanley Avenue. She had never felt so alone in her life. But she knew she had made the right decision.

Caren spotted their car returning and went out to John. Desperate to hear how he'd got on at the interview, she ran down the path.

'Well?' she wanted to know. 'How did it go?'

John shrugged. 'It was okay, I suppose. But there were so many guys after it. Some of them were much younger than me.'

'You're hardly an old-timer.' She noted his dejection.

'It didn't feel that way.'

'Did they say when they'd let you know?'

John locked the car up and walked up the path with her. 'No, they said they'd contact me in due course.'

Caren tried hard not to show how miserable she felt. It didn't sound too hopeful, especially if there were a lot of men out for it.

'Was the pay good?'

'Not bad, but I doubt it matters now.'

'Don't be too down-hearted.' She took his hand.

Suddenly, John grinned. 'Oh, ye of little faith. I got it!'

'What – they told you, just like that?'

'Yep, I was the last one to be interviewed so they made we wait outside while they had a chat and then called me back in to tell me!'

Caren squealed and jumped into his arms. 'That's fantastic! Oh, I knew you could do it!'

'Like hell you did!'

'I did!' She paused. 'Wait a minute! You tricked me, you git!'

'You're so easy to fool.' He kissed her on the cheek. 'Let's go out for lunch to celebrate. I'm starving – all that nervous energy.'

'You mean she left them in reception?' Josie said, her tone incredulous.

'Exactly that, poor mites. They had no idea she wasn't coming back. I haven't been able to get hold of her since.'

Josie was making coffee for Sarah Cunningham, a social worker she had known for about seven years. Sarah had been helping her out at The Workshop since it opened too, and Josie knew if it wasn't for her, some of the women would never have come along. Both known for their persuasion tactics, between them, they were a great team – which is why Sarah had called in especially to see Josie.

Josie handed her a mug of coffee. 'And have you caught up with her since?'

'No.' Sarah shook her head, messy but stylish curls flicking from side to side. 'I've called several times over the past couple of days but either she's not in or she's not answering the door. I'll keep on trying over the next few days but I'm not sure what to do after that. I've taken the case on but I've never had anything like this happen before. She said she wasn't a fit mother and they'd be better off without her.'

Josie sat down at her desk with her drink. She swivelled from side to side on her chair. 'She must have been in one hell of a state to get to that conclusion,' she noted. 'I've been calling for weeks now, only managed to get in a couple of times before the barrier dropped completely. I haven't seen her since.'

Sarah sighed. 'It really gets to you when you can't get through to someone, doesn't it?'

Josie nodded.

'How was she when you did see her?'

'She'd only just moved in so I assumed she was busy, and maybe a little pissed off to be moving into Stanley Avenue.'

'It's not that bad.'

'Not unless you live opposite or next to one of the Bradleys,' Josie retorted.

The next morning, when Sarah Cunningham knocked on her door again, Ruth lay in bed curled up in the foetal position, a photo of her boys in her hand. It was half past eleven and she hadn't got up yet. She ignored the knock but the next one was much louder. She closed her eyes and drew her feet up further. Whoever it was would go away soon.

The letterbox clattered and she heard something drop onto the floor. She wondered who it would be this time – the housing office; the social; the police? Of them all, she was scared of the latter most. It must be a crime to dump your children in an office and run away, like she had, surely? To leave a ten and an eight-year-old to fend for themselves, chuck them into a new way of family life, or worse, into a children's home because no one would want two brothers – she'd heard stories on the news and read them in the papers. Some adoptive parents only wanted one child; they didn't want to take on the responsibility of two. But then again, what did the media know? Maybe they'd got it wrong. She pushed the thought to the back of her mind and imagined Mason and Jamie being put into the loving care of a man and woman who would look after them as their own, not for the money as she'd read about people doing too.

She began to cry again. She'd let her boys down; she'd had to or else she might have killed one of them instead of herself. But what right had she to give her children away, like the booby prize of a raffle? How would they feel later, realising that she had abandoned them? Right now, they were probably thinking that she was coming back for them; she'd had a bit of a breakdown and once she was better they'd be home again.

She leaned forward, picked up an empty vodka bottle and put it to her lips. There wasn't even a drop left for her to devour. On the drawers beside it, she noticed the craft knife covered in blood. She held her wrist up and then dropped it. It too was covered in blood, so were some of the covers around her. She couldn't remember hurting herself last night; couldn't remember the feel of the blade splitting her skin, the blood oozing out. And that upset her, because to take away the pain, she had to feel it. And if she didn't feel it, she couldn't make things better. Hurt heeled hurt. But not this time.

She reached for the craft knife and placed it on her wrist. It would be so easy to draw it across and go to sleep. Really, it was the arm that was a better place. Just above the elbow. She'd seen that on a television program. It bled just as much as slashing at the wrists and looked easier to do as it was fleshier. Simple, clean, and effective. It was perfect. But she knew the blade might not be strong enough to do the job properly. Maybe she needed a Stanley knife for that – or a heavy duty pen knife. Or maybe it didn't have to be heavy duty. Maybe it was the action of drawing the blade across her skin that needed to be heavy duty.

She threw the craft knife across the room. It stuck in the wall before falling to the carpet. Next went the bottle. This too hit the wall but fell without smashing.

She screamed in frustration. 'I can't even break a fucking bottle!'

The following day as Josie drove along Davy Road towards The Workshop, she decided to call into Stanley Avenue and see if she could catch Ruth. But after banging on her door three times with no answer she left, disappointed yet again. She was getting back into her car when she spotted Ruth walking towards her. She went to meet her.

'Hi, Ruth,' she smiled. 'I've been meaning to catch you but you're always out. I wondered if I –'

'No, I'm not.'

'Sorry?' Josie frowned.

'I said no, I'm not.' She looked up at Josie with glazed eyes. 'I'm not always out. I've just been avoiding you.'

'Oh!' Jose was taken aback. 'Well, I'm here again,' she laughed nervously. 'Might I come in for a chat?'

'Please yourself.' Ruth walked through the gate, letting it fall back in place. Josie sighed, opened it and followed her into the house.

'I heard about what happened with your children,' she said. 'I'm really sorry that you felt that way. I wish I could have helped you.'

'What could you have done?'

Josie paused. Ruth's tone wasn't scathing but she was right. What could she have done?

'Maybe I could have talked to you, offered you a friendly ear? Maybe I could have got some help for you.'

'I didn't need help.' Ruth switched on the kettle.

'Do you mind if I sit down?' Josie pointed to a seat at the table.

Ruth shrugged.

As she made coffee, Josie studied her. It was so obvious she'd been taking something. Not heavy drugs but some kind of a sedative to calm her down. Trouble was, it had calmed her down so much that she was acting like a zombie.

'Why give the boys to Children's Services?' she asked once Ruth was sitting opposite her. 'It must have been a hard decision to make?'

Ruth shook her head.

'Was this place getting to you so much?' Josie clocked the sparse kitchen. 'I'm sorry. I could have done more, got you some help with the decorating. I've been so busy lately and –' she stopped herself. 'Hark at me. Ruth, I don't have any excuses. I should have been here for you.'

'You're not my keeper.'

Josie faltered. 'I know, but I do feel responsible for you. Only in the same way I do for all my tenants',' she added hastily as Ruth began to glare at her.

'It isn't easy living my life,' she spat out.

Josie shook her head. 'No, I don't know. Why don't you tell me?'

'So you can go running back to the office and tell everyone my business?'

'I would never do that!' Josie looked horrified. 'What you tell me is confidential as long as it is within the law.'

Ruth opened her mouth to lay into Josie again but she saw the concern on her face. She was being genuine. She felt her shoulders droop.

'I didn't know what to do,' she admitted finally. 'And I was afraid of myself, that I might hurt one of them and live to regret it. Did you know that I'm a widow?'

Josie nodded: she'd seen it on Ruth's paperwork.

Tears misted over Ruth's eyes. 'Me and Glenn were so happy. I could cope when he was around. We had a really great relationship. I lost my soul mate when he died, yet I had to go on with my life. I had two children to look after. They took up all of my time, and I was coping, in a fashion, until I had my breakdown. If it wasn't for my mum and dad, the boys would have been in care.'

'Had you spoken to your parents about how you were feeling?'

'My dad's dead and my mum hasn't spoken to me for ages now – not since I started seeing Martin. She didn't like him.'

Josie sighed. It must be so hard to live the lives of these women.

'I can't have them back,' Ruth said matter-of-factly. 'I can't have it on my conscience that I was the one who ill-treated them; I was the one who didn't look out for them; I was the one who made them into the anti-social thugs they would have turned into. They're a handful now: imagine how they'd be when they got to their teens.' Ruth shook her head. 'It's not fair on them.'

'It's not fair on you, either,' said Josie.

'I don't care about me.'

'But this is –'

'They won't make me take them back, will they?' Ruth rang her hands together over and over. Then she began to pick at the top of the bandage around her wrist. 'I couldn't do that.'

Josie knew that wasn't about to happen. Ruth hadn't even asked about the boys yet.

'But don't you want to know where they are? Who they are with?'

'Yes, but please don't make me have them back.'

It wasn't often in her role that Josie was lost for words. Most of the time she could talk someone around to her way of thinking, but that was easy to do when she wanted them to attend a mother and toddlers club because she knew they were lonely; when she wanted to help them sort the house out, get it cleaned and decorated to an acceptable standard; when she needed a tenant to pay their rent or just a little bit more off their arrears every week to stave off eviction proceedings.

But this was different. She didn't know what to do, what to say, to ease this woman's pain. There were only so many words she knew but none of them were good enough for this situation. Sometimes it was best to sit and listen. Make some sense of it when she had left the property.

'Is someone nice looking after them?' Ruth spoke, her voice barely audible.

Josie nodded. 'They haven't been separated and have gone to live with a foster family who I've met several times. There are three girls there at the moment too. Every time I've visited, there's always been a happy atmosphere.'

Ruth nodded through fresh tears. 'I just want them to be happy.' She began to sob.

Josie felt tears welling in her eyes too. How the hell was she going to deal with this case?

On his first morning at his new job, John had been hoping to sneak out of his house early without Pete seeing him but was dismayed to see him in the front garden. He tried not to catch his eye, knowing he wouldn't be happy with him, but Pete spotted him eventually.

'Hey, John, haven't seen you lately,' he shouted across the street to him. 'You up for a cash in hand job, later in the week?'

'Can't mate,' John shouted back. 'I'm a bit busy.'

'What's more important than making a bit of dough?'

John stopped before getting into his car; he might as well tell Pete now, get it over with.

'I've got a job, mate. I needed something steady.'

Wearing baggy grey joggers spotted with stains and a particularly nasty scowl, Pete crossed the road. As he reached him, he threw his hands up in the air.

'You're deserting me?'

'It's regular hours.'

'I bet you can make more with me in one day than what anyone will pay you for a week's work.'

'It's not that.' John paused. 'I just want to get into a routine.'

'This is Caren's idea, isn't it?' Pete pointed to his forehead. 'She's put ideas into your head. She thinks she's better than anyone else. I can't believe you've fallen for it.'

'Got to keep her happy.'

'By selling your soul to the devil?'

John laughed nervously. 'It's not that bad.'

'You don't need a job when I'm around. She's got a fucking nerve; you should show her who the boss is. Don't you wear the trousers in your house?'

'It's only a job,' John stated. 'We've been through a shit time lately so I'm trying to make things better. What's wrong with that?'

Pete shrugged. 'You've joined the other side, pal, not me.'

'I need the security!' John shouted as Pete walked off.

'Pussy whipped, that's what you are,' Pete shouted back. 'Under the thumb good and proper.'

As John drove off down Stanley Avenue, Pete glanced across the road. Spotting Caren standing at the front window, he shook his head at her slowly, laughing as she moved away quickly. Women! He and John had something good going on; he'd never get half of the gigs without two of them going together. And he'd been wrong about Caren. He thought she'd heed his warning when they'd had their little chat but it seemed not. He wondered for a moment. There must be a way that he could teach the interfering bitch a lesson; something to upset Miss High and Fucking Mighty over there?

CHAPTER SEVENTEEN

Ruth ignored the front door that morning when someone knocked at half past nine. She sat at the kitchen table nursing a hangover: she seemed to have been in constant headache mode for the past few days.

Another knock – why couldn't everyone leave her be!

'Ruth? It's me, Pete.'

Ruth groaned inwardly. What did he want? Because he'd left her alone for a few days, she was hoping he was going to stay away for good.

'I know you're in there. Come on, let me in.'

Ruth dragged herself to the door.

'Hi, I was wondering – Christ, you look rough.' Pete's smiled dropped. 'Are you okay?'

Ruth shook her head. 'I – I –' She felt herself sway, her knees buckle.

Pete stepped in and caught hold of her arm. 'You've gone the colour of pea soup.' He guided Ruth into the living room and sat down next to her on the settee.

Ruth began to gulp in big mouthfuls of air as panic took over.

'You need to calm down. Breathe easy, in, then out. In then, out. Look at me.'

She did as she was told.

'In, then out. In, then out.'

A few minutes later, panic subsiding, she gave an embarrassed smile. 'Sorry,' she eyed him nervously, 'I haven't eaten anything since last night.'

'And that's all?'

Ruth looked away. How could she tell him that she'd drunk a bottle of vodka and taken a few happy-clappy pills? The pills had been prescribed to her a couple of years ago. At the time, she'd stopped taking them because they'd made her act irrationally. Now she'd decided to give them another go – anything to make her feel better.

Pete took hold of her hand. 'You can tell me anything, Ruth. I'm a friend, that's what I'm here for, to listen.'

Latching on to his caring manner, Ruth nodded. Everything came spilling out; about her life, losing Glenn, Martin, and how she hadn't been able to cope with the boys. Forty minutes and two mugs of coffee later, Pete was still there and Ruth felt like a weight had been lifted from her shoulders. Pete was telling her how taxing it had been bringing his own kids up.

'Little bastards they were,' he said. 'Still are, if you ask me. Those twins are evil. I swear they must have mixed them up in the hospital.' He pointed at himself. 'How could such naughty kids come from such a sweet and innocent man like me?'

Ruth giggled.

Pete nudged her playfully. 'Oy! Are you mocking me?'

'No!' Ruth giggled again. Pete nudged her again.

They smiled at each other shyly.

Pete gently wiped the fringe away from Ruth's forehead. 'You have beautiful eyes when I can see them,' he said.

Ruth blushed.

Pete leaned forward and kissed her lightly on the lips.

'So.'

He kissed her again.

'Blue.'

And again.

'Let me make it better for you,' he whispered.

Ruth stared at him for a moment. Up close he wasn't that good-looking but she didn't care about that. Right now, she just wanted to be loved, feel a man's arms around her, comforting her. Surely it wouldn't do any harm? No one would know.

She nodded.

Pete kissed her, gently at first, then more persistent. His hand roamed over her bare legs. Until then, she hadn't noticed she'd gone to the door in only her dressing gown. He pulled the belt undone, his hand finding her breast this time, tweaking the nipple to erection. Ruth gasped as his mouth followed his hand. She ran her hands down his back, pulling out his T-shirt, urging him to remove it. They pulled it off together, then the rest of his clothes. Coming back to her, he knelt down in front of her and buried his head between her legs.

Ruth was in a daze, headache forgotten. She heard a moan and realised it had come from her.

'Does that feel good?' Pete stopped for a second to look up at her. It was all she could do to nod.

He pulled her onto the floor, gazed for a moment at her nakedness before pushing himself into her. She wrapped her arms around him, moving with him as his thrusts became longer and quicker. Then he stopped.

'Turn over.'

Ruth obliged. He pushed into her from behind but this time he didn't thrust. Instead his hand moved over her stomach and down into her pubic hair. He found her clitoris and gently began to massage it. Ruth gasped again. She pressed her buttocks into him, begging him to thrust.

'You want it, don't you?' Pete said, his fingers never stopping.

'Yes.' His touch was so pleasurable. 'Yes, oh, God, yes!'

Pete thrust into her, taking her to a moment where she could forget all her problems. Who cared what was going on in the world while they fucked? She had love; that was all she needed.

Pete bucked for one last time and then collapsed on top of her. 'You are one horny bitch,' he grinned.

As she turned her head to smile at him, Pete smirked. She'd got the nice Pete today but fast, rough and selfish sex was his thing. From now on, he'd show no consideration towards her needs. He'd have her exactly how he wanted.

For the second night in two weeks, Gina heard a commotion in the kitchen. She rushed through to find the girls in a flurry of banging doors and swearing. She swore loudly when she saw Rachel's face covered in blood.

'What the hell has happened now?' Gina marched Rachel over to the sink. 'If this is Stacey Hunter's doing, I'm going right round to her house.'

'It wasn't anyone,' said Rachel. 'I fell down the steps on Frazer Terrace. I'm a right dozy cow at times.'

'This is serious, you two!' Gina sighed loudly as she tended to Claire's face. 'Someone is going to get hurt if you don't stop playing these stupid games.'

'We're not playing games!' Rachel raised her voice.

'Shut up or you'll wake your father.'

'Too late, you already have.' Pete came into the room. 'What's up?'

Rachel knew there wasn't any point in trying to cover anything up now. Dad could clearly see what state she was in.

He rushed across the room. 'Who did this?' he wanted to know.

'That mad cow, Stacey Hunter,' replied Gina. 'I told you she was trouble last week. She needs teaching a lesson. I'm going –'

'No!' said Claire. 'Leave it, Mum!'

Pete tilted Rachel's chin up to inspect the damage but also to look his daughter in the eye. 'Who was it?'

'I told you, I fell,' Rachel insisted.

But Claire had had enough. 'You're right,' she said. 'It was Stacey Hunter.'

Gina watched Pete's face darken. He'd had many a run in with Stacey's step-father, Lenny Pickton, over the years but Lenny had a whole bunch of his cronies and a prison reputation to fall back on. Pete wasn't strong enough to fight him. Lenny's methods were evil, cruel and despicable.

Right now, none of that bothered Pete. His face contorted with rage. 'I'm going to kill him,' he said. 'No one does this to my daughter and gets away with it.'

'Don't be stupid,' said Gina. 'I'll end up with two of you to look after at this rate.'

'Stacey can't get away with this.'

'I said no!'

'Mum's right, Dad,' said Rachel. 'We need to think this through first. There's too much shit aimed at us as it is. We don't want to watch our backs every time we set foot outside the front gate.'

'Me neither,' said Gina, although secretly she was counting

down the days until she could confront Stacey Hunter's mother. She'd rip her hair out before slapping her around. This had all gone too far.

Pete frowned. If he stood up to Lenny, he'd get his head smashed in. If he didn't stand up to Lenny, then his daughters, and maybe his wife, would think he was a coward. Lenny did scare him but he couldn't sit back and let Stacey get away with it.

'I'm going to find him,' he said.

'No!' Three women spoke in unison.

'Leave it be, Dad,' urged Claire, taking hold of his arm. 'For me, please.'

'I can't.'

'He won't stop if you hit him,' added Gina.

'Maybe not, but it'll give me great satisfaction,' said Pete. 'He's had it coming to him for a long time.'

'Let me speak to Maggie Hunter first; see if I can't calm this whole situation down.'

'If she's anything like her daughter, she won't listen.'

'It's worth a shot before you go and –'

'You don't have faith in me, do you?' Pete glared at her.

'Of course I do,' Gina lied, noting the hurt in his eyes. She moved closer to him. 'But I want my family to be safe. If you go after Lenny, it'll start up something bigger. If I talk to Maggie, then maybe things will settle down.'

'I doubt it,' said Rachel.

Pete stared at them all in turn. Suddenly, he shook his head. 'No,' he said.

'But –' Gina began.

'I'm not having it.'

Gina grabbed for his arm as he pushed past her. He was out of the house before she could stop him.

'Pete!' she shouted after him. 'Leave it for now.'

Pete stopped halfway down the path, turned back for a moment. 'If you think that I'd let anyone – ANYONE – get away with doing that to my kids... I'll be back when I've kicked that fucker around.'

*

155

'There's some sort of commotion going on over the road,' Caren told John as he came through from the kitchen.

'Oh?' John joined her at the living room window, in time to see Pete marching down the path towards his car. Gina ran after him, but he screeched off before she had time to get to the driver's door.

'Just another day on the scummy side of the street,' said Caren, unable to keep a smile at bay. It was always good to see Gina and Pete arguing, no matter what trivial matter it was over.

John laughed. 'You shouldn't say that,' he told her, wagging his finger. 'One of these days, you'll slip up and have all the neighbours on your back. And then what would you do?'

Caren watched Gina run back into the house: she looked really upset. If things had been different, she would have gone across to see if she could help, showing genuine concern. But, as it was, Gina wasn't a friend of hers so she didn't really care.

A woman walked past their house. She stopped for a moment at the gate and then pushed it open.

'There's someone here.' Caren watched her for a moment before moving to answer the door.

'It'll be a sales rep trying to flog us something we either don't want or can't afford.' John buried his head in the evening newspaper, not the slightest bit interested.

'No, I'm sure I recognise her but I can't quite put a name to her face.'

'I'm looking for John Williams,' the woman said after Caren opened the door. 'I was told he'd moved into Stanley Avenue?'

'That's right.' Caren eyed her warily. 'And you are?'

'Is he in?'

She was a brassy woman – bottle-blonde hair and make-up that didn't suit the age of her face. Her clothes were stylish but far too tight for her small frame. She had a huge bust underneath her cropped leather jacket and thin legs covered by leggings. Her heels were stacked ridiculously high: Ah – now she recognised her.

'Donna?' she said. 'Donna Adams?'

Donna nodded. 'Yes. Well, I used to be. I'm married now.'

'I thought I recognised you.' Caren moved to one side so that she could step in. 'John!' She waited for him to appear before speaking again. 'It's Donna –'

'Donna Adams!' he exclaimed, a little surprised to see her.

'Hi, John,' said Donna. 'Long time no see.'

'She wants to see you,' Caren said pointedly.

John frowned. He glanced at Caren who seemed just as puzzled at her appearance.

Donna paused for a moment. 'I thought you might like to know now that you're back on the estate again, that you and I have a son.'

Caren paled in an instant. Thoughts of the anguish she and John had gone through to try to conceive a child together came hurtling to the forefront of her mind. Christ, no – it was the one thing she hadn't been able to provide him with. Please don't let this be true.

Donna handed John a photograph.

'I had no idea,' said John looking down at it, realising how it might seem different to Caren.

'Let me see.' She took the photograph from him. Then she almost laughed out loud with relief. 'This is a man!'

'Yes, Sam's twenty-one this year,' said Donna.

'Sam?' John's voice came out in a whisper.

'I thought - I thought you meant a little boy.'

'You thought I'd had an affair!' John looked hurt.

'You can't blame me for being suspicious. When someone comes to your house and tells you that your husband is the father of her son, what do you expect me to think?'

'It was a long time ago,' Donna explained. 'We were only kids. I was sixteen when I found out I was pregnant.'

'Me and you weren't together, Caz,' John added hastily. 'It wasn't a long relationship.'

'It doesn't matter,' said Caren. For some reason, she was immediately suspicious of Donna. 'If you were sixteen, you weren't much more than a child yourself.' She turned back to Donna. 'How did you find out that he was back? Or where we lived?'

'I saw you turning into Stanley Avenue the other day – I was going to follow you but I lost my nerve.'

'How did you know which house we lived at?'

'The car was parked outside,' she said. 'And when I drove past a few minutes ago you were both in the window.'

Caren shrugged. It was a feasible answer: they had been watching Gina and Pete.

'You haven't changed much, either of you,' Donna spoke into the silence that had developed.

'But why now?' John gave the photo back to Donna. 'You could have told me before I left the estate; before I married Caren.'

Donna shrugged.

Caren watched as she spoke to John for a few minutes. Donna had started to look a little awkward at all his questions. Something wasn't sitting right with her – call it gut feeling but she couldn't help thinking that this whole thing was a set up. Why now, after all this time? She decided to play along with it.

'Does Sam want to meet his dad?'

Donna frowned. 'I'm not sure.'

'It's understandable after all this time. I suppose he'll be nervous and... you haven't asked him, have you?'

'Not yet. I – I wanted to talk to you first,' she looked at John, 'to see if you wanted to meet him.'

John had been leaning back on the wall but stood upright again. 'Of course I want to meet him. But I'm a little annoyed that you've come to see me without telling him. What happens now if he doesn't want to know?'

'Well, I –'

'John, why don't you give Donna your mobile number and she can pass it to Sam,' Caren took charge of the situation. 'Then he can decide if he wants to see you.'

Donna smiled at Caren but it wasn't genuine.

As soon as she'd gone, Caren turned to John. 'What the hell was all that about?'

'I'm not sure.' John scratched his head. They moved back to the living room. 'Do you think she was telling the truth?'

'No, but I'm not sure why.' Caren sat down. 'She looked practically distraught when we didn't start arguing.'

They sat in silence as *EastEnders* drew to a close for the night.

'It was a long time ago, Caz,' said John. 'You do believe me?'

Caren smiled. 'Of course I believe you.' Then she frowned. 'But I certainly don't believe her. We need to work out some dates.'

She headed for the kitchen to find a notepad.

An hour later, Pete stormed up the path to his front door. Despite asking around, he hadn't managed to find Lenny and had come home with his tail between his legs. He supposed that was better than coming home with several broken ribs, which is what he'd probably end up with when Lenny got wind that he'd been after him. But he couldn't let it ride again.

He was nearly to his front door when he heard his name being shouted. Turning, he squinted in the dark until the image of John appeared clearer. He sighed; what was up with him now? All Pete wanted to do was curl up in front of the telly and sleep off this godforsaken day.

'You'll never guess who's turned up at our house,' John told him.

'No, but I'm sure you're going to tell me all the same.'

'Donna Adams. You know, she used to be in our year at school?'

'Oh, yeah. Blonde hair, big tits. Skinny legs right up to her armpits.'

John nodded. 'I went out with her a few times before we finished school. Apparently she got pregnant, never told me and now she claims I have a son!'

'Really!' Pete feigned shock. 'What did Caren say? I bet she did her nut.'

'That's where you're wrong.'

'But I thought you and her can't – sorry, *she* can't – have kids.'

'*We* can't.'

'Then how did you get away with that?'

'Ah, Caren's the salt of the earth. She was quite calm about it. Besides, I wasn't with her then.'

'I suppose not,' Pete grunted. 'Look, if you don't mind, I'll catch up another time. I haven't had anything to eat yet and I'm starving.'

'But it's nearly nine. I was just off to the shop,' John tried to make small talk; he knew he wasn't fully forgiven for getting a job.

'What've you been up to?'

'Something and nothing.' Pete walked off.

'Is everything okay, mate?'

'Yeah, why the fuck shouldn't it be?'

'I saw you and Gina having words earlier. Wondered if you wanted to chat about it?'

'No, I bloody don't.'

John shrugged. 'Okay, okay. I'll leave you to it then. See ya.'

As soon as Pete stepped foot into the house, Gina was waiting for him. She gave him a quick once over before throwing herself into his arms.

'You didn't go after him then?'

'I couldn't find him.' Pete shirked her off. 'I tried the pubs and the bookies but he wasn't around – probably keeping a low profile knowing that I'm after him.'

Gina smiled, relief flooding through her. If Pete had caught up with Lenny, she'd probably be visiting him in A&E by now.

'Come on, I'll make you something nice to eat. What do you fancy?'

Pete barged past her. 'I'm not hungry. I just want a beer.'

She went to the fridge and searched out two cans of lager.

'Where are the girls?'

'In their room. Rachel went to lie down with a headache. I sent Claire up to keep an eye on her. I haven't heard a peep out of either of them since. But listen to this. Mum popped round and she said –'

'Leave it will, you, Gene. I'm knackered.' Pete took the can she held out to him. He wasn't in the mood to hear Gina's latest tittle-tattle.

'But I don't have anyone else to share it with.' Gina folded her arms and carried on regardless. 'You know that Ruth across the road? She moved into number thirty-two a couple of months back now?'

'What about her?' Pete tried to stop from snapping; had someone seen him going into her house? No, they couldn't have - Gina was too calm. She would go ballistic if she ever found out.

'Her kids have been taken into care,' she told him triumphantly.

Pete sighed, with relief. 'Is that it?' he said.

'That's big news,' snapped Gina. 'I've been a cow but none of my kids have been taken into care.'

'Why don't you back off for once? Sometimes you don't have the true story and you still go accusing everyone of all sorts.'

'But I want to get to the bottom of this!'

'You're such a bitch,' he told her, before switching off completely.

'I'll take that as a compliment.'

Gina smiled. Already she was looking forward to the showdown with Ruth; she'd try and collar her first thing, when she wouldn't be expecting it.

Needing some fresh air, Ruth ventured out early the next day. She hadn't had a drink the night before because she couldn't be bothered to go and buy some. Instead, she'd cried herself to sleep and ended up with the same headache she would have had with a hangover.

She might have known Gina would be standing at her front gate when she set foot into the avenue. Ruth put her head down, hoping to scuttle past.

'Oy!' Gina shouted. 'I want a word with you.'

Ruth paled - has she found out about her and Pete? She walked a little faster but Gina caught her up.

'It's not what you think,' Ruth began. 'I –'

'Don't come with your excuses,' Gina spat. 'You've had your kids taken off you, haven't you?'

Ruth sighed with relief that the truth about her and Pete hadn't got out but her eyes brimmed with tears. 'Leave me alone. It's got nothing to do with you.'

'You live in Stanley Avenue so it has everything to do with me.' Gina pointed a finger in her face. 'Your business is my business now that you've moved in here.'

Ruth closed her eyes for a moment and pinched the bridge of her nose. Arguing with Gina again was the last thing she needed right now.

'Why don't you get on with it?' she told her. 'Say what you want to say and leave me alone. I'm tired and I have a headache, so if you don't mind?'

'People like you are not welcome in Stanley Avenue.'

'You don't know the full story.'

'I know that you've had both boys taken into care. That means you obviously weren't a fit mother.' Gina folded her arms, warming up for the onslaught. 'You obviously couldn't take care of them.'

'Well, you tell your gossip source that they're wrong. My kids haven't been taken into care.'

'Yeah, right, like I believe you,' Gina said, but her smile slipped a little. 'Where are they, then?'

'If you must spread malicious rumours, then get your facts right. My boys weren't taken into care. I gave them over to Children's Services myself.'

Gina frowned. 'You *let* them take your kids away? That's sick, if you ask me.'

'No one's asking you.' Ruth looked up and down the street, suddenly not giving a damn who was listening in to their conversation or peeking out from behind their curtains. 'I gave my boys up because it was the right thing to do, so don't you, or anyone else in this godforsaken avenue, pass judgement on me because of it.'

Gina was momentarily stunned but it didn't take her long to gain ground again. 'Why, you cheeky little bitch,' she cried. 'I'm going to see to it that you can't walk back to your house without everyone knowing what's happened. Your life won't be worth living by the time you get back from wherever it was you were rushing off to.'

'Leave me alone.' Ruth burst into tears and ran quickly down the avenue. Gina didn't follow her, but her voice did.

'We don't like cruelty cases in Stanley Avenue,' she heard her bellow. 'If we take a vote on it, you'll be banished. Do you hear me? I'll walk you out of the avenue myself.'

CHAPTER EIGHTEEN

Gina Bradley was true to her word. By the time Ruth came back from the shops, she counted no less than six women waiting at their gates for her to pass.

'Bitch!' Mrs Porter from number seventeen shouted across.

Ruth scuttled past, head down.

'Yeah, someone should put you into care, you heartless cow,' said Julie Elliot from number fourteen. 'I've a good mind to slap some sense into you.'

Ruth gulped back tears but she continued. Up ahead, she could see her front door – her sanctuary from preying eyes and heckling women – and wondered if she'd get there without Gina or one of her friends throwing a punch.

Caren was in the garden, clearing a few bits of rubbish that had blown in during the rainy storm they'd had the night before. She stood up to see what all the shouting was about and then sighed - that bloody Gina!

'Take no notice of her evil tongue,' she said as Ruth walked past her garden. 'We're not all out to get you.'

Ruth caught Caren's eye for a moment, noticing the concern as she walked on.

'Don't come past me,' Sheila Ravenscroft shouted. 'You're not fit to tread on the pavement here.'

Ruth ran the last few yards into the house, slamming the door shut behind her. She gulped in air as she tried not to go into panic mode, then dropped to her knees in the middle of the hallway and sobbed. Every day seemed to get worse.

Would she ever get out of this nightmare?

When she heard someone knock at the door half an hour later, Ruth jumped. She couldn't even remember crawling into the corner of the room, but her head throbbed from the number of times she'd banged it on the wall behind her.

The letter box lifted up. 'Ruth? It's Caren, from number twenty-four.'

'Go away,' said Ruth, realising that she couldn't hide now. Caren had already clocked her sitting there.

'I just wanted to see if you were okay?'

'You obviously don't listen to the gossip. If you did, you wouldn't be here.'

'I don't care about gossip. Look, this is killing my back. Can I come in for a moment, please?'

'This is a trick! I know Gina's standing behind you – and some of them other women. If I open the door, you'll all barge in and kick the shit out of me.'

'Ruth, I can't stand the sight of Gina so there's no chance of me playing her stupid games.' There was a pause. 'Come on, what do you say I make you a cuppa?'

Ruth decided to answer the door. She peeped around the frame, eyes red raw, hair messy where she'd been pulling at it.

'I didn't think you knew my name,' she said, her voice barely audible.

'If anyone stands up to that bully, I make it my business to find out their name.'

They went through to the kitchen. 'Sit,' demanded Caren. She put the kettle on, searched around for two mugs and in a matter of moments had made coffee.

'Do you want to tell me the real story behind the rumour?' she asked once she'd sat down opposite her.

Ruth shrugged. 'Most people have already made up their minds about me. What good will it do?'

'I'm not most people.'

'You still want to know what's going on, though.'

'Maybe I do but not for the reason you're thinking. I'm not after gossip.' Caren paused. 'I've watched you since you moved in. I've watched you sink deeper and deeper into a dark hole and it upsets me to think that whatever you have to put up with in your personal life – which you should be able to keep to yourself without it being bawled around the avenue – you have that bleeding Gina Bradley to contend with.'

Ruth's mouth formed into a glimmer of a smile. 'You don't like her either, I presume?'

'She's a nasty piece of work, hell bent on destroying anyone's happiness. If she sees someone smile, she thinks she has the right to wipe it off their face.'

'What did she do to you?'

Caren blew on her drink to cool it down. 'I was unfortunate to grow up with her. I knew her from school. We – that's me and John, my husband – moved off the estate as soon as we could. Growing up on 'the Mitch' made us both want more. We didn't want to end up like the losers on the dole, claiming we had glass backs so that we didn't have to work for a penny.'

'Glass backs?' Ruth hadn't come across that expression before.

'As in you can see right through someone who is putting it on? Swinging the lead; nothing wrong with them really.'

Ruth nodded. 'There seems to be a lot of that around here. I suppose you could say I was one of them.'

Caren tried to backtrack. 'Oh, no, I meant that some people –'

Ruth held up her hand. 'I know what you meant.'

Caren paused again, long enough to take a couple of mouthfuls of her drink. Then she started to talk again.

'I found it really tough when I moved in here too. We – we had everything before John went bankrupt.'

'A business deal gone wrong?'

'Sort of – we lost a major supplier. Not only did they owe us thousands, they took away a lot of his incoming work. John's a plumber by trade and over the years we'd built up a company that allowed us to have a little bit of financial freedom. We had a beautiful house off this estate, and we had a life with no worries.'

'And then you ended up here?' Ruth shuddered.

'My worst nightmare.' Caren nodded. 'But it didn't stop there. That's when I found out Gina and her awful family lived right across from us.'

'And I thought I had it bad when I moved in.' Ruth smiled, warming to Caren.

'What I'm trying to say is that no matter what life, or people like Gina, throw at us, we can get through it. Today will be a shit day for you: tomorrow might be the same. And the day after. But one day soon, it'll get that little bit better; and brighter. Nothing lasts forever.'

'I gave my children away.' Ruth's eyes filled with tears again.

'And you had your reasons.' Caren gave her hand a quick squeeze, ignoring the blood stained bandage around Ruth's wrist. 'You need to work through your problems in your own time and then you'll come out the other side.'

'I – I'm scared that I might not make it.'

'You will – we're all stronger than we think. I know what it's like to move into Stanley Avenue and feel like you don't belong here. Luckily for me, I have John to talk things over with. He picks me up when I'm feeling low. But you don't have anyone.' From a pocket in her jeans, she pulled out a piece of paper she'd written her mobile phone number on. 'The next time something gets you down, maybe you could text me and if I'm free, I'll pop down to see you.'

Ruth wiped at the tears that had fallen and smiled again. 'Thank you,' she whispered.

Caren smiled too. 'Now, don't lose that slip of paper.'

Pleased with herself after most of the neighbours had come out to hassle Ruth, Gina lit a cigarette and leaned on the gate, watching out for Pete. He'd gone out earlier, said he'd pay a couple of bills and then come home and take her for a cheapo lunch in Wetherspoons. Gina was hoping to get him merry enough so that he'd sub her a twenty so she could get some new shoes. She fancied a treat.

Jenny Webster wobbled her heavy frame across to her. Jenny lived in the corner house with her son and daughter from a previous marriage and an Afro-Caribbean man who made Gina's neck ache when she addressed him. Jenny was the same height as Gina: she often wondered how they got it together.

'Can't believe that about Ruth Millington, can you?' said Gina, the minute she drew level with her. 'I didn't know you could do that, give your kids back.'

'Me neither.' Jenny rested her hand on the gate while she caught her breath. 'I'd have given my Leo up a long time ago if I had known,' she laughed.

Gina did too for a moment. 'She's a sneaky piece of work,' she added.

'She is – I've seen some comings and goings at her place already.'

'Oh?' Gina realised she might be about to hear more gossip.

'I don't trust her.' Jenny glanced up and down the avenue before turning back. 'I was going to tell you earlier, then I wasn't sure but I think you should know. I saw Pete going in to see her the other morning.'

'WHAT?' Gina roared.

Jenny nodded. 'It was early, about nine-ish.'

'Did you see what time he came out?'

'Yes, just after ten.'

'And was it the first time you saw him?'

Jenny paused. 'It's not my place to say – I've said enough already.'

Gina clenched her fists. 'Tell me!'

'I've seen him a couple of times. I don't know what...'

But Gina wasn't listening anymore. She was across the road and heading for number thirty-two. Jenny trotted behind her as quick as she could.

'You'd better come outside, Ruth Millington!' Gina hammered on Ruth's front door. 'I know you're in there because I've just seen Caren coming out.' She lifted up the letterbox but she couldn't see anyone. 'I'll rip your fucking head off when I get hold of you. You've had it, do you hear?'

Behind the kitchen door, Ruth sat with her hands covering her ears. Damn that family. If it wasn't Gina spreading malicious rumours and turning the neighbours against her, it was Pete coming to get his end away. Although she knew they shouldn't have done what they did, he had taken advantage of her at her weakest moment and now it looked like she was going to pay for it in more ways than one. Still, at least Gina hadn't found out about that yet. It could only be a matter of time but maybe all this other gossip would keep her off their trail for now. Then she could talk to Pete and see if he would back off.

'You have to come out some time and I'll be waiting.' Gina shouted again. 'No one messes about with my Pete and gets away with it.'

Ruth gasped: Ohmigod, she *had* found out! Were all the women in Stanley Avenue set up as spies? Pete had only called round twice.

Ruth pushed herself further into the corner of the room as the banging on the door continued. Why couldn't everyone leave her alone?

Gina snapped down the letterbox and stared up at the windows. There wasn't a movement from anywhere but she knew Ruth was in. She picked up a brick from the garden and threw it at the large windowpane in the living room. It bounced back onto the garden, narrowly missing her toes.

'Gina!'

Gina turned to see her mum running towards her.

'Leave me alone, Mum. I'm going to get her. She's been –'

'Never mind her. You'd better come quickly. It's your Pete. He's in a right mess. There's blood everywhere.'

'Pete?' Gina stormed into her house. 'Where the hell are you?' She went through to the kitchen. 'Pete!'

Pete sat on the floor, his back resting on the oven door. His face was a mishmash of bruising, swelling; thick blotches of red blood oozed down his cheeks, his neck, over his T-shirt. He was holding onto his ribs.

'You should see the other guy.' He tried to smile but winced in pain.

Gina wet a tea towel with cold water and dropped to her knees beside him. She held it to his nose.

'Is this Lenny's doing?' she asked.

'Ow, Gene, don't be so rough,' Pete moaned.

'You knew full well this would happen if you went after him. He could have killed you. He's a fucking idiot!'

Pete stopped her hand with his own. 'I couldn't let it rest; I knew he'd be after me. But I saw him across the shops. He shouted over, asking how the young 'un was. Then he laughed. I just flipped. No one laughs at me or my family.' He tried to smile again. 'At least I got the first punch in.'

Gina held back her frustration. What was happening to her family? Were they all hell-bent on fighting to get what they wanted? And since when had it started to control their lives, spiral out of control? No wonder people thought they were scum. They gave them enough reasons to think none the wiser.

'We have to stop,' she said after they'd sat in silence for a while. 'All this fighting, it's not good.'

'If we don't stick up for ourselves, people will walk all over us.'

'People do that anyway. We're the Bradleys; people think we're shit. That's why we fight, to get one in before someone knocks us down.'

'It's a beating, Gina.' Pete withdrew the towel from his nose, trying not to retch at the sight of all the blood. 'I'll get over it. I always do.'

Gina rested her back on the unit beside him. 'But what's it doing to us? Our girls have turned into animals. Even I'm ashamed of them at times.'

'They have your temper.'

'What's that supposed to mean!'

'You'll fight over anything. That's hardly a good example to set.'

'Don't go blaming this on me. This is your doing, not mine.'

'I know.' Pete sighed. 'We should try and talk to them, though. Let's catch them when they come in later.'

But later, after school, Rachel and Claire were causing trouble outside Shop&Save. An elderly gentleman had been going about his business when Rachel pinched his tweed cap and raced off with it on her bike.

'Come back, you little cow,' he shouted, brandishing his walking stick and tottering after her.

'Relax, Granddad,' she taunted him, riding by but not near enough for him to claim back his cap. 'You want it? Go and fetch it.' She threw it into a huge puddle of water.

'That's my best cap!' The man bent down and retrieved his soggy possession. He glared at Rachel. 'You're such an awful generation. This would never have happened in my day. You'd have been locked up and dealt with by the local bobby.'

'Yeah, yeah, and I suppose you'll tell me that you fought a war for me too.'

'I'd have never fought a war for a piece of shit like you.'

'Ooh, Granddad's getting brave.' Rachel beckoned to the other girls. 'Come on over, join in the fun.'

'Leave him alone,' said Laila.

Rachel looked over in disbelief; Laila was always the mischief maker. The scowl on her face said she was definitely annoyed about something. Ignoring the man, Rachel rode over to her. She was sitting on the railing with Ashley. Claire was beside her, sitting on her bike, a foot down on the floor to steady herself.

'What's up with you, you moody cow?' Rachel asked Laila.

'Nothing.'

'Yes, there is. You've been like this for days now.' Rachel peered at her closely. 'You're not knocked up?'

'No! And keep your bleeding voice down. I don't want any rumours starting about *me*.'

'What's that supposed to mean?' When Laila didn't say anything, Rachel pushed. 'Go on, tell me what rumour is circulating. Is it about me?'

'Or me?' asked Claire.

'Don't say anything,' Ashley told Laila.

Rachel threw down her bike and grabbed the front of Laila's jacket. 'What's going on that I don't know about?'

Laila still said nothing.

Rachel pushed her away in frustration. 'You're all mouth.'

'You'll have no mouth left when Stacey's finished with you this time.'

'Aren't we supposed to be on the same side here?'

Laila shrugged. Ashley studied her feet, running the toe of her trainers back and forth in the gravel.

Then Rachel understood. 'You two are my bessie mates! Surely you don't want to go back over to Stacey?'

'Yes, she wants us to join her again.' Ashley looked up at Rachel. 'I know you'll probably beat the crap out of me when I say this, but I'd rather have Stacey on side. She hits so hard.'

'Tell me about it,' muttered Claire.

Rachel turned to her with a scowl. 'Shut up, Claire.'

'Look,' said Laila. 'Don't you think it would be better if we all joined as one?'

Rachel shook her head.

'She's going to get us together eventually,' said Ashley. 'Whether you two like it or not.'

'She only thinks she's got everyone on side,' said Rachel. 'Once the others get fed up of her childish ways, they'll soon ditch her. That's why we should stay strong now. We'll all be top dogs again and Stacey Hunter will be nobody. Wouldn't you like that?'

Laila nodded. 'But it's not going to happen. Stacey will keep them all on side because they're scared of getting a leathering. She won't stand for anyone deserting her again.'

Rachel sat down beside her on the railing, quiet for a moment while she thought about things. 'We need to stick together.' She looked at each girl in turn. 'All five of us, including Louise. If we stay like this, she won't break us down but if one of you two falls,' she ran a finger across her throat, 'then the Mitchell Mob will be fucked. Are we in this together?' she asked, holding her breath while she waited for their reply.

'I'm in,' said Claire.

Rachel tutted. 'I didn't mean you, you dope. Laila? Ashley?'

Laila and Ashley looked at each other and after a quick nod of her head, Laila spoke. 'Okay,' she said. 'I want to stay with you two. But if it's a choice between you and her, then I think I'd rather go with her.'

'But –'

'Don't complain,' said Laila. 'If I go with her, I want you to come too. And you, Claire. If we go over, we go over together.'

Claire shrugged a shoulder. 'What do you say, Rach? One for all and all for one?'

'What the fuck do you take me for?' Rachel glared at her. 'I'll never side with Stacey Hunter. Not now, not tomorrow, not ever.'

'But –'

'But nothing,' Rachel interrupted her sister. 'It's either her or me.' She picked up her bike and rode off.

'Rach!' Claire yelled. 'Wait up for me! Rach!'

After pedalling fast to release some of her pent-up aggression, Rachel slowed down and let Claire catch up with her.

'What's up?' she asked when she drew level at last.

'Nothing.' Rachel bumped down three steps onto Rowley Green and headed for home. She didn't want her sister to know how upset she was. 'I'm hungry,' she lied.

As soon as they went through the back door, they could tell something was wrong. It was too quiet – even the television was off. In the kitchen, they found their parents sitting at the table.

'Dad!' Claire swallowed as she took in the state of him.

'Wow, Dad, you did it then?' Rachel grinned. 'You stuck up for Claire and took a beating off Lenny.'

'Sit down, Rachel,' said Gina. 'You too, Claire. Me and your dad have been talking and we feel that the fighting has got out of hand.'

Rachel folded her arms defiantly. 'You talk to us about fighting, when Dad comes home in that state?'

'It's *because* I came home looking like this that I feel the need to talk to you both. Things are going to get even nastier if we don't stop now.'

'I agree,' said Gina. 'Your Dad getting beat up today could be the start of things if you continue to fight with Stacey.'

'You mean he won't hurt you again if we behave, right?' said Claire.

Pete nodded. 'I shouldn't have gone after him; he's too strong for me.'

'You'll always be good enough in my eyes.'

Pete smirked, then grimaced. 'I'm a scrap collector-come-odd-jobs-for-cash-man.'

'We want your word that you two will behave yourselves,' said Gina.

The girls shrugged.

'Promise us!'

'Okay, okay!' said Rachel.

'And you need to back off that Ruth woman, from number thirty-two,' Pete spoke to Gina. 'I heard what you'd been up to earlier.'

'That depends if the rumour is true.'

'What rumour?' Claire and Rachel asked at the same time.

'The one that says she's playing around with your father.'

'Dad!' said Claire.

'It's not true,' Pete lied. He scraped back his chair and stood up. 'We all need to stop fighting, before someone gets seriously hurt. Right girls?'

Rachel stood up and marched past him. 'Fine,' she said.

'I'll talk to her,' said Claire, following on a minute later.

'And you?' Pete stared at Gina once they'd both gone. 'No more from you either?'

Despite her earlier thoughts, Gina wasn't going to promise anything yet, not until she'd spoken to Ruth.

'Right?' repeated Pete.

'All right,' cried Gina. 'I'll keep the peace for a while.'

He pointed at her. 'You need to set a good example for them. They look up to you.'

Gina raised her eyebrows. When had anyone ever looked up to her?

CHAPTER NINETEEN

'Dad looks a right mess, doesn't he?' said Claire as she sat down next to Rachel on her bed.

'Yeah, he's taken a proper pasting. I'm glad he stuck up for you though.'

Claire paused. 'Rach, don't you think they're right, that we should back off?'

'We can't.' Rachel shook her head. 'We're in too deep now.'

'No, we're not. We can always stop.'

Rachel flopped back on the bed. 'If we back down, Stacey will hunt us down and tear us apart. She'll make sure that she humiliates us so that no one will want to be our friends.'

Claire huffed. 'So what? No one wants to hang around with us anyway. Let's face it, Dad's right – we're the Bradleys. Everyone thinks we're scum and that's down to the way we act.'

Rachel said nothing.

'Aren't you sick of it all yet?'

'I hate being the leader of the gang. I hate what it's done to us all. We used to have a laugh over at the shops with the other girls – we used to have fun! Now it's all about who can get one up on the other first. So, yes, I *am* sick of it all.'

'Me too! I dread going out now, wondering who's going to pounce on us next. I want to just have a laugh again.'

Rachel sighed. 'It's never going to happen.'

'But if we don't join in with Stacey and her stupid games, we –'

'Are you mad? She'll never stop coming after us.'

'She will, if we back down!' Claire was warming to her cause now. 'We can do it, Rach. Let's tell Stacey she can be leader again.'

Rachel shook her head. 'It won't work. We'll be a laughing stock.'

'For a week, maybe two, tops. But, you know Stacey; she'll move on to someone else. And we'll be with her then.'

'You think she'll let us hang around with her after what's happened?'

Claire shrugged. 'It's worth a shot.'

'And if it doesn't work?'

'Then we have each other. No one can break that up.'

Rachel knew there was no way Stacey would back down. Even if they went to her and said they wanted to join her gang, she'd laugh them off the estate. Stacey was a power freak; they should have known better than to mess with her. Mum and Dad were right, things had gone too far. The whole family had never been in as many scrapes as they had over the past few weeks.

Rachel knew when she was beat. She couldn't fight the likes of Stacey and win, just as her dad couldn't stand up to her step dad, Lenny. They weren't tough enough.

'What are we going to do?' Claire asked.

From her muffled tone, Rachel could tell that she was crying.

'I don't know,' she told her. 'But whatever happens, it's going to be nasty for a while.'

Things didn't look any better the following morning. Rachel got up in a mood and fell out with Claire, Gina and Pete within half an hour. She slammed out of the house ten minutes later, leaving Claire to face the sombre atmosphere alone.

Pete's right eye had swollen until he could barely see out of it. Gina tried to make a joke about things but it hadn't gone down well. He stormed off after slamming his mug down on the worktop, spraying remnants of tea all over the tiles.

And it wasn't even nine o'clock.

Claire and Gina sat in silence, finishing off their breakfast.

'Things'll get better, Mum,' said Claire. 'They'll both calm down soon.'

'I was talking sense last night, wasn't I?'

Claire nodded. 'But it won't happen, will it? Let's face it; everyone thinks we're shit, so why change a habit of a lifetime.'

Gina felt tears prick her eyes. 'Coming from you, also known as my sensible twin, that doesn't half sting,' she told her.

'I didn't mean anything by it, Mum.' Claire gave her a hug. Gina hugged her back fiercely to stop herself from screaming. What the hell was happening to their family? Anger welled up inside her.

'We have to stick together,' she said. 'No one badmouths us, not without getting what they deserve.'

'But we do deserve what we get at times, don't we?

Gina felt Claire's sobs as her body shook.

'I don't want to fight anymore, Mum.'

'You don't have to.'

'It's not going to be that easy.'

Gina moved back and held her daughter's face in her hands. 'Claire, love, when was anything in life going to be easy for a Bradley?'

By eleven thirty, neither Rachel nor Pete had returned home. Gina hadn't been able to get Claire to go to school either. Bored, she decided to have a walk across to the shops, see if anyone was about for a gossip. She was running low on cigarettes and she could do with some lager for tonight. Maybe, when Rachel and Pete came back, she could persuade them all to have a night in together. She'd get the girls some crisps and chocolates, and a frozen pizza to go with the bag of oven chips she already had. It would do them good to sit down as a family, watch a film together and relieve the tension.

She was there and back in half an hour yet, even as she'd thought about her problems while she walked, things didn't seem any better. She sighed as she got home; maybe soon things would start to improve.

But then, from the corner of her eye she noticed Ruth coming out of her gate. Without thinking of the promise she'd made the night before, Gina dropped her bag and groceries over into her garden and legged it across the road. When she drew level, she slapped Ruth across the face.

Ruth staggered back but stayed on her feet until the second slap was administered.

'Slut!' Gina cried as she slapped her again. 'Stay the fuck away from my Pete.'

Ruth didn't cower. She knew she deserved what she was getting so she wouldn't fight back. Gina slapped her again, grabbing hold of her hair.

'You. Keep. Your. Filthy. Hands. Off. Him!'

'Mum!' Claire shouted. 'You promised! No more fighting and look at you!'

Gina paused for a moment to catch her breath, pointing at Ruth. 'It's all her fault. She's been messing around with your dad.'

Claire gasped. 'Is that true?' she asked Ruth.

Ruth didn't reply. In the background, she could see Caren running towards them.

'Answer her!' cried Gina.

'Stop it, Mum!'

As she was about to hit Ruth again, Caren grabbed her wrist and held it in mid air. 'Enough!' she shouted.

Ruth pulled herself up and leaned on the wall, panting for breath.

'What the hell's going on this time?' Caren hissed. 'Are you always going to act like a child?'

'She started it,' Gina mumbled. 'It was her fault.'

'Ruth started a fight?' Caren looked on in astonishment. I don't think so.'

'Mum, let's go in,' Claire said, 'before you get landed with assault.'

'I – I won't say anything,' said Ruth. She wiped her nose with her hand and pulled it back to find blood all over it.

The black mist was beginning to lift but as guilt began to surface, Gina fought back with her tongue. She pointed at Ruth. 'Breathe a word of this to anyone and I'll –'

'You'll what?' said Caren. 'Pick another fight? Is that all you're good for? No wonder you've never had a job.'

'Hey!' said Claire.

'Leave it, Claire,' said Gina.

'But –'

'I said leave it! Go inside and mind your own business.'

As Claire marched off, Caren held out a tissue for Ruth.

Ruth took it from her. 'Can you help me home?' she whispered.

'Course I can.' But before she did, Caren turned back to Gina. 'Is this how you get your thrills in your sorry little life, by attacking people? Is this how you *all* get your kicks – you, your kids and Pete?'

'No!' cried Gina. 'We –'

'I have never met anyone so nasty, so vicious, so – so animal like in my entire life. You're nothing short of a thug. I should report you for this.'

'You wouldn't dare!'

'I would and you know it, so back –'

'No! Please, I don't want this to go any further,' Ruth broke in.

'But you're bleeding! And look at your eye. You'll –'

'I'll be fine,' Ruth assured her.

'Yes,' added Gina. 'She'll be fine, won't you, Ruth?'

'Oh, get out of my sight!' Caren put an arm around Ruth's shoulder. 'Come on, let's get you home.'

Gina stood in the avenue, watching Ruth stagger off with Caren. As her anger turned to shame, her eyes glistened with tears. She hadn't a clue what had come over her; she just saw red when she spotted Ruth. And now that Claire had seen her, she'd be in trouble with Pete when he finally showed his face again.

Wearily, she gathered up her wits as well as her pride and went back home. So much for a fun night in with the family.

Once inside the house, Caren helped Ruth remove her blood stained jacket. She took it from her and shoved it into the washing machine out of the way.

'You have to report this to the police,' she said.

'I can't do that,' said Ruth. 'I'll have the whole family against me then, as well as all the neighbours. It'll be like signing my own death warrant. I'm going to put in for a transfer.'

'I wish I could. I hate this bloody avenue; everyone is so small-minded.' Caren looked at Ruth, now sitting at the table. Her face was beginning to swell up like a bruised tomato, nerves as shredded as her bottom lip that had split twice. 'How can one family completely rule a street? If it isn't Gina, it's her bloody mother causing grief, shouting her mouth off.'

'I think the neighbours are okay,' admitted Ruth. 'It's just if they all get together with Gina. You were right: she is an animal.'

'So what started it all?'

'She found out that Pete had called around a few times. One of the neighbours must've grassed me up.'

Caren felt her blood run cold. 'He hasn't – threatened you in any way, has he?'

Ruth shook her head, a little too quickly for Caren's liking. She sighed, sat down across from her and reached for her hand. 'Whatever's going on, you can trust me if you need someone to talk to. I'd cut my own tongue off and shove it up my arse before I'd tell Gina Bradley a damn thing.'

Ruth tried to smile at Caren's joke.

Caren squeezed her hand, urging her to talk. 'Did he force himself on you?'

Ruth shook her head.

'You mean you wanted him to?'

Ruth shook her head again.

'So what, then?'

When Ruth shook her head for the third time, Caren backed off. She was upset; it wasn't fair to push her. Still, she wanted to press the point.

'Please, call me if you need to talk. You still have my number?'

'Yes.'

'I can understand if you don't want to but the offer will always be there.'

'She doesn't get it, though.' Ruth looked up through tears. 'No matter what she does, no one can hurt me any more than I've already been hurt. My life is a mess anyway, because of my own doings.' She flicked her thumb towards the front door. 'I don't need them lot out there to tell me how stupid I am.'

'You're not stupid!'

'You don't have kids, do you?'

'Sadly, no. I'm unable to.'

'Oh, shit, I –'

Caren held up her hand. 'It's okay. I've known for a while now. Dodgy ovaries and I ended up having an early menopause. It couldn't be helped.' For a moment, she thought of Donna Adams and Sam. Donna had finally been in touch; surprisingly, it seemed that Sam was coming to visit them next week.

'Then you must hate me for what I did, giving my kids up when you can't have any.'

'We all do things according to our circumstances. It's not my style to judge anyone.' Caren paused. 'Maybe once things have died down, you and I could start meeting for coffee once in a while. I could give you a lift into town, share the odd glass of wine in the evening. What do you say? It'll certainly get that lot out there talking.'

'Why are you doing this?' Ruth asked suddenly.

'It's because I know how shit I felt when I had to move into Stanley Avenue - and I had John to help me out. You wouldn't believe the arguments and rows we had when we first got here.'

Ruth was surprised by this. 'You always look so solid when I see you together.'

'That's because I, unlike Gina Bradley, won't air my dirty washing in public. There were times I could have killed him, especially when he started to spend more time over on the scummy side of the street with Pete.' Caren stopped when she heard Ruth giggle. 'What?'

'The scummy side of the street?'

'Oh.' Caren smiled. 'That's my nickname. I shouted it out in temper to John once and it stuck. It's appropriate, though.'

'It is.'

'And if that bloody Pete knocks on your door again, tell him to sling his hook.'

Ruth's smile faded.

'He's a bully too. I think that's where Gina gets it from. She doesn't control that family as much as she likes to think. He does; the tosser. He tried it on with me too.'

Ruth's mouth gaped.

'He threatened me. Said he'd get me if I stopped John from hanging around with him. Well, I stopped him and nothing happened to me.'

'Yet,' muttered Ruth.

'It's too late now. And besides, he moved on to you, didn't he, the bastard?'

Ruth nodded.

'But he won't be coming in again, will he?'

Ruth shook her head. 'I just hope he gets the message.'

'Maybe he won't come round now that someone has blabbed. And I'll get John to fit you some more security on your door, if that's ok?'

'I don't have any money until next week. I can't pay you until then.'

'We don't need money.' Caren waved the offer away. 'Have you any idea of the junk he pulled from our garage before we had to move? He'll have something lying around doing nothing.'

'Thanks,' Ruth said again.

Caren smiled.

'No, really. I mean it. You didn't have to step in this morning.'

'I *wanted* to. Someone has to stand up to that foul-mouthed cow. Although, I must admit, I'm not a fighter. If she had a go at me, I'd have done the same as you.'

'She's got a hard hit.' Ruth winced.

'There is one thing, though.' Caren splayed out her fingers. 'I'd have been annoyed if she broke one of my nails. Hey, I've had an idea.'

Gina stood on the back step, puffing heavily on a cigarette. Although there was a wind blowing and the weather had turned colder overnight, she wasn't about to go inside the house; she knew she'd have to face the music after what she'd done.

She took another long puff. What the hell had gotten in to her? One minute she was telling her family to back off and behave; the next she was fighting hell for leather in the middle of the street. Some example she was setting! She recalled every detail of the incident in slow motion in her mind. Ruth had looked like a cornered animal. She hadn't fought back at all and there was only one reason she could think of for that – she must have a guilty conscience.

A few minutes later, Gina took a final drag of her cigarette before stubbing it out, letting out a sigh along with the smoke. Maybe Caren was right: maybe she was fit for nothing except fighting. Gina Bradley – not an exam to her name, not a penny earned by hard work. And if truth be told, she had too much time on her hands. There was nothing to do with her days; they all rolled into one.

She had no purpose to her pitiful life. Pete went out to do some kind of cash in hand job most days. Even the girls went to school occasionally. But what did she have? Nothing. Every day was the same. Every day in the future was doomed to be the same – unless she did something about it.

Claire was in the kitchen when she finally went inside. She gave her mother a filthy look.

'I'm sorry, love,' said Gina. 'I don't know what came over me.'

'Then why did you do it?' Claire asked. 'It was horrible to see you laying into her, in front of everyone, not bothering how much you hurt her.'

'It's only the same as you and Rachel having a go at Stacey or one of the other girls you've been fighting with lately.'

'No, it's not. We're not that nasty.'

Gina opened her mouth to snap back an answer but she closed it instead. Her fight wasn't with her daughter.

'I don't know why I did it,' she admitted moments later after they'd sat in a stony silence. 'That's the honest truth.'

'Then maybe you should do an anger management course or something.'

'Anger management?' Gina laughed. 'You must be joking. Living in this house, I'd never get a chance to learn how to be calm. Besides, it's not in my make up.'

'But have you any idea how embarrassing it is to see your mum beating up a defenceless woman in the middle of the street? To have another neighbour pulling her away?'

'Okay, okay!' Gina had heard enough. 'It's me who should be lecturing you about these things.'

'I didn't start the fight this morning!'

'No, but you'll probably start another one sooner than I will.'

Claire had no answer to that.

Gina left her to sulk in the kitchen. In the living room, she thought about what Claire had said. She hadn't realised how she would look through her child's eyes - she hadn't actually thought any further than punching Ruth's lights out.

She ran a hand through her greasy hair and sniggered. Anger management indeed. But deep down inside, she knew it was what she needed. She had to get rid of all her pent-up aggression or it would ruin her. She'd end up in real trouble – she might even end up in prison – and then where would she be?

Maybe it was time to see if she could get some help, start setting an example to her children instead of being an embarrassment. It was never too late to change, right?

And she knew just the person to go to.

CHAPTER TWENTY

'I never expected to see you sitting in my office.' Josie smiled at Gina. 'It's obviously not a call you're making lightly. Trouble at the mill?'

'Isn't there always?' Gina tried to make light of her mood. It had been easy to make out she was nipping across to the shops this morning and sidle into The Workshop and ask to see Josie. She'd thought of the idea last night; her cosy family night in had disintegrated when Rachel and Pete had given her as much of a tough time as Claire had over the fight with Ruth. Rachel dragged Claire out with her and Pete stormed off to the pub fifteen minutes later, saying she was stifling him. She'd sat and cried for over an hour before deciding that she needed to get help. But now she was here, sitting in Josie's tidy office, she didn't really know where to start.

'So who do you want to talk about? Pete? The girls?' Josie paused. 'Or is there anything I can help you with?'

Gina glanced up and was embarrassed to find her eyes had filled with tears. 'I don't know where to start. I'm so angry, all the time. I'm arguing with Pete; my girls have gone haywire because I let them get away with stuff. When I do decide to talk to them, I go and...' Gina stopped. She didn't want to alert Josie to the trouble she'd made with Ruth. 'Let's say I let myself down.'

'You're bored, Gina. Your life is empty, your children have grown up and are no longer dependent on you, and you don't feel that you fit in anywhere. And, being frank, you don't, do you?'

If anyone else had spoken so harshly to her, Gina would have followed it with a torrent of abuse. But she knew that Josie was telling the truth. And hadn't Caren said something similar yesterday?

'I feel like I'm not in control anymore,' she admitted. 'I feel like no one listens to me. I feel – I feel invisible.'

'And that's what makes you so angry?'

Gina nodded. 'I suppose.'

'I still think it comes down to boredom.' Josie swivelled on her chair slightly. 'Look, I could really use you right now. I've been asking you to visit The Workshop for months. There are lots of things you can do here to stop you from taking your frustration out on other people. Come and help me.'

'Me?' Gina looked taken aback. 'What would you want me here for? I've just said no one listens to me. I can't –'

'You are part of the estate.' Josie ticked off a list with her fingers. 'You know how easy it is to be dragged down. You'd be great with some of the kids groups, even the teenagers.'

Gina sat wide-eyed. 'No one has a good word to say about the Bradleys. How can that be to your advantage?'

'I'm crying out for help – there's obviously no way I can pay you, I have to make that clear from the start – but you'd be perfect because of who you are.'

'Now you're talking crap.' Gina sat back in her chair.

'No, I'm not. I think it would work for both of us.' Josie reached for her diary and flicked through it quickly. 'How about you give me a week? You come to the centre, say a couple of hours every morning, and I'll get you involved with different groups. At the end of the week, if you're still here,' she smiled kindly, 'maybe you can choose an area where you feel you could make a difference and come on a more regular basis? I can be around for you, if you like? I could introduce you to people; let you get the feel of the place. It'll become familiar to you after a few days. More importantly, it'll give you something to look forward to.'

Gina felt her spirit lifting. Could she find a purpose here, fit in and do something useful? Maybe she'd stop getting into so much trouble if she was involved with other people. Maybe she could even make a few friends.

But then reality kicked in. Pete would take the piss out of her for volunteering - in his eyes you never did anything without payment. And Rachel and Claire would probably be mortified that she'd be working with some of the kids from their school. They'd start moaning about street cred and that she wasn't home for them when they needed her.

But, no matter how much grief she was bound to get from her family, she knew that she needed this more. She nodded at Josie.

'Okay, then. I'll give it a go. A week, you say?'

Josie's smile made it all the more meaningful. 'Great! I'm sure you'll find it worthwhile. And, like I said, I need all the help I can get here.'

Gina grinned. 'As long as you remember, I'm as mad as the colour of my hair.'

Caren had dropped John off at work and taken the car to do a shop at the supermarket. When she parked up outside her house afterwards, the first thing she noticed was the Bradley girls sitting on their garden wall. Hmm – no school again, she shook her head. Then again, they were wearing their uniforms underneath their coats and it was lunch time. Maybe she shouldn't be so judgmental. She gathered together a few bags of groceries from the boot of the car.

'Damn and blast and bugger!' She grappled helplessly as the handle split on one of them, her groceries falling to the tarmac. She knew the twins would be laughing at her. But then she noticed a pair of trainers in her line of vision and heard one of them speak. She stood up quickly, surprised to see one of them holding out the damaged bag and the other putting things back into it.

'You'll have to carry it by the bottom,' said Claire, 'but it should hold.'

'Thanks,' said Caren.

'I'll take it in, if you like,' offered Rachel.

A bit taken aback, Caren nodded. 'Okay.'

'I don't know why you don't have it delivered,' said Rachel. 'I bet it's so much better ordering online and then getting it delivered for you.'

And a luxury I can no longer afford, thought Caren. Gone are the days when she could order all she wanted over the internet and not worry about the cost.

'But this way I get to see all the bargains and BOGOF's.'

'BOGOF's?'

'Buy One Get One Free,' said Claire. 'BOGOF's.'

They trooped around the back of the house and Caren let them into the kitchen. Claire put the broken shopping bag down onto the table. Rachel added the two that she'd brought in as well.

'Thanks,' said Caren. 'That was good of you to help me.' As they turned to leave, something inside her softened. 'Would you girls like a coffee?' She pulled out a packet of biscuits. 'And a BOGOF custard cream?'

Several minutes later, they were chatting around her kitchen table. Rachel's foot was tapping away to a tune on the radio. Claire was telling Caren about her latest favourite band.

'Your nails are so lovely,' she said, pointing at Caren's hands. 'Are they real?'

Caren nodded. She splayed her fingers to display them to their full glory. 'They're hard work to keep like this but,' she curled up her fingers now to inspect them for herself, 'it's worth it. I love them. I go ballistic whenever I break one.'

Rachel splayed out the fingers on both her hands. They were bitten down, dirt under the tiny rims. 'I'd love to have nails like yours. As soon as mine get long, they start to snap off.'

'But you bite them, don't you?'

Rachel nodded. 'With a life like ours, you'd bite them too.'

Caren smiled inwardly. If only they knew how different, or difficult, life would be for them in ten years time. Then she wondered...

'I'm having a nail party,' she told them. 'Would you like to come?'

'What's a nail party?' asked Claire.

'I've started doing manicures and beauty treatments on a mobile basis. And to get to know the neighbours a little better, I'm going to do free manicures for the evening. I'll get a few bottles of wine and some nibbles. If I have time, I'll do everyone's nails. If not, some will have to settle for a hand massage.'

'We could both come?' asked Rachel.

Caren nodded. 'Yes.'

'What about Mum?'

'She can come too – I suppose.'

Claire giggled. 'You don't like her that much, do you?'

'Is it that obvious?' Caren tried to make light of it. 'You're right. We're not exactly the best of friends but, yes, if she wants to come, she can.'

Rachel shrugged in a non-committal manner. 'We might be busy.'

'No, we bloody won't!' Claire nudged her sharply. 'I fancy having my nails done, especially for free.'

'What about my nan? Can she come too?'

Caren sighed inwardly - and Nan made four. Four Bradleys under one roof. Her fun party atmosphere was beginning to sound like a disaster waiting to happen. Maybe they wouldn't all be able to make it.

But this wasn't about making enemies. This was about breaking barriers down for Ruth and, now that she had them here, trying to get these girls to realise there was more to life than causing trouble. Caren decided to kill two birds with one stone. She opened the kitchen drawer and pulled out a pile of envelopes.

'Would you two like to post these for me? I've already written them out.'

'There isn't one for us,' said Rachel as she flicked through the names of all their neighbours.

'That's because I didn't think you'd want to come,' Caren admitted.

Both girls looked at her.

'I've enjoyed your company today. What do you say?'

Both girls looked at each other.

'Yeah,' they replied.

'Great!' Caren picked out a blank invitation, quickly wrote their names on it and shoved it into an envelope. 'These will be like gold dust. Every woman in Stanley Avenue has been invited but no one else has. I'm hoping once word gets round the estate that I might get a few clients. But this will be a one-off free party.' She gave the envelope to Rachel. 'And you two are invited.'

Caren smiled – how easy was that! Suddenly, her plan to engage Ruth with the women in the avenue had taken a turn for the better. By having Rachel and Claire go on about their invite to the party, Gina might be curious enough to turn up. Then she could really get going on Ruth's return from the dark side. Once Ruth had a friend or two, everything might not seem so black.

Later that evening, Rachel turned the corner out of Stanley Avenue onto Davy Road. She was heading for the shops, a little earlier than usual as she and Claire were hoping to stick to their promises they'd made to their mum and dad. Rachel had sent a text message to Laila and Ashleigh saying that they needed to talk. Claire had nipped back home because she'd forgotten her phone.

'Frigging hell!' She blurted out as someone came out of the shadows. She held onto her chest. 'Laila, bird, you nearly gave me a heart attack.'

Laila stood in front of Rachel, not realising that, although she appeared to be alone, she wasn't. Behind her, she could see Claire running to catch up.

'What's up?' Claire asked as she drew level with them both. She looked from one to the other.

Laila chewed at a fingernail.

'What's up?' said Rachel, although she'd already guessed.

Laila swallowed. 'I don't know how to say this, because I know you're my mates, and I know I'll probably get a good bollocking off you, and I'll probably deserve it for giving up on you, but I don't want to be in the Mitchell Mob anymore. I'm joining Stacey.'

The words were said so quickly that it was hard to decipher where one sentence finished and the next began. Laila stood there, her breath coming in short bursts. She clenched her fists in readiness for the fight to come.

After a few seconds, she realised nothing was going to happen. She dropped her hands.

Claire placed a hand on Rachel's arm as she took a step nearer to Laila.

Rachel looked back with a smile. 'It's okay; I'm not going to do anything.' She looked next at Laila. 'We were coming to tell you that we're not fighting anymore.'

'What?' Laila frowned.

'We've had enough – of all the fighting, of all the ganging up on each other. We were coming to tell you and Ashleigh first and then go and find Stacey – see if we could have some sort of truce.'

'Are you mad? She hates you.' Laila pointed at Rachel. 'Especially you. She's only waiting for us all to go back to her and then she's going to beat the fuck out of you.'

'I'd like to see her try!'

'Rachel!' said Claire. 'We promised.'

'Promised who?' said Laila.

'Never you mind,' snapped Rachel.

'She'll find out eventually,' said Laila. 'Stacey always does.'

Suddenly Rachel clicked in. 'You're the snitch in the camp! While Stacey gathered together the rest of the mob, you were in on it all the time!'

'Not all of the time.' Laila looked down at the pavement for a moment. 'She's too hard for me, Rach. I can't deal with her by myself. You two will always have each other. Stacey doesn't like that. You know she wants to be top dog –'

'More like top bitch,' Rachel spat out.

'I wouldn't let her hear you saying that.'

'She doesn't bother me,' said Rachel.

They all knew she was lying.

Across the street, music started up from inside the Reynolds' house. Someone inside had cranked the volume to full.

'So what happens now?' Laila shouted above the noise.

Rachel got out her phone. 'I'll text Ashley, see where she is. Then we'll have a meeting.

Caren paced up and down the living room. It was nearly half past eight and Sam was supposed to have arrived for eight. Surprised that he was coming at all, she now had her doubts reaffirmed. Something was wrong.

'He's not coming, is he?' John said.

Caren was about to reply when the doorbell rang. John glanced at her before going to the door. Donna came into the living room first, followed by a man who fitted the image of the photograph they'd been shown last week.

Caren stood up, unsure how to greet him. 'Hi, Sam.' She held out her hand. 'I'm Caren, John's wife.'

Sam shook her hand slightly before slumping down on the settee.

'Can I get you anything to drink?' said John, for want of something to do.

'Lager.' Sam's eyes flitted around the room before turning to watch the television.

'We'll have coffee,' said Donna.

Before Caren could offer to help, Donna beat her to it. She watched her follow John into the kitchen, realising too late that it left her sitting with Sam. She smiled at him as he caught her eye. He raised his chin slightly in acknowledgment before staring intently at the next product that came on.

Bloody typical, thought Caren. An advert for panty liners.

'John says that you live over in Graham Street?' She made small talk. 'Have you got your own place?'

'You have to have kids to get a decent shack on this estate, so I live at home with the olds,' Sam replied, without taking his eyes from the box. 'I ain't got any kids. Well,' he sniggered. 'None I'll admit to, anyway.'

Caren smiled but inside she was horrified. Suddenly all the suspicions she'd had began to rise to the surface again. Surreptitiously, she studied him. Sam was supposed to be twenty-one but he looked younger than that. His eyes were blue: John's eyes were brown. His hair was blonde: John's was dark brown. And Donna's hair was bottle blonde: her roots were dark. He was quite small: John was tall. At a guess, Donna was around five foot four, give or take a heel; neither small nor tall. It wasn't easy to surmise.

Sadly, she realised, Sam's whole demeanour spelt out loser. This didn't look good; it looked suspicious. Was John being set up to believe this was his son? And if so, what on earth for? She couldn't put her finger on anything.

John and Donna came back into the room, carrying two mugs apiece.

John placed his down on the coffee table.

'Why didn't you use a tray?' Caren asked.

'I didn't know where they were kept.'

Donna giggled. 'Like father, like son. Sam isn't domesticated either.'

'John's not too bad.'

'Sounds like you're under the thumb mate,' Sam snorted.

John smiled a little. 'Where do you work, Sam?'

'I don't.'

'Oh, I see. Finding it tough to get something? I did too. I haven't been at my current place for long but I hated every day that I didn't have a job.'

Sam shook his head. 'I don't want a job.'

'But what do you do with yourself all day?' questioned Caren. 'This estate hasn't got a lot to offer.'

'I do a bit of this; a bit of that.'

'Maybe you could put a word in at your place for him, John.'

'I'd be pleased to, if anything else comes up.'

'I'm happy as I am.'

'Yes, but –'

'I hear you've set up a mobile nails business,' Donna interrupted Caren purposely.

'There's no money here, if that's what you're after,' Caren snapped.

'Caren!' said John. 'Donna didn't mean anything like that.'

'Sorry.'

'I heard you went bankrupt,' said Sam.

'You hear a lot of things about us, don't you, Sam?' said Caren. 'I wonder where you get your information from.'

Sam folded one leg over to rest it on his knee, nudging the coffee table in the process. A mug fell to the floor, hot coffee splattering everywhere.

'For Christ's sake.' Donna sat forward and pulled a tissue out of her pocket. She began to dab at the flooring. 'You're such a clumsy bastard.'

'It's okay.' Caren stood up, face like thunder. 'I'll get a cloth.'

'Stick the kettle on again, Caz, and make Sam another.'

Caren couldn't help herself when she sighed loudly. Why was it

192

always her that had to do everything?

But Sam misunderstood its meaning. 'Don't bother,' he retorted. 'I can see I'm not wanted here.'

Donna stood up too. 'I think we'd better go. Maybe we could call again? Perhaps next time it won't seem so... *awkward*.'

The minute John had seen them both out, he rounded on Caren. 'What the hell's wrong with you? You were out to have a dig from the moment he walked in.'

'She's playing you, John. They both are.'

'What do you mean?'

'Sam isn't your son.'

'Why wouldn't he be?'

'He looks nothing like you. In fact, he's the total opposite.'

'No, he isn't!'

'Why can't you see what they're doing!'

But John wasn't having any. 'You had no intention of making him feel welcome, did you? You'd already made up your mind before he got here. You didn't want him in our house, so you went out of your way to be spiteful.'

'*Spiteful?*' Caren hissed. 'Why were you so long in the kitchen with Donna?' Caren watched John's mouth drop. 'You were gone ages and left me having to make small talk with your so-called son. What were you discussing back there in the kitchen?'

'Nothing! I was showing her the coffee maker we brought with us.'

'Like I believe that!'

'What do you think I was doing? Getting re-acquainted with her over the kitchen table?'

Caren's eyes filled with tears. 'No,' she said. 'I didn't think that.'

Suddenly the rage was gone. John drew her into his embrace. 'I'm sorry,' he said. 'I'm really disappointed. It didn't go as well as I wanted it to.'

That's because he's not your son, she wanted to add. But instead, Caren stayed quiet. She'd had enough for one day. Besides, until she figured out what the hell was going on, it was as well to keep it to herself. She'd do some digging of her own.

And she knew exactly where to start.

CHAPTER TWENTY-ONE

'So how are you feeling now?' Josie asked Ruth as she sat in her living room. After trying on four separate occasions over the past week, she'd finally managed to get in for another visit.

'So, so,' said Ruth. In actual fact, she hadn't set foot outside the door since the fight with Gina. Luckily, Caren had kept to her word and, instead of taking her shopping, she'd brought some essentials back for her when she'd feigned illness. Quite frankly, she looked too much of a mess to go out in public so it must have been easy for Caren to agree rather than try and persuade her to get a little fresh air.

'Have you been to see the boys?'

'No, I don't want to upset them.'

'I'm sure they'd be pleased to see you rather than be upset.'

'How would you feel if your mother left you in an office for someone else to look after? I'm not going to be the most popular of people.'

'Maybe not, but I bet they'd like to see you.'

'Am I allowed to see them, after what I did?' Ruth ran a hand through her hair, pulled at it. 'Why did I do it? Why did I give them away?'

'Because you couldn't cope at that particular moment in time,' Josie tried to appease her. 'It doesn't mean that you'll never be able to see them again.'

'You have an answer for everything.'

'It comes with the job, I'm afraid. I'm nosy too – are you going to tell me how you got that black eye? I heard there was a bit of trouble with the Bradleys earlier on in the week.'

'Oh? I never heard anything.'

'And you got those bruises by keeping yourself to yourself?'

'That's none of your business.'

'I know,' said Josie, 'but humour me. Like I said, I'm nosy.'

Ruth smiled; she couldn't help it. No matter what, Josie always made her feel at ease. She had a way about her that felt like she enveloped you in a fluffy blanket and smothered you with enough hope and optimism to get you through the day.

'I'm fine,' she told Josie.

Josie raised her eyebrows questioningly.

'Really,' reiterated Ruth. 'I'm fine.'

'So Gina didn't hit you?'

'No, I didn't say that! Please! You won't say anything, will you? I deserved what I got.'

'Why would you think that?' Josie pointed to Ruth's face. 'She's an animal for doing that and she needs locking up.'

'I'm not going to grass on her!'

'I know you're not, and I wouldn't expect you to either. It's just that sometimes I wish someone would give her a taste of her own medicine, make her hurt for a while. Honestly, that woman and her family have been the bane of my life for a –' Josie stopped. 'I'm sorry, Ruth. I shouldn't have said that to you. My feelings got in the way. It was unprofessional.'

'It's true, though, she isn't a nice woman.' Ruth grimaced. 'Mind, I made a mess of my life too.'

'You talk as if it's over.'

'Newsflash – it is.'

'No, it isn't. There's always hope, no matter what.'

Ruth had to stop herself from laughing aloud manically. Josie Mellor was always so positive. She always thought she could bring out the best in people. It was a good trait to have, but it was wasted on her.

Optimism was something she'd given up on a long time ago.

'This party was such a good idea,' said Caren to Rachel and Claire. They were in her kitchen getting things ready for the evening ahead. 'I can't believe how many women are going to come.'

'It's the talk of the avenue,' said Rachel. She was putting glasses out on Caren's worktop.

'I reckon it'll be the talk of the estate,' added Claire.

'I hope it is. I...' Caren frowned. 'How do I tell you apart?'

'I'm Rachel,' said Claire.

Rachel nudged her. 'I'm Rachel.'

'No, I'm Rachel.'

'No, I am!'

Rachel touched her nose with her finger. 'There's really only one of us.'

'Yeah, she's a ghost.'

Caren shrugged, none the wiser.

Claire pointed at her jumper. 'I'm always in red or white. Rachel is always blue or black.'

'And I have a scar, here.' Rachel pointed to the side of her face.

Caren passed them a multi pack of crisps. Then, surreptitiously, she watched as they filled the bowls set out on the worktop. Since moving into Stanley Avenue, she'd always felt intimidated by them – more to do with their surname rather than their behaviour – but as she watched them chatting away, she had to admit that maybe she'd been wrong. Or maybe she'd judged them, as other people did, on the outfits they were wearing. They wore hoodies and tracksuit bottoms, with trainers. Their hair was short, faces void of make up. Yet, if they made more of themselves, they could be real beauties.

She remembered what she wanted to ask them.

'Do either of you know Sam Harvey?' she asked, trying to keep her tone light.

'Yeah,' said Rachel. 'Why?'

'He's been asking to do some odd jobs. I wanted to check him out.'

'He'll make money any way he can. He's work-shy.'

'What makes you say that?'

'I don't think he's ever had a job in his life.'

'He is only eighteen,' said Claire.

Caren froze. 'I thought he was older than that.'

Claire paused and looked at Rachel for confirmation.

'No, he's younger than our brother. Danny is twenty-one.'

'Have you ever met his parents?'

Rachel helped herself to a handful of nuts. 'I don't know what happened to his old man but his mother, Donna Adams? She's a right slapper. She works in the massage parlour in town. Red Lace, it's called. I think she does more than massages, if you catch my drift.'

'Not a very stable life for a child to be brought up in.'

'That's probably why he turned into an idiot,' said Rachel.

'And you're sure he's only eighteen?' Caren pressed one more time, hoping she didn't sound too suspicious.

'Positive.' Rachel grinned. 'You're not after a toy boy, are you?'

'In my dreams.' Caren glanced at her clock on the wall. 'Right, you two, thanks for your help. I'm off to have a bath now so I'll see you back here in an hour?'

Once the girls had left, Caren wondered what was going on. If Sam was only eighteen, then he couldn't be John's son unless he really did have an affair. And if he wasn't John's son, then what were he and Donna up to? Were they after money thinking that John would pay up because of all the missed years? Fat chance they had of that.

As soon as the party was over, she'd have a word with John, try to put things to him delicately because he probably wouldn't believe her, and then she would see what happened next. In the back of her mind, she hoped that whatever games were going on between Donna and Sam were finished. Sam had clearly been unwilling to play the doting son and Donna throwing cow eyes at John every two seconds had been another dead giveaway; it was a strange predicament.

What had they on John?

An hour later, Claire stood examining her nails while she waited for Rachel to come downstairs. Her sister had been choosing an outfit for the past half hour, something Claire had found highly amusing as she'd done the same – usually they'd grab whatever clothes were close at hand, clean or dirty.

'Are you sure you're not coming over the road, Mum?' she asked.

'No,' said Gina. 'I can't be bothered.'

'But wouldn't you like to be pampered, make the most of what you've got?'

Gina waved a hand from her head to her feet. 'I'll never be able to make anything out of this blob. It's too late.'

'But it's free,' Claire tried to entice her. 'When have you ever missed out on anything that's for nowt?'

Gina didn't bite. Instead, she lit a cigarette.

Rachel joined them a few minutes later. She wore a bright blue T-shirt over a black long-sleeved T-shirt, dark jeans and ballet pumps. Gina's eyes nearly popped out on stalks. She'd got them each a pair for Christmas but she'd never seen them on either girl yet.

'At last!' Claire sighed. 'There'll be no time for us if we don't get over there soon.' Then, as they got to the door, she stopped. 'Wait! I'm going to put my pumps on too. They're better than wearing these manky trainers.'

Rachel tutted. 'Hurry up then.'

'Looks who's talking. I waited ages for you to get ready.'

Rachel sat in the chair that Claire had vacated. 'Are you coming across, Mum?'

Gina sighed. That was the trouble with having twins; sometimes things had to be explained twice.

'No, I'm not,' she replied. 'There's bound to be something interesting on the telly.'

Rachel was old enough to catch the sarcasm. 'She's not the enemy.'

'I never said she was.'

'She's trying to bring everyone together for a laugh. She'll do your nails, if you want her to.'

Gina curled her fingers into a fist so that Rachel couldn't see what a state hers were in.

Claire appeared, saving Gina from snapping a reply. They grabbed the bottle of wine Gina had got for them and in a flurry of giggles, they were gone. For a few seconds, she sat in silence until curiosity won her over and she ran upstairs. She stood in the bedroom window, hidden behind the grimy nets, watching as Rachel and Claire knocked on Caren's front door. She saw Caren open it and smile, taking the wine from Rachel as they went in.

Over the next quarter of an hour, she watched most of the neighbours troop into Caren's house: Julie and Sheila, Mrs Porter and Jenny Webster. Each time the door opened, she heard the music filter through until it closed again. Then Gina gasped, her mouth hanging open at who walked up the path next. That bloody bitch Ruth Millington had been invited.

Gina fumed in silence. This was Caren's doing. She knew it would wind her up to see Ruth having fun with the neighbours – her friends! It was as if Ruth belonged in Stanley Avenue.

Her mind made up in an instant, she reached for her mobile phone and rang her mum. If Ruth was good to go, then so was she.

The party was in full swing at Caren's house. Before John left them to it, he'd helped to rearrange the furniture in the living room. What could be pushed back was now around the walls. They'd also borrowed dining chairs from next door and brought in the chairs from the patio set. Looking around, Caren realised that most people who had been invited were there. She picked up a bottle of nail polish from the coffee table. 'Ruby Red. Who'd like this one?'

'Me!' shouted Rachel, practically pushing Claire over to get up.

'Hey, look out!' Claire narrowly avoided spilling her drink. She watched as the liquid settled in the glass again.

'She's a live wire, that sister of yours,' Wendy remarked once Caren and Rachel had gone into the kitchen.

'No, she isn't!'

'Relax, honey, it was a compliment. She's nice – and so are you, when you want to be.'

Claire was amazed when some of the other women in the room nodded their heads in agreement.

'I thought everyone thought we were scum.' She became hostile as the other women began to laugh. 'That's not fucking nice!'

Wendy smiled and tapped Claire on the thigh. 'We're not laughing *at* you. We're laughing *with* you.' She waved a hand around the room. 'Everyone in here is known as scum. But we're not, are we ladies?'

'No, we're not,' said a lady with purple hair, a nose ring and a tattoo covering half of her arm.

'Absolutely no way,' said another, wearing a dress short enough for a five-year-old girl. Her hair had been bleached so many times it resembled white candy-floss, black roots peeping through. She wore red lipstick. Claire tried to remember her name but decided to call her freaky instead. She looked scary but at least she was smiling.

'Well, I think they're right!' one dared to say.

A murmur echoed around the room and a cushion was flung at the culprit.

'We are! But we make the most of what we have.'

'And we stick together.'

Claire grinned, finally realising the woman was joking. Then everyone laughed.

'You're new, Ruth.' Wendy turned to her next. 'Tell us how you see us all.'

Ruth coloured instantly as all eyes fell on her. Oh God, if she had known she'd be the subject of interrogation, she wouldn't have come.

Well, I, erm, think... I...' she stumbled over her words. 'I don't know you well enough to comment really.'

Wendy glared at her before folding her arms and pulling back her head. She laughed, as did the other women.

'I'm sorry, love, I'm pulling your leg. We only heard what her mother,' Wendy jerked a thumb in Claire's direction, 'had to say about you. And 'scum like us' should really find out the whole truth before taking up a stance.'

Ruth lowered her head. She knew they were referring to the fight she'd had with Gina. She still had the remains of the bruising.

'I wish Mum would change,' Claire admitted, helping herself to a few crisps. 'You might not think it but she can be really cool at times.'

'Yeah, right,' said Julie Elliot. 'And I've got myself a sugar daddy.'

'It's true. She really does care; she just doesn't know how to show it.'

'No, she's more interested in spreading rumours around than love. Isn't she, Ruth?'

'Maybe they aren't all rumours,' Claire said.

Ruth gulped. The spotlight was on her again. Why did they insist on doing that? There was no way she'd admit to sleeping with Pete, especially in front of one of his daughters.

'She shouldn't have had a go at you like that,' said Wendy, noticing her discomfort. 'And, I for one, am sorry that she did – *and* that I joined in.' She picked up a wine glass, a smidgen of liquid left in its bottom, and raised it in the air. 'So, how about we toast to new beginnings?'

Everyone raised their glasses. 'New beginnings.'

'New beginnings,' Ruth joined in cautiously, not exactly sure if she was being swept into some sort of gang ritual to be explained later.

Back in the kitchen, Rachel sat opposite Caren at the table while she painted her nails. She'd already had her hands massaged; something she'd never had done before yet had instantly loved.

Caren finished one hand and Rachel gasped. 'That colour! It makes my nails look really long.'

Caren smiled. 'You have a lot to learn, my dear. Do you ever wear make-up?'

'No, I'd end up looking like a dog's dinner.'

'Have you never experimented?'

Rachel shook her head. 'We haven't got anything to experiment with, although we could lift some.'

Caren looked up momentarily.

'I mean we could buy some,' Rachel said quickly. 'I just don't know what to pick. There's so much of it.'

Caren stopped for a moment before painting Rachel's thumbnail. 'Would you like me to show you afterwards, give you a makeover?'

'Would you?' Rachel felt excitement fizz up in her stomach. 'I'd love to know how to do it all. Some of the girls at school look like shi – look awful but some of them look really nice.'

Caren smiled. 'Let's finish these nails and before I shout anyone else in, I'll do you a quick makeover. No doubt Claire will want me to do the same for her?'

'I suppose.'

'Right then, go and ask her. And see if anyone wants any more wine?' she shouted after her.

Despite her earlier freak out, Ruth was beginning to enjoy herself now. The women in the group were making a conscious effort to get to know her. They'd asked questions about her boys but not in a nasty way, not trying to blame her for it, but in a women united kind of way. One of them, Denise, had even spoken of her miscarriage and her breakdown trying to cope with her four-year-old son afterwards. Half of the women were either alone or in unhappy relationships. And every one of them knew horror tales of kids that had gone into Children's Services and why they'd had to. It was as if they were trying to let her know that what she'd done, what she thought was so wrong, was in actual fact right for her, as well as Mason and Jamie. Tears pricked at her eyes as she dared to bring their faces to the front of her mind. Wendy noticed and came to comfort her. As Ruth cried, she held her.

'Pass me some tissues,' she pointed to a box. Claire passed a couple over to Wendy and she gave them to Ruth. 'Feel better now?' she asked after a minute or so.

Ruth nodded.

'Good. Let's change the conversation and get on with having a good girlie night in. Let's up the tempo of the music and have a sing song.'

'I have a karaoke machine,' said Claire.

'Oh, we don't need any machine to sing, now do we girls?' Wendy grabbed an empty lager bottle and held it an inch away from her mouth. 'This'll do. You can hear my voice over anything.'

As the women in the living room danced and sang along to an Abba CD, Caren was running around her kitchen. She'd moved the table to one side as best she could in the space provided and told Rachel and Claire to sit back to back. As she added foundation to one and then the other, she wouldn't let them look.

'No peeping!' Caren cried, catching Rachel trying to see her sister as Caren swept blusher over her cheeks. She handed her a small black case. 'Find me some brown mascara, would you?'

Rachel dived into the case. 'Why have you got so much?'

'I used to be a rep, selling it for parties, that kind of stuff. Most of it is old and out of date, but it's great for experimenting on. Help yourself to anything you like. It'll go back upstairs and be forgotten about after tonight.'

'Have you finished after you've put mascara on?' asked Claire, trying desperately not to laugh as Caren added colour to her eyelids.

'Nearly,' said Caren. 'The piece de resistance is always your lippie.'

'Hurry up,' urged Rachel. 'I'm dying to see what we look like.'

'I reckon we'll look like the ugly sisters from Cinderella.'

'Hey,' Caren said and tried to look hurt by Rachel's remark. 'I'll have you know that I'm good at creating something out of nothing. Anyway, I'm done now.' She stood between them. 'Seeing as you look identical, even with make up on, you can look at each other. On the count of three. One. Two. THREE!'

Rachel and Claire turned to face each other and gasped.

'Ohmigod!' said Claire. 'You look *amazing*.'

Rachel sat wide-eyed. She pointed at Claire, no words coming from her at all.

'Say something!' urged Caren.

'I feel so – so grown up,' said Rachel.

'Wow!' Claire clapped her hands in glee. 'I can't believe it's us. Why haven't we done this before?'

'Maybe because you're hell bent on causing trouble across on the square. There are other ways to get attention. I'm sure the boys will be queuing up soon.'

'Do you think?'

'I don't think so – I know so!'

Rachel turned to Caren and smiled shyly. 'Thanks,' she told her.

'My pleasure,' Caren smiled too, glancing from one to the other. 'You really do look great.'

'We'll have to practice,' said Claire.

'Just use the tricks I've shown you. Accentuate what you have and always make the most of everything. Then you can –'

'Bleeding hell, what have we here?'

Caren turned to see Barbara in the doorway. Behind her mother was Gina.

'Nan, Mum, look at us!' exclaimed Claire. 'Don't we look gorgeous? Caren has made us up. She's given us loads of freebies too.' She twirled round. 'What do you think?'

'It's such an improvement!' Barbara nodded. 'Although I've always thought my granddaughters were gorgeous.' She winked at Caren. 'I don't suppose you could do anything with me to hide these wrinkles. Or this one behind me?'

'Mum!' said Gina.

'Mum!' said Rachel, spying her too. 'You came across!'

'I had no choice,' Gina fibbed. 'Your nan dragged me across.'

Barbara tutted. 'I did no such thing. You wanted to –'

'Here, you lot,' Wendy shouted, appearing at the kitchen door. 'If you're not careful, we'll all be pissed in here before we've had our nails done. We've eaten all the crisps too.' She held out a bowl in *Oliver* style. 'Please, miss. Can we have some more?'

'Let me join you in the living room for a break first,' said Caren. 'Besides, I need to show off my work. Come on, girls. In you go.'

Gina lagged behind, standing in the living room doorway. Inside, the women were either talking or laughing. As everyone was having fun, the music had gone off momentarily. No one even noticed that she'd come in. She couldn't even take pride in the fact they were too busy admiring her girls.

'You look so grown up,' said Ruth, joining in freely now she felt more confident with the women. 'Your mum had better watch out; the boys will be going wild.'

'Their mother is right here,' snapped Gina. 'I hope you, of all people, weren't insinuating that my girls were going to get knocked up now that they look like tarts.'

'Give over, Gina!' said Barbara.

'Mum!' said Claire and Rachel in unison.

'I – I didn't mean that at all.' Ruth's temporary good mood crumbled in a second.

'Calm down, Gina,' said Wendy. 'The atmosphere was great until you showed up. So either go back out with the chip on your shoulder or leave it at the door and come and join in the fun.'

Gina knew when she was beat. Somehow, in a couple of hours, Ruth seemed to have won over all her friends. Why hadn't she come across right away rather than take an age to get ready? By the time she'd finally left her house and called for her mother, nearly an hour had passed. It was only just after nine but the party had started long ago. The women were all enjoying themselves so she'd have to do the same, even though inside she hated the thought of having to mingle with Ruth. She hoped Ruth wouldn't speak to her or else she'd have to keep herself in check. She wasn't finished with her yet.

She perched on the arm of the chair next to her mother. Caren passed her a glass of wine and she smiled politely. Might as well get the night over with as quickly and pleasantly as possible – drink would make her feel a little bit better about it.

'Let's crank the music up again,' said Wendy. 'Then, you, my lady,' she pointed to Caren, 'can do me next. But don't worry; I won't expect a pedicure as well. The smell would knock everyone out if I took off my shoes!'

As Claire chose another CD to put on, Rachel heard her phone go off in her pocket. It was a text from Laila. It was short and sweet.

Gone with Stacey. So has Ashley. Hope 2 c u around. L&A

Rachel put her phone away and sat quietly as she digested the news. Fuck, they were in trouble. There was only Louise left now to go over to Stacey. Once Louise heard from Laila or Ashley, Rachel knew she'd join Stacey. She couldn't blame her: if she was Louise, she would join Stacey too. It was too dangerous to be alone – or even around her and Claire now that Laila and Ashley had gone over as well.

She watched Claire as she began to dance, holding onto Nan's hands, swinging her around gently. Nan was laughing and Claire looked so happy.

Maybe it would do them good to stay low for a while, watch out for each other. But would Stacey then think she'd won, without even fighting for top position? And could Rachel back down? For Claire it would be easy: she'd do whatever she told her to do.

What should she do next? Should she fight for the leadership and risk the wrath of Mum and Dad? Or should she back down and let Stacey win? Rachel didn't know if she could let that happen. She was a Bradley through and through – and no one got the better of them now, did they?

CHAPTER TWENTY-TWO

Gina was awake early the next morning. She nudged Pete who was lying on his back and snoring like a train; he turned over in his sleep. She cuddled up into the duvet. The clock said half past five; she needed some sleep before she decided what to do. Today could be the start of a different life for her.

The nail party at Caren's last night had turned out to be a disaster for her, but she seemed to have been the only one who hadn't enjoyed herself. Rachel and Claire had stayed over there when she'd finally found time to excuse herself without fear of being accused of breaking the party up. They'd come in an hour later, for once high on life and not alcohol, thankfully. Gina had been lying on the settee in a sulk and told them to shut up as they were still singing. They'd tried to pull her up to join in their duo but she'd refused. Even when Pete returned home from the pub with fish and chips, she hadn't managed a smile. She knew the reason why. It was because she'd seen the inside of Caren's house. Ever since she and John moved back, Gina had imagined how their home would be, but her imagination was way off with this one. It had felt like walking into a television advert for a furniture store. The house was spotless; it was modern and fresh and inviting... it was all she'd ever wanted.

And all her so-called friends had been there – another thing that had annoyed her. They'd all been quick to accept invitations when something was free, she'd realised as soon as she'd walked into the living room, yet they seemed like they were really enjoying themselves. Gina couldn't remember a time when the women in the avenue had got together like that. Sometimes there would be an impromptu barbeque when the weather was promising, where everyone's families would join in for the night. But there had never been anything planned.

Worst of all, Rachel had told her they were going to make it a regular thing; go to a different house each month. And Claire had upset her by saying that it was obvious they couldn't come there though - their house was too old-fashioned and even with a good clean wouldn't be inviting enough. Gina had cried the minute they'd gone to bed.

The girls had startled her too – they'd looked so grown up after their makeover. The worry of one of them getting pregnant had popped into her head straight away - she didn't want either of them to end up in the same predicament as her, pregnant by the only fella she'd ever slept with. Gina wanted much more than that for her girls.

And now it was Monday morning, the first day of her challenge to spend a week with Josie at The Workshop. Josie had been true to her word and arranged five, two hour sessions, one each morning this week, with different groups so that if she liked it, which she doubted already, she could decide which area she'd like to volunteer in. She hadn't told anyone about her plans. Pete would go mad if he knew she was doing something for nothing. And even though, after joining in last night in a fashion, Rachel and Claire might think better of her for having a go at something, she wouldn't tell them either. She wouldn't tell anyone until it was over. She would do the week to keep Josie happy; then she'd either go back to being boring Gina or show an interest in something. She would have to wait and see how she got on. This morning she'd be helping out with the mother and toddlers group. Tomorrow was the self-assertiveness group. Wednesday and Friday mornings would be spent at the community house with the teenagers and Thursday was pensioners' coffee morning.

Gina glanced at the clock again: ten minutes to six. She decided to get up and make a cup of tea. It was far more productive than lying in bed trying to get back to sleep. Besides, she needed to find some clean clothes if she was going to go out of the house. Leggings, what-used-to-be-white T-shirts and baggy cardigans weren't called for today. That was if she decided to go at all. She had more than three hours to change her mind yet.

*

'Did you leave a window open?' Caren asked John when they got home that evening. She frowned; she could have sworn she heard music coming from their house. But that was impossible.

'I don't think so.' John sighed. 'Neither did I kick the wheelie bin over. There's rubbish strewn everywhere. Bloody kids!' He made his way up the path and stopped dead in his tracks.

'What's wrong?' Caren felt the hairs on her neck rising. She shuddered involuntarily.

'Some fucker's broken in.' John turned to her. 'The back door's been forced open.'

Caren followed him into the kitchen. Breakfast cereal scrunched underneath their feet. A four pint bottle of milk had been tipped over the kitchen table, left dripping onto the seat covers. Every drawer had been pulled out and smashed up, the contents thrown to the floor.

'Christ, what a mess,' said John.

Caren's hand covered her mouth. A mess was an understatement: it was a pure act of vandalism. And after they'd worked so hard to make it into something decent.

'Don't touch anything. I'll check upstairs and then I'll ring the police.'

Being careful where she stood, Caren went through into the hallway, trying to ignore the lines of aerosol paint stretching from one end to the other. Framed pictures and the hall mirror had been thrown to the floor and smashed. Something, she dreaded to think what, had been crushed into the carpet.

'They've been in every room,' John told her when he joined her a few minutes later. 'It's as if we've been hit by a tornado. The portable TV's gone; so has my laptop. The rest is mess to clean up.'

Caren stepped into the living room, tears pouring down her face. There were spaces where their television and stereo should have been. Both settees had been slashed, the stuffing pulled out in lumps and strewn around. Paint had been thrown over the fireplace and over the carpet. The aerosol can had been used in here too, around the middle of all walls and the door.

Caren crumpled as John pulled her into his arms.

'Who would do something like this?' she asked him.

'I don't know. Let's hope the police get some clues.'

When the police arrived, PC Mark White crunched through the kitchen. He pointed to the open door. 'Any windows broken?'

'No, just the door that's been forced. We'd been out for something to eat – two hours at the most – and we get back to... to this!'

'Have they taken much?' PC Sandra Morton asked, getting out her notebook.

John raised his hands in exaggeration. 'The usual stuff – we'll have to make a list. If I could get my hands on the little bastards, I'd break them too.'

'It's easy to put it down to the kids on this estate. There's not much for them to do so they get their kicks out of petty crime and vandalism. But in my experience, they usually take smaller items, things they can offload quickly to make a bit of money. Other than that, on an avenue like this, with no real easy access out if you come home early, I'd say you were targeted.'

'Targeted?' Caren cried. 'No one would do this to us!'

'Sadly most people have enemies, Mrs Williams.'

Caren noted it was said kindly, not spitefully. As the policeman checked the door in the kitchen, she hovered in the doorway, not wanting to enter yet not wanting to go back into the living room. None of it felt like her home anymore; she felt violated. Suddenly she retched. Covering her mouth with her hand, she managed to get to the kitchen sink where she threw up.

Afterwards, she steadied herself on the worktop as she tried to gain her composure. She wondered about the neighbours but knew they probably wouldn't have heard a thing: they were both in their eighties. She wondered if it was something else the thieves would have known before they'd broken in. Then she wondered about the women who had been at the nail party on Sunday – no, it couldn't have been any of them, surely? But could she rule that out altogether?

'I suppose it could be kids, getting their kicks out of breaking and entering,' PC Morgan said. She held up the plug that had been cut from the wire to the microwave. 'I could understand more if they'd taken things to sell on but blatant vandalism? Nothing like this ever makes sense. Do you have a spare key that you give to anyone?'

'No.' Caren tried to focus on anything in her kitchen that hadn't been ruined. She glanced around: there was nothing. Someone was hell-bent on making them suffer. So far, all she could see was it costing them money; at least they were insured. But it didn't take away the fact that someone had been into their home when they weren't there.

PC White came back into the room. 'I'll arrange to get what I can fingerprinted and we'll go from there. If you can provide your prints, we can eliminate you and then see if there are any different ones that might match up on our database.'

'Do you think you'll find anything?'

'It's possible,' he said. 'But from what I've seen so far, I very much doubt it. It's more likely that you're not going to find out who did this.'

Once the police left, Caren and John tried to get their house back into some sort of order.

It took Caren a long time to settle down when they finally went to bed. John spooned his body around her. Every window and door had been shut and checked, yet still she lay staring ahead into the darkness, listening to the sound of the house settling.

Damn it – she'd just started to get used to being back on the Mitchell Estate and now this had to happen. Her imagination working overtime as she heard a clank of a radiator, Caren sat up in bed. But John pulled her down again.

'Relax,' he said, his voice husky with sleep. 'You're safe now.'

'There's no way I'm leaving the house until you've changed the locks.'

'Try to sleep.' John kissed the back of her hair. 'You'll feel better about it tomorrow.'

'Are you out of your mind? How can I ever forget what's happened today?

John pulled her nearer into him. 'The only way I can make you feel safe is to hold you. I don't know what else to do.'

Caren squeezed his hand. Being so wrapped up in herself, she hadn't given a thought to John and how he would be feeling.

'I'm sorry,' she whispered into the silence, even though she hadn't got anything to feel sorry about.

She lay awake for ages wondering who would do such a thing.

On Thursday morning, Gina made her way to The Workshop. It was her fourth session and the one she was looking forward to the most. Monday had gone okay as she'd helped out with the mother and toddler group. She'd panicked at first, thinking she'd be a glorified babysitter while the mums went off to attend classes. But the mothers and the toddlers stayed together, interacting with each other. It hadn't taken long to get into the swing of things, even though most of the time she'd been making tea for the women.

On Tuesday, she'd helped out at the self-assertiveness class. That had been tougher than she'd imagined. After listening to a young woman from Adam Street talking about the abuse she'd suffered at the hands of her partner, Gina found herself in tears and thanking her lucky stars that even though her family were a little wayward at times, they all looked out for one another.

Josie had been true to her word and stuck by her side. Gina had thought she'd be an irritant but found, to her surprise, that she'd had a laugh with her. On mutual territory, they even shared a smile or two.

This morning she was helping out at the pensioners' coffee morning in one of the back rooms. By chance, she was topping up the tea urns when she heard a snippet of conversation from outside in the corridor.

'Yeah, we trashed it good and proper,' the voice said. 'It was a total wreck when we'd finished.'

'Did you come away with owt to sell on?'

Gina peeped around the door frame. She thought she recognised the voice. Yes, she was right. It was Sam Harvey.

'A few bits,' he continued. 'I sold them on to Lenny. The place was rich-looking; she was a stuck-up cow considering she lived in

Stanley Avenue. She got what she deserved.'

Stanley Avenue? Gina wondered if they were talking about Caren and John. Pete had told her their place had been trashed on Monday evening.

'I bet Pete won't be too pleased.'

Pete? Gina held perfectly still. *Pete who?*

'I'm not walking away if I can make a quick buck.'

'But he paid you, didn't he?'

'Yeah, fifty quid but only to pretend I was the bloke's son. There was stuff there for the taking too. I wasn't going to leave it. Plus if I've been lax with my prints, I've already been there so they'll rule me out.'

Gina stayed quiet, hoping to hear more but when she peeped around the frame again, Sam and his mate were walking away. She frowned, trying to make sense of their words. Why would Pete set someone like Sam up to visit Caren and John? It must be Caren's place as it was the only one she'd heard of lately that had been done over in the avenue. Apparently, it had been trashed beyond recognition. And although they didn't particularly get on, she didn't deserve that.

The urns topped up, Gina went back to the group, wondering what on earth was going on.

On Saturday, Rachel received a text message from Louise. She and Claire were in their bedroom. They'd been in there every evening since last weekend and hadn't wanted to go out that afternoon either, feeling safe but putting off the inevitable. They would have to face Stacey and the gang soon.

'Who's that?' asked Claire nervously, already dreading her sister's reply.

'Louise.'

'Oh.'

'She wants to meet us on the square in half an hour.'

'But we'll get lynched if we go out!'

'Not necessarily. Louise is still on our side, remember. Maybe some of the others have swapped back again. We might not be on our own.'

'I doubt that very much.'

'Well, we'll soon find out.'

Outside Shop&Save half an hour later, Claire glanced up and down Davy Road but there was no sign of Louise.

'What time did she say she'd be here?' she asked Rachel.

'Ten minutes ago. We'll give her ten more.'

'Maybe we should go now. We did promise not to fight.'

'Yes, I know, but it's only an excuse, isn't it?'

'What do you mean by that?'

'We have to fight, to survive. Stacey will kill us if we don't.'

'She won't *kill* us.'

'Maybe she'll get the message that we're not interested in gangs anymore.'

'It doesn't ring true, though. Think about it. You were hell-bent on being the leader of the Mitchell Mob when Stacey came out of juvie. We've both been fighting all the girls who've swapped sides and then... then we stay in for a week. It doesn't make sense. It seems like we're scared of her.'

'*You* are scared of her.'

'Of course I'm scared!' Claire shook her head. 'But I'm not frightened by any of the others. I think we should finish off what we started or take a beating from Stacey and get on with it. We don't have to hang around with any of them afterwards but at least we'd have street cred.'

Rachel looked away then, pretending to look out for Louise. She knew Claire was right; it was killing her to know that Stacey thought they'd chickened out. And she knew Stacey wouldn't settle until she'd knocked them both down and taken back her crown.

Rachel sighed and lit up a cigarette that she'd lifted from Mum earlier. It looked wrong with painted nails. Since the nail party, she and Claire had spent a couple of hours over at Caren's house learning more make up tricks. Caren had shaped their eyebrows and showed them how to style their hair a bit softer. The result had made them both feel feminine. It'd had a soothing effect on them, far more than any lecture from their mum and dad would have done.

Finally, Louise appeared in the distance a few minutes later.

But instead of joining them, she shouted to catch their attention. She beckoned to them with a wave and sat down on a wall to wait for them.

Rachel sighed. 'She keeps us waiting for near on twenty minutes and then she wants us to go over to her?'

Claire put her arm through Rachel's as they walked towards her. 'Chill out, Rach. At least she wants to know us.'

'What took you so long?' Rachel couldn't help but say when they reached her.

Stacey stepped out from behind the wall, the rest of the girls too.

'What's going on?' asked Claire. Pulling out her arm from Rachel's, she balled both hands into fists in readiness.

'She's done what I asked her to.' Stacey narrowed her eyes. 'What the fuck have you done to yourselves?'

'We thought we'd make an effort for once,' said Rachel. 'I see you couldn't be bothered.'

Stacey laughed. 'You look like a pair of hookers.' She pointed at Rachel's hands. 'You're wearing nail varnish!'

'What's wrong with making the best of what you've got?' Claire spoke out.

Stacey laughed again. 'No one could make anything out of you two – you're Bradley scum, remember?'

'It's better than being Hunter scum,' taunted Rachel.

Stacey took a step nearer to her. 'Say that again and you're dead.'

'What, the part about you being scum? Or the part about you being Hunter scum? It's the same thing either way.'

'Rachel!' Claire warned.

As Rachel turned to address her sister, Stacey punched her in the face. Rachel did her best to fight her off when she came at her again but she was too strong. Claire lunged at them, grabbing Stacey by the hair. While the rest of the girls watched, she managed to pull them apart.

'Stop it!' she cried. 'We don't want to fight anymore.'

'Who cares what you want.' Stacey pulled out a knife.

Three of the girls behind her stepped back, worried looks

flitting between them.

'You didn't say anything about a knife!' said Laila, standing her ground.

'Shut the fuck up,' said Stacey.

'Put it away!' said Rachel. 'It's not part of what we are.'

Stacey waved the knife about in front of her. 'You have a new look. Well, this is the new me. It's fair now, don't you think? Two against two. You and Claire.' She stabbed at the air in front of her again. 'Me and my knife.'

'Back off, Stacey,' Ashleigh spoke out.

Before anyone could dissuade her, Stacey lunged forward. She slashed the arm of Rachel's jacket.

'Watch it!' Rachel looked down at the damage. But not before she'd seen the glint in Stacey's eyes. It was the look of someone who wasn't in control.

Claire nudged Rachel's arm. They turned and ran.

CHAPTER TWENTY-THREE

Caren was in the kitchen wading through a pile of ironing. When the house had been trashed, some of their clothes had been taken from the wardrobe and thrown out of the back window, landing in the garden. Washing them again had meant a bigger pile than normal.

She heard a knock at the door and opened it to find Gina. 'You're the last person I expected to see,' she spoke first.

Gina looked embarrassed but stood her ground. 'I wanted to come across, see how you were doing after the break-in and –'

'You've come to gloat!' Caren folded her arms.

'No! I wanted to see if there was anything I could do to help. I heard it was a right mess.'

Caren baulked. '*You* want to help *me*?'

Gina nodded. Since Thursday, she hadn't been able to get Sam Harvey's conversation out of her mind. She needed to know why Pete had given him fifty pounds to say he was John's son. By coming across and chatting to Caren, she might glean a little more information. Then she'd decide whether to tell her or not. This might be something she wanted to keep from her.

Caren smiled faintly. 'You could come in rather than stand on my doorstep, I suppose.'

Gina nodded. 'Yeah, ta.'

Claire ran across Davy Avenue and into Winston Green. Behind her, she could hear Rachel close on her heel. She glanced behind them, only to see Stacey and the others on their tail.

'Come on, Rach,' she urged. 'They're catching us.'

'Wait for me, Claire! I'm going as fast as I can!'

'No way!' Claire jumped down two steps, levelled out and then three steps onto the green in between the houses. She could hear

Stacey screaming out obscenities as she tried to catch ground. They legged it over the grass, across Graham Street and back into Stanley Avenue.

Rachel yelped: She'd caught her shin on the bumper of a parked car as she ran past it. Claire turned back to help, saw she was on her feet and continued to run. When she reached Stanley Avenue, she had never been so pleased to see her house up above.

As Rachel caught up with her, they slowed their pace. Stacey stopped at the top of the avenue. There were only three girls with her now.

'I'm going to kill you, Rachel Bradley,' Stacey yelled. 'I'm going to rip your fucking heart out.'

'Yeah right! When you're strong enough!' Rachel bent over and leaned on a wall as she caught her breath for a moment. When she looked again, Stacey was running at them. She turned quickly and ran, bumping into Ruth up ahead in her haste.

'Sorry!' she said, but didn't stop.

Further in front, Claire had made it and was halfway up the path to the house. But Stacey had caught up quicker than they'd anticipated. As Rachel got to the gate, she yanked her back by the hood of her jacket.

'Claire!' She held out her hand to her sister in front.

Claire saw the knife still in Stacey's hand and screamed. 'No! Leave her alone!'

Stacey plunged the knife into Rachel's back.

Although Claire could hear herself screaming, time seemed to stand still. She watched helplessly as Stacey thrust the blade into Rachel's back again and again.

Rachel dropped to her knees on the path.

'Leave her alone!' Claire jumped on Stacey but she lashed out with a fist. Losing her footing, she fell down the path, landing with a thump against the gate.

Stacey glowered at her. 'You'll be nothing without her,' she said. Then she plunged the knife into Rachel's chest.

'Rachel!' screamed Claire.

*

Ruth saw the girl grab hold of Rachel and pull her back by her hood. Bloody typical, she thought: the Bradley twins were up to no good again. She continued on her way until she heard Claire scream. The hairs on the back of her neck stood up when she saw the girl had a knife. Without a thought for her own safety, she ran over.

'Stop her!' Claire screamed to Ruth.

Stacey stepped away, for a moment standing with a bewildered look on her face. Then she threw down the knife, pushed past Ruth and ran onto the street.

Ruth watched her go, for a moment wondering if she was dreaming. But Claire's screams were real; there was blood all over her hands.

Hearing Rachel gasping for breath, she knelt beside her on the damp path.

Rachel's head lolled to one side.

'Rachel!' sobbed Claire. 'Oh, God, she's going to die, isn't she?'

Ruth didn't want to think about that. 'Go and get your mum.' As Claire ran into the house, she took off her coat and, ignoring the cold weather, removed her jumper. She pressed it to Rachel's chest. Rachel groaned, causing Ruth to burst into tears. She could see whatever she did would be hopeless. Blood was covering Rachel at an alarming rate: the knife must have cut through a major artery.

Claire came running out of the house moments later. 'There's no one in!' She got out her mobile. 'Do something. DO SOMETHING.'

Ruth knew there wasn't time for an ambulance.

'Go and get Caren,' she said. When Claire didn't move, she shouted. 'Claire! Fetch Caren. NOW!'

Gina sat down at the table. Apart from the faint smell of paint in the air, the room was fairly void of any reference to the burglary. The conversation she'd overheard with Sam Harvey spoke of all the rooms being trashed. They must have been busy to get it painted so quickly.

'Did they make a lot of mess?' Gina wanted to know.

'Did they ever! They went into every room. Paint tipped over the rug, aerosol paint sprayed everywhere, food chucked out of the fridge. They even emptied our wardrobes and threw the clothes out of the bloody window! It was pure vandalism; it's going to take forever to put right. I cried for –'

'Caren!' Claire burst into the kitchen through the back door. 'You have to come – Mum!'

'Claire! What's going on? Are you okay? You look like you've seen a ghost.'

Claire pointed to the door. 'Rachel – she's been stabbed. Outside.'

They all ran out of the kitchen and across the road. Gina saw three girls outside her gate. As she got nearer, she spotted Ruth, Rachel's legs to her side. Nearer still, she saw her cradling Rachel in her arms.

'Rachel!' Gina pushed Ruth out of the way and took her place. Rachel's arm flopped around as she pressed her body to her chest. 'Stay with me, Rachel. Stay with me.' She looked back to the street. 'Where's the ambulance?' she screamed.' Where's the fucking ambulance!'

'I rang for it as soon as I saw what happened,' Ashley told her, openly crying. 'I saw what happened. Oh, God, she isn't going to die, is she?'

Gina ignored her, turning on Ruth who sat on her knees beside her. 'You had no right to touch her!'

Ruth shivered. She stared down at her hands, her body, her jeans; they were covered in Rachel's blood.

Caren tried to take control. 'Claire, where's your dad?' She turned to John who had followed them across. 'John, go and look!'

'He's not in the house,' Claire sobbed. 'Mum, do something!'

'I don't know what to do!' Gina cried.

'Mum,' Rachel spluttered, her voice barely audible.

Gina stroked her hair. 'I'm here for you, baby,' she said. 'I'm here for you. You're safe now.'

Caren sat down beside Rachel. She took off her jumper and gave it to Gina. Gina removed Ruth's top, soaked through to dripping, and pressed that one to Rachel's chest.

Rachel groaned.

'I'm sorry,' Gina told her over and over. 'I'm sorry.'

A scarlet bubble appeared at the corner of Rachel's mouth.

'The ambulance is on its way,' Gina told her. 'You hang on in there.'

Blood began to trickle from her mouth. Rachel coughed and more appeared. She coughed again.

'Mum!' screamed Claire. 'Do something. She's dying!'

'No, she's not,' said Gina. She stroked her daughter's forehead. 'Now you listen to me, Rachel Bradley. We're made of strong stuff. You're not going to die, do you hear? Don't you fucking dare!'

But Rachel didn't hear anything. She didn't see anything either. Life slipped away from her. Her arm flopped to the floor.

'NO!' cried Gina. 'No!' Tears poured down her face as she held Rachel to her.

'Rachel!' Claire dropped to her knees next to them.

Caren's hand covered her mouth; her blood ran cold. She looked back to see John standing by the side of the three girls who had come into the garden. Ruth sat in shock a few feet away. By now, a few neighbours had come out too.

Gina looked at Ruth with so much hate. 'You let her die, you bitch,' she yelled. 'Not content to steal my husband, you let my daughter die!'

'But I –' Ruth tried to explain.

'I hate you. This is your fault. You let her die!'

Claire grabbed her sister's hand. 'Rachel, wake up. Rachel!'

Caren gently pulled Claire away and hugged her, hoping to comfort her, knowing that Gina needed to hold Rachel for the moment. And then, amidst the chaos and the sound of an ambulance in the distance, silence fell on Stanley Avenue. Gina rocked Rachel in her arms. Caren hugged Claire. Ruth sat on the garden, holding her hands in the air, staring at the blood. John stood in shock, three teenage girls crying by his side.

'She's not dead,' Claire sobbed. 'She can't be. I was talking to her just... She can't be dead.'

Caren let her ramble on. She wondered how Claire was going to fare without her twin. Gina was going to have a tough time as her mother, but Claire was the other half of Rachel.

'Where will your dad be?' she asked.

'I don't know.' Claire stared at Rachel, fresh tears falling fast. 'She's dead, isn't she?'

'Let's wait until the paramedics look at her,' Caren replied. 'Look, they're here now.'

'I'm going to try Dad's phone again.'

'He's probably shagging his latest conquest somewhere,' Gina said, never taking her eyes from Rachel, wiping the hair from her forehead.

The ambulance drew up, the sirens dropping off as it parked up. 'Excuse me, love,' said the paramedic as he sat down next to Rachel.

'There's no point,' Gina said. 'She's dead.' She slapped his hand as he reached to check Rachel's pulse. 'Don't you fucking touch her!'

'Mum, let him help.' Claire dropped to her knees beside them. 'He needs to look.'

Gina looked at Claire and gasped. Then she held out her hand. 'Rachel,' she smiled.

'No, I'm Claire!' She moved away, horrified.

The paramedics took over and Gina looked around her. This was a dream. She was going to wake up in a moment. There was Claire sitting beside her and there was Rachel, lying... lying... Gina stared at Rachel before turning to Claire. Oh, there she was.

'Rachel,' she whispered.

'It's me, Mum, Claire.' She pointed at the lifeless body of her sister, paramedics all over her. 'That's Rachel.'

Gina frowned. She looked at Rachel, and then back at Claire. 'Rachel,' she whispered. 'Rachel.'

'No.' Claire shook her head vehemently and then she ran.

'Claire!' As she ran past, Caren grabbed for her arm but Claire thumped out at her.

'Leave me alone,' she cried. 'I don't want to be here.'

Once the police arrived, everyone was moved from the garden as a murder investigation got underway. Barbara had been asleep until she'd heard the sirens but she rushed across. She stayed surprisingly calm after she'd learned that her granddaughter had been murdered, realising that as a mother, Gina needed her help. She needed her strength. The police said it would be some time before they would be let back into their property so she took them all across to her house.

Although John had gone home, Caren had stayed with Gina, not really wanting to be there but feeling the need too. She was worried about Claire; she'd been gone a couple of hours now.

She was worried about Ruth too. Ruth had gone into a stupor since Rachel's death. After the police had arrived and taken their details, Caren had walked her home. All she'd repeated was 'I couldn't save her.' And no matter how many times, she'd reiterated that it wasn't her fault, Ruth had continued, changing to 'I should have saved her.'

Caren had cried with her as she'd made cups of tea. Once she thought Ruth was going to bed, she'd gone back to Barbara's. It had seemed eerie seeing the white tent and the hustle and bustle outside Gina's house. There was a small crowd, several vehicles and lots of police around. She'd been told someone would need to question her soon. She wished there was more that she could tell them. What a dreadful chain of events. It was such a young age to die.

She'd been at Barbara's house for no more than five minutes when Pete burst into the kitchen. He rushed over to Gina.

'They just told me. She…is she… She can't be –'

'Where were you, you bastard?' Gina's legs gave way as she slumped into his arms. 'I called you and called you and…'

'I'm sorry,' he sobbed, holding on to her tightly. 'I didn't know what had happened. I'm sorry.'

'Mr Bradley,' said PC Andy Baxter. 'If I could–'

'That bitch Stacey Hunter stabbed her,' said Gina, the words she spoke making her cry again. 'She was home, Pete. She was running up the path but she pulled her back by her hood.'

'But she's just a kid! They're both kids.'

'Kids have weapons too, unfortunately,' said Andy.

'Rachel didn't have a knife, did she?'

Gina gasped. 'Did she? Did she have a knife?'

'I'm not sure,' said Andy. 'We'll know more later.'

Pete wiped at his eyes. 'Did you see what happened?'

'No, I wasn't there.'

Pete looked at Caren who was standing in the doorway. 'Were you there?'

'No, Gina was over at mine.' When Pete frowned, she explained. 'Gina offered to help me with the mess we'd been left in because of the break-in. I suppose when Claire didn't find anyone here, she ran across to get me.'

'You didn't hear anything before that?'

'Sorry, no.'

'No one heard them fighting?'

'She did – that fucking Ruth Millington,' Gina cried out. 'It's all her fault. She was the first person to get to Rachel. She should have stopped the bleeding.'

'There was too much,' said Caren.

'Blood everywhere.' Barbara shook her head from side to side before breaking down.

Gina glared at Pete. 'You should have been here.'

Pete wiped his eye with the back of his hand. 'I'm sorry, Gina.'

'She was too badly injured to survive.' Andy rested a hand on Pete's shoulder. 'I'll leave you for a moment and then I'll need to take a statement from you.'

Noticing how sad he looked, Caren followed him into the kitchen. She closed the living room door and sat down at the table.

'Are you okay?' she asked him. 'I didn't think this sort of thing would upset you.'

Andy sat down next to her. 'Every case is different but it's terrible if you know someone personally. I knew all the Bradleys.' He laughed half-heartedly. 'Who doesn't know the Bradleys? But Rachel was a child; just sixteen.'

'It's Claire I'm worried about,' said Caren. 'She's going to be so lost without her sister.'

Andy nodded. 'This isn't going to be an easy case. The witnesses are all teenagers. They'll be frightened of Stacey Hunter and her family.'

'Claire saw it all, though.'

'Yes, we'll gather what forensic evidence we can from Rachel's body, as well as the knife that Stacey dropped, and the garden area.'

'It's a terrible thing to happen. It's going to hit the family hard.'

'It's going to hit the estate too. Another murder to bring us down; remind people how shit it is on the Mitchell Estate.'

'It isn't all that bad,' said Caren.

Andy raised his eyebrows questioningly.

'It isn't!' Caren shook her head. 'I remember when I had to move back, I cursed the day I set foot in Stanley Avenue. But slowly the people around here, they got under my skin. They made me into a better person – and I wanted to help them.'

Andy listened as Caren continued.

'Rachel and Claire were trouble but did anyone give them a chance because of who they were? They always had the Bradley reputation to live up to. Maybe I could have won them around; maybe I couldn't. Or maybe it was them that won me around, I don't know. But I changed – I accepted what I have. And...' Caren's voice held a shake, 'until today I thought that no one could take that away from me.'

From behind them came a voice.

'Caren?'

Caren looked up to see Claire. She tried desperately to hide her shock as she saw the innocent face staring back at her. It was literally like seeing a ghost of Rachel, a terrible reminder of what had happened.

'I don't know what to do,' Claire said, her tears falling again. 'I don't know –'

The living room door opened. 'Claire!' said Pete.

Claire ran into her Dad's embrace. 'She's dead, Dad,' she cried. 'What am I going to do?'

'I don't know,' said Pete as he hugged her close. 'I don't know.'

Two doors away, Ruth sat on her sofa, one hand wrapped around the near-empty bottle of vodka, the other turning a craft knife over and over.

She staggered into the hall, knocking into the doorframe as she did. She cursed loudly, rubbing at her arm, but she managed to negotiate the stairs, even if she did have to crawl up the last two steps.

She threw herself face down on her bed. The room had long ago started to spin. But when she closed her eyes all she could see was blood. Rachel's blood; lots of it. Thick, dark blood, the worst kind. She pecked at the scar on her arm. She needed to see her own blood instead, to take the pain away.

'Argh!' Ruth screamed. 'It's so unfair!' She plunged the craft knife into the open wound, tearing at her skin.

Then just as suddenly, she stopped. It had made her realise how much pain Rachel must have been in when the knife went into and through her vital organs.

Ruth threw the craft knife down to the floor. 'I should have saved her,' she cried. 'I should have saved her!'

CHAPTER TWENTY-FOUR

Gina spent the next few days in a haze. Half of Rachel's school turned out to see where she had died, along with lots of local people. Bunches of flowers lay in front of the garden wall, stretching from their gate and halfway to next door's driveway. Teddy bears, small and large had been left, a T-shirt with dozens of messages written on it in blue biro. An odd photograph; an odd candle. Gina had been across to look at them a few times, finding comfort in some of the words of tribute. Other times, she couldn't bear to look at them.

Everyone was saying what a lovely girl Rachel had been – well liked and great fun. What a bunch of liars, Gina had wanted to shout. It was always the same; someone taken down in their prime and no one having a bad word to say about them. Well, not in public anyway – behind closed doors, she knew what everyone would be saying, what they were thinking.

They hadn't been allowed home yet. They'd been over to get a few belongings but until the forensics had finished their job, they'd had to stay at her mum's house. From the window of the spare room where she and Pete were sleeping, Gina gazed down onto the avenue, watching two council workers picking litter up from the pavement. One of them stooped to read a card. He leaned on his brush and then beckoned his colleague over. They read the words together, and then with a shake of their heads, continued on their way.

Gina wiped away tears pouring down her face. Once Rachel's body was released to the coroner, they were planning on giving her a great send off. She'd asked Claire what she thought Rachel would like to wear; each of them had also chosen something to put into the coffin. Claire wanted to give Rachel her favourite baseball cap but knew that Rachel would prefer her hair to be spiked up and styled. She'd also asked Caren if she could do her make up. Caren had looked relieved when Gina stepped in before she'd had time to answer and said that it would be the undertaker's job.

Pete had chosen a family photograph. It had been taken a couple of years ago when they'd all gone to Dorset for a week's holiday. Gina was going to give her the teddy bear with 'I love Mum' embroidered on its T-shirt that Rachel had won at the fair when she was seven. It was dirty and grubby now and it had an ear missing where Danny had pulled at it with her. Gina knew that Rachel would be comforted to have that near to her. And it had to go with her – she couldn't bear to look at it now that Rachel had gone.

Behind her, there was a knock at the door. Pete opened it and came into the room with two mugs.

'I thought you might like a cuppa,' he said, placing them down on the bedside cabinet. He perched on the end of the bed, looking everywhere but at Gina. They sat in silence for a moment. It had been ten days since Rachel had been murdered, yet the question of Pete's whereabouts had remained unanswered long after Gina had held her while her life slipped away. She was going to have to force it out of him.

'Where were you?' she asked outright.

'I was down the pub.'

'No, you weren't. Mum phoned The Butcher's Arms and they hadn't seen you since the day before.'

'I – Christ, I can't remember now. Besides, it doesn't really matter in the big scheme of things. We've far more important things to think about.'

'Like who to invite to the funeral? Michelle? And Donna? And Tracy?' As she turned to face him, Gina couldn't even take pleasure in the look of bewilderment that flashed across Pete's face. Michelle Winters had been the first affair she'd found out about. Donna Adams had been his second or was it his third? Tracy Tanner, however, had been a guess because of her reputation. But from the look of guilt that flashed across his face, she had hit the jackpot.

'You selfish, two-timing piece of shit!' she cried.

'I'm sorry,' he said, 'it was just a fling!'

'While your daughter was dying, you were fucking Tracy Tanner!' Gina leaned forward and thumped his chest. 'Have you any idea how I felt? I knew what was going on when your phone was switched off. Everyone else knew what was going on when I couldn't get hold of you. Where were you when I needed you?'

'It didn't mean anything!'

'So why did you do it?'

Pete paused and sighed. 'Because I could, okay? She was there - you weren't and we just –'

'Don't you dare fucking shift the blame on me! You have the nerve to screw around and you think it's okay to say it's *my* fault?'

'You're right.' Pete looked shamefaced. 'I'm stupid and thoughtless and should have known better by now.'

'No, *I'm* stupid and thoughtless and should have known better by now. I should have kicked you out after I found out about the last tart.'

'We'll sort it, love.' Pete stretched across the bed for her hand. Gina snapped it away and glared at him.

'Don't 'love' me. We *will* sort it. Once the funeral is over, there are going to be changes around here, whether you agree with them or not.'

Caren left her house to walk the few metres down to see Ruth. As she drew level with Barbara's house, she stole a look at the windows, wondering how Gina was coping with things. She hadn't seen her out and about for a couple of days.

She knocked on Ruth's front door; there was no answer. She hadn't seen her for a couple of days either – usually by now, she'd have gone past her window at least once – and she hadn't answered her phone today. She'd tried several times without any luck.

She knocked again: still no answer. She peered through the living room window but couldn't see anyone. Not one for giving in, she tried around the back, pummelling on the door.

'Ruth? It's me, Caren!'

'In here.'

Caren opened the door to find Ruth sitting at the kitchen table. Her head lay on the surface, one hand clasped around an empty glass. There was a half empty bottle of vodka beside her.

'Jesus, Ruth, what time did you start drinking this morning? Or haven't you stopped from last night?'

Ruth's head popped up a second. 'I can't remember,' she slurred.

Caren sighed and switched on the kettle. 'I'll make coffee – black. Lots of it for you, my lady.'

'Don't want any coffee.'

'Tough luck. And you're having no more of that, either.' Caren took the bottle of vodka and put it away in a cupboard.

'Hey, you can't do that,' Ruth griped. Wincing, she held onto her head. 'You can't tell me what to do.'

'And I can't sit around while you drink yourself to death either. Honestly, you have to take –'

At the mention of death, Ruth's face crumpled.

'I'm sorry. It was only a slip of the tongue.'

'It was my fault she died,' sobbed Ruth.

'No, it wasn't.'

'I let her die.'

'No, you didn't.'

'But if I had got to her sooner,' she sat up, 'she might not have lost as much blood and –'

'Bloody hell, Ruth, how long are you going to sit here wallowing in self-pity?' Caren spoke firmly. 'Rachel died. It wasn't your fault – get used to it.'

'But –'

'You can't keep blaming yourself for her death. Neither can you keep feeling sorry for yourself. You haven't lost Rachel: Gina has.'

'Yes, but –'

'Ruth, snap out of it!'

Ruth sniffed. Tears intermingled with snot; she wiped it all away with the back of her hand.

Caren pulled a tissue from her pocket and gave it to her. Secretly, she wanted to slap her. She felt her patience slipping away again. It was hard to talk to Ruth when she was drunk.

'I suggest you sober up and get a grip.'

'I'm not drunk!' Ruth slurred even more. 'Where's my vodka?'

Caren made her strong black coffee and plonked it in front of her nose. 'Drink this and get yourself washed and changed. You smell, Ruth. When was the last time you had a shower?'

'I don't know.'

'I think you should –'

'Stop telling me what to do!' Ruth shouted.

Caren held up her hands in surrender. 'Have it your way,' she said. 'Drink yourself stupid. But don't expect me to come round and check on you later. I have my own life to live.'

'Fuck off... and leave me alone.'

Caren frowned but she did exactly that.

Claire lay on her side, curled up on the camp bed set up in her nan's bedroom for her. She hadn't slept much since Rachel had died; it still didn't seem real that she'd gone. And at the hands of Stacey Hunter too. What a nasty, vicious bitch. Who would have thought she would go that far to get even?

Claire could see the attack every time she closed her eyes. Stacey had been caught almost immediately after the assault and was now remanded in custody until the date of a court hearing. Even that tiny thought didn't console her. She was all alone. She had lost the one friend she thought she would have for life. Rachel was her twin, her equal, her soul mate. For her, she was irreplaceable.

No one knew how to behave around her since it had happened. Her mum was treating her like a five-year-old; her dad barely talking to anyone. Twice she'd gone around to Caren's but had come away before she knocked on the door. Aunty Leah had been around for a fair but was keeping away now, probably unsure what to say. Claire had even thought about knocking on Ruth's door. Maybe she'd understand. She had been with Rachel at the end too.

She closed her eyes, concentrating to see if she could feel her sister's presence, cuddling into her back, bringing her closer, trying to protect her.

'I'm here,' she whispered into the room. 'Please come back for me. I can't do this by myself.'

Suddenly, she heard screaming outside. She ran to the window. Down below, she saw her mum. She was standing in the middle of the street.

'Mum!' She ran outside quickly.

Gina had dropped to her knees in the middle of the road.

'They took her away,' she cried. 'They took my baby away.'

Barbara appeared in her dressing gown. 'Gina, come on in.'

'She's gone, Mum. I don't know what to do without her.'

'You still have me,' whispered Claire.

But Gina ignored her.

Caren was next to come out. 'Let me help get her inside,' she said to Barbara.

By this time, a few more neighbours had appeared on their doorsteps. But as they turned to go back into the house, Gina spotted Ruth silhouetted in her doorway.

'You!' She shouted over to her. 'You were useless at looking after your own kids and you were useless at looking out for mine.' She prodded her own chest. 'I would have saved her,' she screamed. 'I would have, but – but you...'

Caren looked over at Ruth as they helped Gina back into her house but she had disappeared. Damn – she'd have to go and check on her after she'd settled Gina again. She sighed. How had she managed to become chief babysitter?

CHAPTER TWENTY-FIVE

The day of the funeral dawned on a cold December day. The sun was high in the sky, but the wind was bitter with it. Ice from the morning frost was still under foot. Gina put on a black suit that she'd bought especially for the occasion; so too did Pete. Everyone else had been told to dress in bright colours. She was sure it was what Rachel would have liked.

Claire had new clothes too. She'd surprised everyone by buying a black and white dress. It came just above her knees and she'd teamed it with black knee-length boots with a slight wedge heel. Gina had also treated her to a fake-fur coat. Wearing her make up the way Caren had demonstrated, plus a bright pink lipstick, Gina realised that she didn't just look different; she looked individual. If it hadn't been such a heartbreaking occasion, she would have told her how lovely she was. She would have complimented her on her choice, how she'd put it all together, the colour of her freshly-painted nails. But she couldn't say anything because she was burying her other daughter. Rachel had been so much the life and soul of the twins, it was hard to put into words how much she was missed once they'd been able to return to the house. With only Claire, there had been quiet.

All of a sudden, Gina realised how selfish she was. With tears forming in her eyes, she smiled and beckoned Claire over. She held her face in her hands and kissed her nose.

'I may be burying one daughter today,' she smiled through the tears, 'but I still have you. You look beautiful, so grown up.'

Claire swallowed and hugged her mum. 'I can't do this, Mum. I can't say goodbye.'

'Yes, you can. We all can.'

Pete knocked on the door. 'The cars are here,' he said softly.

'We'll be down in a minute,' Gina told him, keeping her back towards him until he'd gone. Then she spoke to Claire.

'Rachel will always be with you, in your thoughts and in your memories,' she comforted, wiping away her tears and pointing to her chest. 'She'll be right there, in your heart, no matter how far away you go. You need to make her proud today, and so do I.'

'No more fighting?'

Gina squeezed her eyes tightly together for a moment. Could she get through the day without laying into someone? If anyone said a bad word about Rachel, she'd be right in there. If anyone mentioned Stacey Hunter or her family, she knew she'd be the same. It would be so hard to keep her word.

But she would do it.

She would do it for Claire.

'I promise.' She smiled. 'No more fighting. Let's get through this the best we can.'

Caren and John were waiting in their doorway for everyone to come out of the house. The hearse had arrived a few minutes earlier but so far there had been no sight of the family. Suddenly, the front door of number twenty-five opened. Caren gave John's hand a squeeze as she held back her tears. Just the sight of a coffin was enough to reduce her to pieces. This funeral seemed so meaningless. It shouldn't have happened.

'They're coming out,' said John. They saw Pete walk down the path and chat to the undertaker in the second of three black cars. Caren blinked away more tears as Pete stared at the coffin in the hearse, and put a hand to the glass for a moment before turning his back to it and wiping at his eyes.

John locked their front door and they walked down their path to the pavement.

Gina came out, holding onto Claire's arm. There were lots of family members behind them; Claire's brother, Danny, other people she didn't know but could recognise as Pete's parents, and a brother and sister on Pete's side.

'Christ, I haven't seen Dave Bradley for years.' John reached for Caren's hand. 'I'd forgotten there was a sister too.'

They stood in front of their gate until all the Bradley family were on street level. Then they got in their car and waited for the cortege to pull away from the kerb. Then they would follow on, just like half a dozen more cars that were waiting.

Like a lot of neighbours who wouldn't be going to the funeral but wanted to pay their respects, Ruth came out to watch. Unlike the other neighbours who were mostly on the pavement, Ruth stayed in the doorway of her house. Somehow it made her feel protected from the outside world. She didn't want to intrude, but neither could she stay indoors and pretend that she didn't care.

She watched Gina get into a car, followed by Pete and Claire and a young man she assumed to be Danny. Then the rest of their family followed. The engines started and suddenly the street erupted with the sound of music. Ruth popped her head out as everyone turned towards the Reynolds' house. Despite the cold weather and as a mark of respect this time, their front door was wide open, all the windows too – the sound of Robbie Williams singing *Angels,* so apt for the day.

Ruth wiped at tears that slid down her face as the cars moved off.

She should have saved Rachel.

As the funeral cortege pulled out of Stanley Avenue and onto Davy Road, Gina felt Claire grip her arm tighter. She followed her daughter's gaze out of the car window. There were people dotted here and there, waiting at the side of the pavement. An elderly man took off his cap as they passed. Gina saw two shop workers and the manager from Shop&Save standing in a line. One by one, as they passed a car, an engine would start and moments later, another car would join in at the back of the procession. Some cars had only teenagers in them.

'Do you know any of them?' Gina asked Claire.

Claire could only nod.

'It's such a tragedy,' said Leah, Gina's sister. 'Someone dying so young always upsets people. Rachel hardly had chance to live her life before...'

Claire began to cry.

Gina's heart broke again. She'd been determined to keep it together until after the funeral. But seeing Claire in so much pain was more than she could take. She pulled her into her embrace and they cried together.

'What am I going to do without her, Mum?'

Ever since she'd come to live in Stanley Avenue, Ruth had fallen deeper and deeper into a hole. First she'd lost the boys through her inability to look after them. Then she'd started to drink again. Martin had come back and although he'd taken advantage of the situation, wanting a roof over his head rather than be back with her, he'd gone almost as soon as he'd arrived. That had left room for that business with Pete Bradley – and look at the beating she'd received because of that.

She'd had one ray of sunshine when Caren took an interest in her. The nail party had been a success and a couple of the women had continued to be friendly to her afterwards. One of them had even invited her over for coffee – not that she'd taken up the offer yet.

And then Rachel had died. In the back of her mind, Ruth knew she could have been one of any neighbour to be first on the scene that afternoon. But Gina hadn't seen that. She'd just seen Ruth meddling in her business yet again.

Today had been the last straw. Ruth had really wanted to go to the funeral. She'd wanted to explain to Gina that she knew how empty she'd be feeling. She'd lost her children too. But it was better to stay away. It would have sparked off another fight.

But seeing all the Bradley family together, supporting their own, no matter whether they got on with each other or not, it made Ruth realise she'd completely lost her way. Worse than that, she couldn't think of anything she could do to make amends.

Back in the kitchen, Ruth took out two bottles of vodka she'd bought the day before. She twisted the top from one and, not bothering with a glass, swigged back a large mouthful. Wiping her mouth, she coughed. Then she poured half of it into a large glass and fumbled for her tablets. There was only one thing left to do.

But first she needed a notepad.

*

As the funeral cortege drew up in front of the chapel at the crematorium, Gina imagined how a movie star must feel at a film premiere. There were no paparazzi, no screaming crowds, no flash photography, but everyone was looking at them – and ironically she could glimpse a red carpet inside the chapel.

'There must be two hundred people here,' said Pete, glancing around at the groups standing in silence. 'I barely know any of them.' He peered through the window.

'Good old Mitchell Estate, give anyone a good sending off,' said Barbara fondly.

The driver came round and opened the door. Gina stepped onto the tarmac. The crowd began to move forward. She noticed a few familiar faces amongst them: Josie Mellor and Matt Simpson - the caretaker from the Workshop - Cathy Mason, Andy Baxter. She spotted some of the regulars from The Butcher's Arms, and the manager of Shop&Save was just driving past in his car to park up. But mostly there were teenagers everywhere. Groups of girls in tears; groups of boys standing stoic. There were people from Stanley Avenue too. But even as she wondered if she'd come, Gina knew who she was really searching out.

Her eyes raced around the crowd and beyond, finally seeing Maggie Hunter in the distance. She prickled but realised she needed to catch the woman's eye. When she did, she watched Maggie lower hers to the ground. Gina waited for her to lift them again and gave her a small nod in acknowledgement. Mother to mother, she understood her pain. They were both suffering for the actions of their daughters and Maggie had lost her daughter in a way too. Stacey would be locked up for a good many years to come. Gina couldn't stay bitter at the thought that Maggie could always visit her daughter; always see her when she was released. What had happened would change Stacey too. She needed help; maybe she would get it, and maybe she wouldn't accept it – who knew? But it would be a long time before Stacey came back to the Mitchell Estate, if she ever did.

Maggie Hunter nodded back before disappearing behind a crowd of teenagers who had only just arrived.

Claire took her hand. 'Come on, Mum.'

Gina looked at the coffin in front of them by the chapel doors, even now not wanting to believe that one of her daughters was lying inside it. The family had said their final goodbyes last night and Gina felt more at peace now. She'd kissed Rachel's cold forehead and left her in the hands of the angels – she wasn't sure whether God existed or not. But she hoped that Rachel had gone to somewhere far better than here. And she hoped to see her there someday in the future.

By her side, Claire took a single red rose from the undertaker. Gina gave her hand a quick squeeze as they waited for everyone in the funeral party to get out of their cars and stand behind them.

'I feel sick, Mum,' whispered Claire.

'Me, too.' Gina took hold of Pete's hand on her other side. Danny stood to his side.

The notes from the chorus of *We are Young* rang out from inside the tiny chapel, their cue to move forward. Gina knew that some people wouldn't have heard of the band *Fun* but the song had been Claire's choice. It meant a lot to her.

With her remaining daughter hanging onto her arm, Gina swallowed, blinking away tears. Finally, she managed to put one foot in front of the other and go in.

By the time they were back in Stanley Avenue, Gina was drained of emotion as well as tears. She'd refused to have the wake anywhere but the house – didn't want Pete getting drunk and shouting his mouth off about the Hunter family. It would only cause more ill-feeling.

Quite a few friends had come back to the house for the wake. It was nearing six thirty now; most people had gone but a few of the neighbours were there.

'It's been a tough day for you, our Gina,' Barbara stopped her on the way back to the kitchen with a pile of empty plates. 'You look worn out.'

'I'm knackered, Mum,' she admitted. 'But I'll keep on going until everyone has left.'

Claire was in the kitchen, sitting with Caren and John. They were laughing about something, and instantly stopped when they saw Gina.

'It's okay,' said Gina, understanding their guilt.

'Claire was telling us about some of the things she and Rachel got up to.'

Gina smiled. 'About the times they got into scrapes or the 'just plain silly' times?'

'A bit of both actually,' said Claire. All of a sudden, her laughter changed to tears. Gina rushed over and hugged her.

'It's okay to be happy, love. Rachel wouldn't want us to be sad all the time.'

'I miss her, Mum,' sobbed Claire. 'I can't live without her.'

'Yes, you can. Things will seem different for a while, that's all.'

'But you don't understand. I feel like I'm missing my shadow.'

Pete staggered into the room. He burped loudly, noticing the scowl that came from Caren.

'What's the matter with you lot?' He wiped his mouth with his hand and sniggered. 'Cheer up, why don't you!'

'Don't be so disrespectful!' snapped Gina.

'It was a joke, for Chrissake...' Pete raised his hands in surrender, splashing lager from his can over the floor.

'I can't believe you're wasted. Go upstairs and sleep it off,' Gina told him coolly. 'You're embarrassing.'

'Hey, Miss Fancy Pants,' Pete staggered towards Caren. 'Did you enjoy seeing Sam Harvey?' he stopped within inches of her face.

'Get away from me!' Caren pushed him, trying not to heave at the stench of his breath.

'You think you're so high and mighty across the other side of the road. Well, I showed you, didn't I?'

'Showed me what?'

'Did it shatter your perfect life when you found out John had a kid when you failed to give him any?'

'That's enough,' warned Gina.

'It's – it's none of your business,' said Caren, the word failed hanging in the air.

'But I want to hear. How much did Sam coming back on the

scene ruin your happy marriage?'

'We have a strong relationship – something as stupid as that wouldn't have torn us apart.'

'You are so stupid,' Gina said to Pete.

'Huh?' Pete spun round to face Gina, staggering slightly but keeping his balance.

'I *know*, you sad bastard,' she snapped.

Pete frowned as he steadied himself again.

'I knew too – that Sam wasn't John's son,' said Caren. 'One minute Sam was there; the next he never turned up when he arranged another meeting. The girls had told me his age and I was deciding what –'

'I don't mean that,' Gina interrupted. She looked pointedly at Pete, 'I mean that I *know* who Sam's father is.'

'What's going on?' John was looking from one to the other in confusion.

'Claire, tell them how old Sam is,' said Gina.

'He's eighteen.'

'But Donna told us he was twenty-one,' John said to Pete.

'He tried to trick you,' said Gina.

'Sam's your son,' Pete said to John.

'Liar!' Gina screamed. 'Sam's your son!'

'What?' Caren cried.

'Yuck!' said Claire. 'You mean I've kissed my own brother!'

'So,' John tried to link the pieces together, 'if Sam isn't my son, then why did he turn up with Donna to say that he was?'

'He paid Sam fifty quid to pretend that he was your son, thinking it would cause arguments between you, take away what you had and maybe spilt you up. But once Sam, being the loser that he is, saw your house and what he could thieve, he decided to rob it too.'

Pete looked confused. 'I didn't tell him to do that.'

'I overheard him talking when I was at The Workshop. All the damage he caused is down to you.'

'My God, you piece of lowlife.' Caren shook her head in disbelief. 'Have you any idea how we felt after that burglary?'

'That stupid little fucker,' said Pete. 'If –'

240

John stood up quickly. 'Why, you –' In his haste, the chair scraped across the floor as he lunged at Pete.

'John, no!' Caren pulled him back.

'I'm warning you,' John pointed at him. 'Stay away from me and stay away from my family.'

Gina left them to it. What did she care? Pete had done his worse by her. The neighbours were already standing in the doorway, coming to see what the commotion was about. This new revelation would be all around the estate tomorrow.

'Is it true, Dad?' Claire asked once John and Caren had gone. 'Sam is your son?'

'Of course it's true,' said Gina. 'Your dad can never keep his dick in his trousers.'

'That's because you never give me any – you're like a lump of lard.'

'Zip it,' she told him. 'For years I've put up with you and your inconsiderate ways, your philandering and your selfishness; letting you get away with everything. Good old Gina – why should I give a fuck about her? Well, you were right about one thing. I must have been dim to put up with it. But at least I can make amends for my stupidity now. I want you out of this house.'

'You can't make me –'

Gina launched herself at him. 'Get out of my HOUSE!'

Pete wrestled to grab her wrists as she pummelled at his chest.

'I hate you, you useless piece of shit. If it wasn't for you, we –'

'Stop it!' yelled Claire. 'STOP IT!' She began to scream at the top of her voice, taking a step backwards, and another and another until she touched the wall behind.

Everyone stopped as Claire pointed a finger at her mum and dad.

'You two,' her hand shook visibly, 'that's where we get it from. Rachel's dead and you're *still* fighting. I hate you. I hate you *both*.'

Pete turned away from them. Even drunk, Claire's words had got to him.

All at once, Gina saw herself through her child's eyes. They had to stop all this rage escaping. It wasn't good for any of them. Suddenly, she knew what she must do – the *only* thing she could do. But first she needed to comfort her daughter.

'I'm sorry, love.' Gina put out her arms. 'Come here.'

Claire slapped them away and pushed past her. 'I hate you. I hate him. I'm leaving and I'm never coming back!'

CHAPTER TWENTY-SIX

Dear Mason and Jamie
I am sorry for letting you down. I love you so much but I know that you will be better off with people who love you and can take care of you and make you happy. I hope that you find that and I hope that you will always look out for one another. Lots of love always, Mum
x

Dear Gina
I am so sorry that I couldn't save Rachel. She was so young and didn't deserve to die like that. I hope you can find it in your heart to forgive me. I never meant to hurt you. I felt so helpless watching her slip away, knowing that I couldn't do anything to stop the blood. I hope that Claire will find peace, as I hope you will too, one day.
Ruth

Dear Caren
Thank you so much for being my friend. You were there for me when I had no one to talk to. I'm sorry to let you down but I can't see a way out apart from this. The dark cloud is back. No one will miss me anyway.
Ruth

Ruth picked up another photo. It had been taken when Mason was two; Jamie was a baby. They were sitting on a bench either side of their dad. She ran a finger down the image of Glenn, remembering his smile, his laughter, the way he made her feel. Tears dripped onto the glass. God, she loved him so much.

Another photo. She was holding a newly born Mason, Glenn had his arm around her. She topped up her glass with vodka and drunk it quickly. Her eyes were getting weary now as she brought the photo closer. It had been such a happy time. But Ruth didn't smile through her tears.

Paper balls were strewn across the kitchen floor. She'd started to write notes to the boys and given up many times before finally settling on what she had written. In simple terms, she loved them and she needed them to know that. What more was there to say? She was sorry but they wouldn't care about that. She'd already ruined their lives; she had no right to ruin them further. They weren't her children now. Someone else was looking after them.

She picked up another photo: another faded memory. Ruth was standing by the edge of the sea, her hand trying to keep her skirt from flailing around in the wind. She remembered how she and Glenn had walked hand in hand into the cold water, then ran out laughing as the waves took their breath away.

'Glenn,' she sobbed. How had she survived for so long when life wasn't worth living without him? Gina was right when she'd told her she was bad through to her core. She grabbed a handful of tablets and washed them down quickly with vodka, coughing a few times in her haste.

'Not long now, Glenn,' she slurred. Her head touched the table and the glass fell from her hand. 'Tired... Not long now.'

Gina left it until eight o'clock before she went around to Caren's house. Claire hadn't come home yet but Gina had a sneaky feeling where she might be.

'Is she here?' she asked Caren when she answered the door.

Caren nodded, pressed a finger to her lips and then beckoned her in. Gina followed her through to the living room. Claire was curled up asleep on the settee. Even closed, her eyes seemed swollen. She looked so young; so fragile.

'They both told me how much better it was over here than at our house,' said Gina sadly. 'You made a real impression on them.'

'Oh, please,' Caren waved the comment away with her hand. 'All teenagers think someone else's mum is better than theirs.'

'You *are* better than me, in every way.'

'No, I'm not. I've made mistakes too. I just don't go round

broadcasting them to everyone.'

Gina tried to look offended but failed. She smiled shyly; she knew exactly what Caren meant. They went through to the kitchen and sat down at the table.

'Can I ask you something?' she started.

'Sounds ominous,' said Caren.

'What do you see when you look at me?'

Caren stared at her. 'Are you trying to trick me?'

'No, I'd like to know.'

Caren paused for a moment. 'Last month I would have said that I see someone in a loveless marriage, who's under the thumb where her husband is concerned; who hasn't got any control of her kids and who isn't bothered how she looks or what anyone else thinks of her.'

'Wow, don't hold back.' Gina almost grunted.

'Like I said, a month ago I would have said all that. But now, you're changing.'

'*Changing*?'

'Last month, you would have taken great pleasure in telling me what Pete had set up with Sam Harvey. But instead, you kept it to yourself rather than blurt it out.'

'I used it to get even with him!'

'Only because you've finally realised he's a loser and that's a massive step in the right direction.'

'Watch it,' she said. 'I have a great upper cut.' But Gina was smiling.

'And you volunteered at The Workshop – now that I *am* impressed with.'

'It was only a few hours... but I really did enjoy it. I enjoyed the days with the babies but really I loved hanging round with the kids. The ones in their early teens, you know, thirteen or fourteen.'

'I think you should continue with it. They'll listen to you. Maybe you can make a difference on the estate – especially now.' Caren reached across the table and squeezed Gina's hand. It took them both by surprise but none of them moved. 'Through Rachel's death, maybe you could talk to the kids about gangs and fighting and belonging. It all comes down to peer pressure to conform.

Make them see there's more to life.'

Gina didn't know what to say.

'I think it's what you need right now,' Caren continued. 'I like Josie Mellor, she's a good sort. I – I thought about offering to volunteer myself actually.'

'You?' Gina sat back in amazement.

'Yes, I have some free time until I get my business up and running. Maybe I could help out.'

'Well, I have to admit, you've changed too.'

'I had to, being back on the estate.'

'Was it tough, to lose your house like that?'

Caren sighed. 'It was the worst thing that ever happened to us. But me and John got through it – it's always a good sign if you can do that.' She laughed and held up a hand. 'And look what we got instead!'

'Yeah, worn out flooring, chipped doors and damp patches.'

'And nuisance neighbours.'

They smiled at one another.

'How about letting me help you get through this?' Caren suggested.

'It's worth a shot.'

'How about me,' Caren paused, 'and Ruth?'

Gina sighed. 'I can't.'

'It wasn't her fault what happened with Pete.'

'I know.'

'But you blame her.'

'I don't really.'

'So, help her. She's grieving too.'

'It's not the same.'

'Of course it's not the same,' said Caren. 'But she has lost two children in a way. What she did was so brave, hoping to give her boys a decent chance somewhere else.'

'But to give them to Children's Services? That's beyond cruel.'

'Can't you see, Gina? Imagine how low she must have felt to have no other choice than that. No one to talk to; no one to get her through it.'

Gina lowered her eyes. She hadn't thought of it like that. In actual fact, until now, she'd never thought of anyone but herself.

'She needs friends,' Caren pushed. 'We all do.'

The kitchen door opened and a sleepy Claire came in. Gina smiled and patted her knee. As big as she was, Claire sat in her lap and wrapped her arms around her mum's neck.

'Would you like a coffee?' Caren asked.

'Please.' Claire nodded.

Caren flicked on the kettle and then picked up her phone, only to find it switched off. She must have forgotten to turn it back on after they left the crematorium. 'Let me give Ruth a quick ring,' she said, 'see if she's okay. She looked a bit upset this morning.'

'And then shall we go home afterwards?' Gina asked Claire.

Claire nodded. 'Mum, can I change bedrooms and sleep in Danny's old room?'

'Of course you can, love. Although, I have plans that we need to discuss tomorrow.'

'Ruth? Hi, it's Caren. Just ringing to see how you are.'

'Am fine.'

Caren sighed. She sounded drunk again. 'Do you want me to pop round for a while?'

Silence.

'Ruth, are you okay?'

Gina and Claire looked up at Caren.

'Ruth?'

'I... want to... time to... time to go. I want to –'

'You're not making sense. Christ, Ruth how much drink have you had tonight?'

'I – I... No, I – Glenn. I –'

'Ruth?'

'I – s'over.'

'RUTH!'

Caren didn't give her time to reply again. She ran out of the house and down the avenue towards number thirty-two. 'Ruth!' She banged on the front door. She raced to the window and banged on there too. 'Ruth! It's me, Caren.'

'Does anyone have a spare key?' Gina had come running up behind her with Claire.

'I don't know. Claire, run round to Mrs Ansell's and see if she has one.'

Claire took off and Caren went to try the back door. 'Ruth!' She tried the handle. 'It's open.' She looked at Gina. 'Should I go in?'

'Of course you should. Something spooked you on the phone.'

Caren knocked and went in. 'Ruth?' She gasped as she spotted the array of things on the kitchen table. A blister-pack of painkillers sat next to an empty bottle of vodka. She noticed the writing on the notepad and picked it up.

'Oh, God,' she covered her mouth with her hand as she read it. 'We need to find her! RUTH!'

Both women checked downstairs but didn't find her. Caren ran up the stairs two at a time. Into the bathroom, into the back bedroom and then into the front bedroom. Ruth lay on the bed, another vodka bottle on the floor beside her.

'Ruth?' Caren shook her but there was no response. 'Ruth? Talk to me. It's me, Caren. Talk to me! Gina – in here!'

Ruth moved her head and muttered something unintelligible.

'Get her to her feet and walk her around.' Gina pulled on her arm. 'We need to keep her awake.'

Claire appeared in the doorway. 'Ohmigod, is she okay?'

'She will be,' said Gina. 'Ring for an ambulance.'

'No.' Ruth muttered again. 'No – blance.'

'You don't have any choice in the matter.'

'No...' said Ruth. 'No choice.' Her head flopped to the side.

'Ruth!' Caren slapped at her face and took another few steps around the room, dragging her along with Gina. 'Ruth. Stay with us, Ruth!'

CHAPTER TWENTY-SEVEN

Josie pushed opened the gate to number thirty-two Stanley Avenue. As she walked up the path to the front door with trepidation, she wondered what sort of welcome she would receive. Was it too early for a support call? Would she be accused of poking her nose in again? Would she even be allowed in?

But she needn't have worried at all.

'You look better than the last time I saw you,' she smiled widely as Ruth led her into the living room. 'How are you feeling now?'

Ruth smiled too. 'I'm feeling good, thanks,' she acknowledged.

In actual fact, Ruth was feeling exceptionally well. It had been two weeks since her suicide attempt. She wasn't self-conscious about it, more embarrassed by the fuss she'd caused. People around her had been so nice, kind even, afterwards. She'd had her stomach pumped and a stern lecture off a doctor half her age. But the nugget of information that she'd left the hospital with – hope and a reason to survive – had re-enforced how precious life could be.

Josie held up her hand. 'I've got the paperwork you requested. Sorry it's been a while for me to get it to you.'

'Oh, that. I don't need it anymore.' They moved into the living room and sat down before Ruth replied. 'I've decided to stay here,' she said.

'Here?'

'Yep.'

Josie shook her head. She frowned and then she smiled. 'I'm shocked. I thought you hated living in Stanley Avenue.'

'I did, but the grass isn't always greener and all that malarkey.'

'I'm glad because I would have only been able to get you transferred into a flat anyway. And I think you'd be better staying in a house, in case things change in the future.'

Ruth knew she was referring to the boys coming to stay. Last week, she and Josie had gone to see the social worker with a view to meeting up with them for a one-off visit to start off with. It wasn't going to be easy. She didn't know if they'd want to see her again and rejection would hurt like hell, but she felt she had to give them the choice and then to stand by their decision.

'I'm scared of it not working out,' she told Josie, unaware she was wringing her hands.

'But you'll never know if you don't try and that would be much worse,' said Josie.

'I don't mean for me. I mean for them. What happens if one of them doesn't want to see me? Jamie might be able to be won around because he's younger but Mason probably won't ever forgive me. And it's not just that, it's upsetting their new routine by imposing myself on them again.'

'Imposing yourself on them?' Josie sounded shocked. 'You're their mother!'

'Yes, but I gave them away.'

'Only because of how you were feeling at the time. Now you're back on the straight and narrow, anything's a possibility.'

Ruth sighed. 'I suppose so. I'll just have to take one step at a time.'

'Talking about steps,' Josie stood up. 'I'd better be making a move. I can see my work here is done before it's even started.'

Alone with her thoughts again once Josie had gone, Ruth flopped back in the settee and hoisted her feet up onto the coffee table. She rested a hand on her stomach, feeling the tiny bulge that had started to form over the past week. Now wasn't the time to tell Josie, or anyone else: she needed to be sure there weren't any side effects from her suicide attempt first. Not for another couple of weeks at least, or until she could hide the little life growing inside her no more.

What a predicament to be in. She wasn't sure if the father was Martin or Pete, but she knew she wouldn't be making the same mistakes with this one. She was going to be a better mother to this child, try her best and give her or him her undivided attention. And now that she had a friend in Caren, she didn't feel so alone.

*

Ruth took the plate of chocolate muffins through to the living room and slid them onto the coffee table. She wondered if Gina and Caren would like the cake that she'd made especially for them or would it be over the top? She had never hosted a coffee morning before.

She'd been surprised when Caren had told her she'd invited Gina along too. Surprised because Gina Bradley was the last person she'd thought would want to walk through her front door, even with an invite. It would be the first time she'd seen her since she'd been taken away in an ambulance.

The knock on the door had her heart pounding in her chest. She checked her appearance quickly in the mirror, smoothing down her hair.

'Hi,' said Caren, handing Ruth a carrier bag. 'We have cake, biscuits and more cake. And before I go home, I'm going to have one of everything.'

'I fear we have enough cake to last us a month.' Ruth smiled shyly as Gina hovered in the doorway. She beckoned her in.

Coffee made, Caren started the conversation off.

'How are you feeling today, Ruth?'

'I feel a little delicate, I suppose, but other than that, I feel great.'

'You gave us a real fright,' said Gina, wanting to join in but not sure how much she should say.

'I think I frightened myself a lot more.' Ruth picked up a cake and began to nibble at it before replying again. 'I had no idea that I was going to do something so stupid.'

'It's stupid, all right,' said Caren. 'But I happen to believe that suicide is really brave. Just think how hard it must be to end your life. I can't imagine throwing myself in front of a train or hanging myself.'

'Or taking tablets and getting blotto, like I did? I suppose it was the easy way out but I wasn't thinking of anyone but myself. It was selfish, really.'

'It might have felt like that, but it was a cry for help.'

Ruth shrugged.

'Did you want to kill yourself?' asked Gina.

Caren tutted. 'Trust you to come out with the one question I needed an answer to but wouldn't have dared to ask!'

'I'm a Bradley,' said Gina. 'It's my job. Unless,' she glanced at Ruth, 'unless you don't want to talk about it.'

Ruth shook her head. 'It's okay. I've thought about nothing else since.'

After Caren and Gina had found Ruth near unconsciousness that night, at the hospital she'd had her stomach pumped out and stayed in overnight to be observed. What she'd found out while she was in there had been her saving grace.

'The worst thing was that I can't remember doing it,' she admitted, her cheeks colouring. 'I must have been so drunk that I wasn't thinking straight. I was really upset about not going to Rachel's funeral and you blaming me for it.'

'I'm sorry,' Gina said quietly.

'No, I'm not blaming you,' Ruth said quickly. 'But I think, in a way, I was still grieving for the loss of my family.'

Ruth launched into her past. When she'd told them about Glenn and how devastated she'd been by his death, how she'd thought she was being punished by losing him and how she found it hard to cope with life without him, Caren and Gina finally understood why she had given her boys over into the care of the local authority.

'That's some story,' Caren said, wiping a tear from her eye. 'And I thought my life was over when we lost our house. What a wuss! Have you ever thought about getting the boys back?'

'Lots of times, but I know it's not the right thing to do.'

'Says who?' asked Gina. 'A bunch of social workers? They don't know what's best for you.'

'They're not interested in what's best for me,' said Ruth. 'They're interested in the welfare of Mason and Jamie, and so they should be. They are the most important people in all of this mess. I – I miss them so much but I think what I did was for the best.'

'Maybe for now, but you should see what you feel like in a few months when you're more able to cope.'

Ruth nodded. She had been thinking about her future a lot over the past week.

'How's Claire doing?' she asked to take the heat away from her.

'She's starting to attend school on a regular basis. Seems she doesn't want to waste her life now. I think she might be finding her feet more as an individual.'

'Wow, that's great.' Caren picked up a biscuit and raised her cup in the air as a toast. 'I do hope she settles down. It must be so hard for her.'

Gina felt her eyes brim with tears. 'It's so hard to be in that house every day without her. Everywhere I look, there's a reminder of her.'

'But that will be a great comfort in time,' said Caren.

Gina wasn't so sure. 'It feels so empty now.' She smiled. 'I hadn't realised how much she and Claire argued. The noise was deafening but the silence without it is so much worse.'

'I was such a bad mother,' she added, moments later.

'I bet you weren't.' Ruth smiled. 'We always feel that everyone else's life is perfect, that we're the only ones that aren't doing it right?'

'Human nature, I suppose.'

Caren held up her cup. 'Any chance of another.'

Ruth stood up. 'I have a bit of Tia Maria left if you fancy adding a tot to it? There's enough for the two of you.'

'Aren't you having any?' Caren teased.

'No.' Ruth placed her hand on her tummy discreetly. 'I think I need to look after myself a bit better from now on.'

She rejoined them minutes later with fresh drinks. She gave them each a mug and then raised her own high in the air.

'Here's to new beginnings,' she toasted, smiling shyly.

'And new friendships,' said Caren.

Gina laughed and raised her mug in the air too. 'And here's to no more fighting for survival!'

EPILOGUE

'Is that the last of everything?' John asked as he packed another suitcase and a box into the back of his car.

'I think so,' said Gina. 'Everything else has gone ahead in the van – unless Claire has anything to come.'

'I'm done.' Claire came up behind her. She placed both of her hands on Gina's shoulder and rested her chin on them. 'Feels strange, doesn't it?'

'Yeah.' Gina saw her mum walking towards her. Across the road, Ruth was rushing over. Some of the neighbours were already standing on the pavement. Surely they weren't all coming to see them off? Oh, God, she was going to cry.

'Bleeding hell, I'm only moving a few streets away.' She waved her hands in front of her face and blinked back tears.

As everyone crowded around to say goodbye, Gina noticed Pete in the doorway.

'Ready to go then?' Caren asked a few minutes later.

Gina held up her hand. 'Give me a minute?' She made her way back up the path.

'You off then?' he asked.

She nodded, seeming a little shy with him.

'You don't have to leave.'

'Yes, we do.'

Pete stepped down to her and took hold of her hand.

'Please stay.'

Gina had never seen him looking so forlorn. He looked like he hadn't eaten much for days – actually she knew that he hadn't. My God, she realised. He really was going to miss her. But she wasn't backing down now. The hardest decisions had been made. She turned to leave.

'I'll always be around,' he told her.

But I won't always need you.

'I know,' she replied.

Claire was already in the car. Before she joined her, Gina stopped and looked back at the house.

'Goodbye, Rachel,' she whispered. She continued to stare, as if she expected the ghost of her daughter to run across the garden and stop them from leaving.

'Goodbye, Stanley Avenue,' Claire said as John drove off.

Gina smiled at her daughter and squeezed her hand. Good riddance more like, she thought. She'd lived her life on Stanley Avenue, moving only from number twenty-eight to number twenty-five. Moving to a flat in Harrison Court was a whole new journey for them both. She was frightened, yet excited; nervous yet intrigued. Could they make it on their own?

Caren thought they could. Ruth thought they could. Her family thought they could. Even Josie Mellor thought they could.

So she'd have to give it a damn good try – even just to prove them all wrong. She'd never done anything on her own before; neither had her daughter.

'Here's to our future.' She smiled at Claire. 'We're finished with the scummy side of the street. From now on, it's Happy Road for me and you.'

ABOUT THE AUTHOR

Mel Sherratt has been a self-described "meddler of words" ever since she can remember. After winning her first writing competition at the age of 11, she has rarely been without a pen in her hand or her nose in a book.

Since successfully self-publishing *Taunting the Dead* and seeing it soar to the rank of number one best-selling police procedural in the Amazon Kindle store in 2012, Mel has gone on to publish three more books in the critically acclaimed *The Estate* Series.

Mel has written feature articles for The Guardian, the Writers and Artists website, and Writers Forum Magazine, to name just a few, and regularly speaks at conferences, event and talks.

She lives in Stoke-on-Trent, Staffordshire, with her husband and her terrier, Dexter (named after the TV serial killer, with some help from her Twitter fans), and makes liberal use of her hometown as a backdrop for her writing.

Her website is www.melsherratt.co.uk and you can find her on Twitter at @writermels

Printed in Great Britain
by Amazon